THE VOICE OF A MUTE

The Voice of a Mute

Christopher J.A. Graham

Christopher J.A.
Graham Books

Table of Contents

CHAPTER 1

The Mighty Mawkin

It was a muggy late-summer afternoon, and the only thing to make it more worthy of a long nap for Dowyr Mawkin was the fact it was visiting day at the orphanage. He put off leaving his bed in the bunkroom for as long as he could, laying on his back, head hanging over the edge to stare at the wall. Only the most comfortable of positions.

His lounging was interrupted as one of the younger Sisters, Naiya, came to stand over him.

"Time to join the others," she said, and the effort to sound patient was palpable.

Fine, he hand-signed, taking a moment to let the blood rush out of his head as he sat up. *I'm still not getting adopted.*

"You never know."

He gave her a blank look. She sniffed and strode away, motioning for him to follow.

They entered the visiting room, deceptively spacious from its high ceiling, and painted to be warm and colorful, but it had been decades since the last paint job. The colors were faded, and in some spots washed away altogether. It was a depressing sight, as were the rest of the orphans. The Sisters certainly did their best to lighten their mood, keep the place tidy and presentable, but only so much could be done for a place that was built with the soul of mud. And yet some might say it still looked prettier than Dowyr himself.

It had been years since he came to understand that any effort on his part to get adopted was futile. Nobody wanted the ugly, mute 14-year-old. Just a reality he had come to accept. He didn't want anyone either.

Taking to his chair in the corner, Dowyr tilted his head back to stare at the ceiling while trying to ignore the sounds of the other children happily interacting with the prospective parents that came through. He wondered what kind of life he could have if he could channel an Emogic of some kind; a power that was gained from having an Apex of Emotion, which was a somewhat rare one-time event that occurred when experiencing an intense or abnormal amount of emotion associated with one of the 32 different Emogics. Dowyr had read everything there was to know about each from the books at the library, one of the places he spent most of his time when not trapped in the orphanage, even when there was nothing left to read.

He imagined what it would be like to fly using the Emogic of Happiness. The first thing he'd do is fly somewhere warmer like the southern nation of Arkonia. Winters in Elyssanar were much too cold for his taste. Unfortunately, the odds of him having an Apex of Happiness were probably near zero. The soul of mud was far too oppressive. Perhaps he could have an Apex of Loneliness, which would've been almost as good due to its power of teleportation.

Visiting time wore on, but for all of Dowyr's daydreaming, he only found himself more and more bored. He almost wished some pastor or other clergyman would walk in and try to argue him into accepting Heaven or Elysium or whoever. At least then there would be someone to talk to for a while. But none did. It had been months since the last. He wondered if he'd scared them all away, but no, he was sure some newly determined clergyman would come again. The religious types in Elyssanar were relentless. Which, as far as he could tell, meant everyone. All the more reason to fly south to Arkonia, which the clergy often spoke against as being full of heathens.

Leaning back in his chair, Dowyr tried to tilt his head even further to stare at the wall, albeit unsuccessfully. The chattering of adults and children washed over him.

Nothing to do, nothing to doooo, he thought, wishing he had something to sketch on.

And that's when the Apex of Emotion hit.

He felt nothing when it occurred, but something about his boredom changed. There was an energy of it within him, as though he could reach into himself and take hold of it, shape it, and make it go somewhere and do something. Not even aware of what he was doing, he reached in and pulled it out, channeling it. The Boredom flowed outward, permeating the air around him in the form of a gray mist. If he hadn't been so focused on the dusty ceiling, he would've seen it.

So stupid, he thought. *I'd rather have an executioner come in and chop my head off.*

When the executioner's face came into view, a giant of a man looming over him with an axe at the ready, his instincts forced his legs to jump, causing the chair to fling back and crash to the ground, bringing him with it. With the floor having dealt a solid blow to his head, his accidental channeling was cut off. The Emogic energy vanished, and the executioner went with it as though he had never been.

Dowyr blinked in confusion, then gasped in realization. *An Apex... of Boredom?* he thought. It had to be. There was no other emotion he was feeling so strongly.

"Are you alright, Dowyr?" Naiya asked from afar as she hurried over to him.

Yes, he signed. *Accident.*

Naiya helped him to his feet. "After how much time you've spent sitting on that chair, I never would've thought... well, never mind. Maybe instead you should try tal—" She caught herself mid-word and sighed. "Try... interacting?"

Dowyr looked past her, seeing some of the prospective parents looking his way curiously. He held back from sticking his tongue out at them and signed, *I'd rather not.*

"Of course. You'd rather leave for the afternoon altogether, wouldn't you?"

It was difficult to hide his grin. *It's like you can read my mind. Can I go to the library? I'll be back in time for dinner.*

"I thought you had already read everything? Well... how many times have we let you skip visiting days this month?"

Does that really matter?

"I suppose not, but then I'll have you on dish cleaning duty after dinner."

Deal.

He dashed off to put on his sandals and was out of the orphanage before any of the other Sisters knew.

The city of Elyssanar—which the country was named after—was relatively quiet at this time of day. Most people stayed in their homes, avoiding the summer heat, but there were still a number of carts rolling down the streets, children playing tag, and the usual old geezers playing a game of Kings in the shade. They waved as Dowyr passed, and he waved back. One shouted after him if he had time for a game, but he shook his head. Any other time he might've taken them up on it—they were the only people he knew outside of the orphanage that he actually liked and got along with—but he intended to test out his new Emogic powers, and the temptation to use them for cheating would be too strong.

Turning down another street, Dowyr reached the library with its large stone pillars holding up its grand façade. He weaved in between them like a snake and went past the entrance, having never intended on entering in the first place. The market was his true destination, a less conspicuous place to test his Emogic.

Right as he cleared the last pillar, he ran into someone who had just rounded the corner, a man in clergyman robes, and with an all-too familiar face. Pastor Orson. Of all people to run into, it had to be the worst.

"Oh, excuse me!" Orson said with sincerity, then upon recognizing Dowyr, added, "Ah... it's *you*. Dowyr, if I'm not mistaken?"

Dowyr took a step back and signed, *Dowyr Mawkin.*

Orson gave him a cold look. "Still going about using that filthy moniker? Hmph. Isn't it a visitation day? You shouldn't be sneaking out, whatever your excuse."

This is what Dowyr loathed about the man. He assumed the worst, and what he assumed was law. He was never mistaken, there was no talking back, no explaining the situation, no correcting him, and he made you know it. So, being the only reasonable course of action, Dowyr tried to run. His plan went well for all of two steps before Orson grabbed his arm and yanked him back.

"I think not," Orson said, and began dragging him in the direction of the orphanage. "I'll be sure to teach the Sisters how to deal with you appropriately. The Sentinels do not smile down upon disobedient children."

As if he knew anything about what his imaginary Sentinels thought. For all that was written in The Five Sentinels—the primary religious text of Elyssanar—there was nothing about 'disobedient' children and what the Sentinels themselves thought of them. Dowyr would know, he had read the entire thing, and he never forgot a single detail of any book he read. Not even the Snakes—the Sentinels' evil counterparts—had anything to say about delinquents.

An idea came to him. If he was a Boredom Emogician as he suspected, he should be able to use his Emogic to escape. Boredom's powers were telepathy and sensory manipulation, and using the latter should make for an easy escape. If there was someone he didn't mind testing it on, it was Orson.

Recalling what he'd read about how to channel Emogic, he took a calming breath and tried to ignore the hand grasping his arm. Instead, he turned his focus inward, feeling the Emogic energy churning within him, and mentally willed it to come into his control, the way all Emogics were channeled. Some were harder to control than others, and he had to mentally coax the Emogic into his grasp as though it were a bit sluggish to obey, but still it came, and he channeled it out. It appeared as a gray floating stream, which he then pierced Orson with. The man wouldn't have seen the Emogic; only other Emogicians of the same type or an Empathy Emogician could see the channeling.

With the Emogic touching Orson, Dowyr felt a clear sense of possibility of what he could do with it; telepathy, or sensory manipulation. He focused on the latter and then imagined, in the perspective of Orson, that he broke free and began to run. As expected, Orson let go of his arm for real and ran after the illusion. Dowyr maintained his channeling at him, having his fake-self run faster. He gasped when Orson went beyond ten meters and could still channel all the way to him.

So I'm above Class 1, he thought with some giddy excitement.

After aiming a rude gesture towards the old fool, he started running in the opposite direction, still channeling. After about ten seconds, his stream of Boredom stretched thin and slipped off of Orson. That sealed being at least Class 2, probably even a bit higher, earning an excited leap forward.

Still, he wanted to be sure of exactly how powerful he was. The power measurement of an Emogician scaled logarithmically, and the more powerful, the less chance of someone having an Apex to reach such strength, and some Emogics were rarer than others. He could likely be the only Boredom Emogician in the country.

There were a few ways to know where he fell along the Class scale, such as a trained Empath to sense it outright, but without one he resorted to testing how many people he could channel to.

Before he could start doing so, he nearly tripped over a stray dog that was lying down in the shade of a building. The shaggy mongrel was panting hard and looked like it hadn't eaten for a few days. It looked at him with frightened eyes and made a low whine.

It's okay, Dowyr signed, backing away slowly. He wondered if Boredom worked on animals and channeled to the dog, but he couldn't sense any sort of telepathic possibility. That much was expected; an animal's thoughts were incompatible with a human's, unless you were able to channel the Emogic of Peace. At least he could tell that sensory manipulation would work, so he made the dog hear the voice of one of the other orphans as though it came from him.

"*I'll go get something for you to eat, okay? Wait right here.*"

Running off and reaching the market, he came across a tired looking fruit merchant and looked through what he was selling. A colorful variety of apples, pears, and oranges. Dogs could eat apples, right?

"Good day for some fruit," the merchant said absently, waving a straw hat at himself to cool down.

Dowyr nodded in agreement and again channeled out his Emogic, piercing the merchant with it, but this time he focused on the possibility of telepathy. The mind of the merchant opened up to Dowyr's own.

...looks like an orphan, the merchant thought. *Ugly kid. Probably can't even afford anything.*

"*Ugly!?*" Dowyr channeled sensory manipulation using the merchant's own voice. "*Who are you calling ugly, ugly? I am the Mighty Mawkin!*"

The merchant's eyes widened. Dowyr continued channeling and imagined himself disappearing. Gasping, the merchant leapt to his feet, eyes searching wildly. Dowyr grinned and jumped in place a few times, but there was no further reaction from the bewildered merchant.

Satisfied, Dowyr grabbed a couple apples and made it seem to the merchant that they were still there. Deciding the dog could wait a bit longer, he began to channel at each person he came across. Even at this blistering hour of the day there were plenty around to do so. As he pierced them with the Emogic, he felt the distinct possibility of either telepathy or sensory manipulation. Not knowing whether that was enough to test his limits, he decided to go with telepathy for them all. One by one their minds opened up to his own, but he didn't let his own thoughts go into theirs. No reason to raise suspicions.

That man was worried about his work, that woman was worried about her husband, that kid just wanted to play with friends. Dowyr continued striking new targets with his Emogic.

Seven, eight, nine. This wasn't so bad. The voices clamoring in his mind were fairly easy to ignore too.

Ten. Not much more difficult. Any Class 2 would be able to channel at this many without issue. How many more?

Eleven, twelve, thirteen. That woman was having an affair, that man was planning to cheat his business partner, that kid just wanted to eat cake. Dowyr didn't even know what cake tasted like.

Each new target felt like it was taking a fair bit more effort to channel at, but still manageable. All the voices just became background noise.

Fourteen. Getting close. Why was that guy so desperate for a shovel?

Fifteen. His heart pounded. Was this what it was like trying to run a marathon? There was no way he could go much further, but he wanted to know for sure.

At sixteen it took twice as much effort, and the streams of Emogic visibly trembled. Suppressing the voices became impossible and they flooded his mind with an overwhelming force. Any more and Dowyr thought he'd instantly collapse from the effort. He was ready to as it was and cut his channeling, letting the streams of Emogic vanish along with all the voices.

Fifteen must be my limit, he thought, holding his head which suddenly felt dizzy. *That makes me Class 2.2 according to the books. Not bad.*

He chuckled to himself and slowly began walking back to where the dog had been. Maybe now that he had a way to communicate with people besides signs he could get adopted. The thought made him laugh out loud and stumble, earning a few odd stares from passersby.

No, there were better things to do than that. With the power of telepathy and sensory manipulation he could leave the orphanage and be on his own for good. So long as he found the right people to trick, getting enough money to leave the country would be easy, and then off to Arkonia he'd go. Pastor Orson had preached it was full of sinful unbelievers a number of times, which made it all the more fitting for Dowyr, even if they did have weird ideas about names. As long as it didn't snow there, that was good enough for him.

Upon reaching the dog, he found it lying still, eyes closed. It gave no reaction even when he nudged it with his foot. It wasn't breathing. Dowyr stood over it, unsure what to do. He looked around to see if any adults were paying attention and might do something, but none were. There was barely anyone else walking the streets. He hesitantly took a step back, then put one of the apples next to the dog's snout. He had meant to eat the second apple himself, but thinking about his appetite, he realized it was gone. He put down the second apple and made himself walk away. For some reason his heart was racing even faster than when he was channeling to all those people.

Returning to the orphanage, he was careful about going back in. Pastor Orson might have come to inform the Sisters of his whereabouts. Opening the door a crack, he looked around and found no sign of him. Entering, he tried to be discreet about making his way back to the bunkroom. Nobody paid him any mind, and soon he was collapsed back on his bed.

Snakes, he was exhausted all of a sudden. Where had that ache in his bones come from? His muscles felt like jelly. Had channeling at sixteen people really taken that much out of him? It must have been that. Dowyr had read that if an Emogician drained themselves all in one go, it took an entire day to fully recover. It certainly felt like he needed an entire day.

The door opened and Naiya strode in, eyes set on Dowyr. He sat up and prepared a stream of Boredom. At least, he tried to. His focus was slipping and he couldn't maintain channeling.

"There are some people here looking for you, Dowyr," Naiya said. "They say you've had an Apex of Emotion. Are you okay? You look exhausted. What happened?"

Snakes, Dowyr thought. *How did they know? An Empath? But how would an Empath have known I was—*

Orson. The bastard must have gone straight to the Academy of Emogic to report him. Of *course* he'd know; once Dowyr's channeling to him stopped, the fake Dowyr would've simply vanished into thin air. *Stupid, stupid, stupid, stupid, stupid!*

Two men strode into the room, their attention focused on Dowyr. His instincts made him jump up and try to run, but exhaustion got the better of him. They grabbed him, and there was little he could do as one hoisted him over his shoulder. He felt like he was falling asleep and cursed his body for being so pathetically weak.

"Don't worry, ma'am," the man holding him said. "We'll take good care of him and make sure he won't get himself hurt."

"Nooooooo," he tried to say, but it was just an unintelligible groan before he slipped into unconsciousness.

CHAPTER 2

A Rozbury Roommate

Dowyr laid on the top of a bunkbed staring at the gray slate ceiling of his room at the Academy of Emogic, the view from a small frosted window letting him know it was early morning. The only thing that kept the room from being indistinguishable from a prison cell was how nicely furnished it was, with a dresser, padded bench, and padded chair. The room even had a surprisingly clean private bathroom with running water, a luxury the orphanage never had. There was also the fact he could leave the room. Just not the building. It was expected that those who went through an Apex of Emotion needed to be educated on everything concerning Emogic, so he was confined to the Academy until he was 'properly trained'. Might as well have been a prison for that. He already knew everything books had to say on the subject, and he understood how to channel. What then was the point of being a mandatory student?

He sat up with a groan. His torso was sore like someone had carried him too roughly, but he had no recollection of the event. Everything was a blur beyond getting back to the orphanage after testing his Emogic. That bothered him. He remembered everything. The Sisters said he had a perfect memory, and some clergymen tried to convince him it was a divine gift from Heaven. He retorted with asking if Heaven gave him his ugliness and inability to speak too. Some of them even had the gall to say yes.

More unnerving than the lack of memory was that he couldn't channel. There was something blocking his attempts to bring the Emogic out, which meant there was an Indifference Emogician channeling at him somewhere, or some kind of Indifference emitting device. Dowyr remembered reading some years ago about the Academy's discovery of being able to take an inanimate object and inject it full of Emogic, but he had never seen such an object in person, at least to his knowledge. They must have used something filled with Indifference to keep the newer Emogicians from harming themselves or others, but for Dowyr, it only made the possibility of communication all the more difficult.

On a related note, there was the matter of the snoring coming from below to attend to. There was another kid on the bottom bunk. Snoring didn't usually bother Dowyr, but at the moment he found it annoying to the point he couldn't think straight.

Shut up, shut up, shut up, shut up, Dowyr signed. He looked over the edge of his bunk and blew at the sleeping boy's face. The boy didn't stir, so Dowyr jumped down and pinched his nose shut, jerking back when the boy awoke with a gasp.

"What was that for?" the boy asked.

Dowyr blinked, unsure what to do. *You know signs?* he signed.

The boy stared at him, face blank.

Dowyr pointed at himself. *D-O-W-Y-R.*

"Are you deaf?"

With a roll of the eyes, Dowyr pointed to his mouth and shook his head, then to his ears and nodded.

"Oh, you just can't speak?"

This sucks, Dowyr thought, but he nodded, then pointed at the boy and tried to imitate his snoring.

"Ohh. Sorry, I didn't know I had a new roommate. I must have been asleep when you got here. My name's Weynon Rozbury."

Weynon looked about Dowyr's age, maybe even a year older. His short hair was sandy blonde, which nicely complimented his amber eyes. He might even be considered handsome if his ears weren't so lopsided.

Dowyr moved back as Weynon got out of bed and went to the dresser. From the top of it he grabbed one of two journals and a thick paper-wrapped charcoal and held them towards Dowyr.

"Can you write?" Weynon asked.

Finally, I have a voice, Dowyr thought, gladly taking the journal and opening to a blank page to write his name and age on. He wondered for a moment whether he should omit his fake last name, but it had always proved to be an effective test of someone's character to him due to being a religious slur, and he wanted to see what Weynon's reaction would be.

Weynon took a single look and smiled. "Nice to meet you, Dowyr. I'm only twelve, but I hope we can get along. Did they tell you your Emogic yet?"

Dowyr blinked, mildly surprised by such a friendly reaction and also that he was two years younger than he looked. The question wasn't out of the ordinary though, as people who went through an Apex of Emotion often didn't know what emotion they were going through at the time. Dowyr shook his head and wrote, *No, but I've already figured it out anyway. Boredom, Class 2.2.*

"Really? I didn't know Boredom was an Emogic. Cool. I'm a Class 3 Peace Emogician, a Druid."

Dowyr took an involuntary step back, nearly stumbling. *This kid's a powerhouse.* And a surprisingly ignorant one at that if he didn't know Boredom was an Emogic. But Peace Emogicians—'Druids' being their nickname, and there was one for every Emogic—had the widest range of capabilities. When channeling, they could calm an angry mob, could listen to the land and communicate with animals and plants—plants!—and lastly could use the emotion that nature gave off, if in great enough amount. Out of the 32 Emogics, only six had been proven to exist in nature so far: Anger, Depression, Fear, Happiness, Sadness, and Love. Of those, only Happiness wasn't terrifying at Class 3 or higher. Unless flying counted as terrifying too. Perhaps it did, for some.

"Don't be scared," Weynon said, "Even though I still need to learn how to use my Emogic, we can't channel in here. I don't know how, I've only been here since yesterday afternoon and was told I'd have my orientation today. But can you tell me what Boredom Emogicians do? And what are they called?"

Dowyr wrote, *Mind Intruders. If we get to channel eventually, I'll show you.*

Weynon blinked. "*Mind* Intruders? I don't know if I want you to show me."

Dowyr grinned, but before he could write a reply, the door opened.

A slender middle-aged woman stepped into the room and smiled at them both. "Good morning, students," she said in a soft, smooth voice; the sort of voice that sounded directed at children who needed to be put to sleep. It reminded Dowyr of the way clergywomen would talk to congregations and made his ears want to burrow into his skull. "I am Aelyss, an instructor here at the Academy. We're so happy to have you. Breakfast is being served in the mess hall, and afterwards will be your orientation. If you would please follow me."

Dowyr shared a look with Weynon, but quickly followed after Aelyss. He was starving, and whatever they had here must be better than the slop at the orphanage. Weynon was right behind him, and they walked down a wide, white-marbled hallway. Lightstones embedded in the ceiling and walls glowed a little brighter as they passed. The doors of other student rooms were spaced evenly across the way on both sides. Many such students were walking the hall too, hurrying along to breakfast or classes. They all looked older, mainly young adults, but even a few that looked well into their thirties. Apexes of Emotion were rare among children to early teens, so Dowyr doubted he'd meet many students around his age.

He tried to reach within and channel, but still found himself blocked off from his Emogic and grunted in annoyance.

Heaven is stupid, he signed. *Hell is stupid, the Sentinels are stupid, the Snakes are stupid, they're all just stupid, stupid, stupid.*

He chuckled to himself as people gave him odd passing stares. They probably had no idea he was blaspheming in front of them. Nothing about their ridiculous religion mattered to him. If Heaven and Hell were real, or any of the Sentinels and Snakes for that matter, they never showed it. As far as he was concerned, this life was demanding enough as it was without the need to worry about pleasing gods or whatever came after. Perhaps that was because the local clergy were so demanding to be pleased. Not that he obliged. Sure, the pastors and teachers at the mandatory church services and classes he was forced to attend tried to make him change his ways, but they so flagrantly flaunted hypocritical teachings and ideas not even found in The Five Sentinels that it was child's play to dismiss nearly everything they said. If they wanted to use a book to rationalize their actions or moral foundation, they at least ought to know the book inside and out. So many clergymen who tried to teach him only seemed to know half of what he did, if not less.

They turned down another hall where a faint mass of voices could be heard. The noise grew until Aelyss brought them to a large series of arches that opened to the mess hall, where a myriad of men and women, ranging from teenagers to middle-aged, sat at tables eating and chatting with one another or waiting in line to get food. A number of long counters stood at the far end of the room where the people lined up, and beyond them was the largest kitchen Dowyr had ever seen. Cooks and kitchen servants darted around to replace empty platters on the counters. Each new platter looked like a work of art, with all the colors of a rainbow in fruits and vegetables purposefully placed to draw the eyes towards the center. The art pieces were quickly ruined once hungry hands got a hold of them, and despite Dowyr's own grumbling stomach, he shed an invisible tear for them.

Other platters were far plainer. There were a couple with large bowls of various stews, one purely for mashed potatoes, another for steamed vegetables, and the last Dowyr could make out held a variety of breads and cheeses. There was no meat to be seen, which was well and good in his mind. He had never tasted meat, and did not intend to. The closest to it he had tried was salmon, which he quickly decided was not for him.

"Go ahead and get in line," Aelyss said. "An orientation leader will be here soon to show the new students around and give you your schedules."

Aelyss disappeared back into the hall, leaving the two boys gawking at the scene.

Weynon turned to Dowyr, looking a bit pensive. "You can go first."

Dowyr could barely make out his voice, but he nodded and moved towards the line, stepping lightly. He never liked loud crowds of people, and usually felt like he was getting in someone's way when trying to navigate through them. The line moved slow, allowing him to grab a little of everything, not even worrying if he would be able to eat it all. Recovering from channeling too much the evening before had taken its toll on his stomach. His hands were starting to tingle from hunger.

They sat in the emptiest corner of the room and ate in silence, though the rate at which Dowyr stuffed himself was anything but silent. Weynon looked as if he wanted to ask a question, but Dowyr hadn't brought the journal to respond and still couldn't channel. That hardly mattered to him right now, as this food was *so much* better than what was served at the orphanage. Satisfied hums were the only thing worth being communicated at a time like this.

Though once his mouth acclimatized to the tastes, he did think about teaching Weynon how to sign, wondering if he could channel the knowledge straight into his mind. The books he read said Mind Intruders could do things like that, and it would make the process much faster, but he hadn't the slightest idea of how it was done. Perhaps there was another Mind Intruder that could teach him, or an Empath that had experience with Boredom.

When Dowyr finished eating, Weynon stared at his empty plate in disbelief.

"My mom always said I ate too fast," he said. "I think she was wrong now."

Dowyr gave him a toothy grin, but it was short-lived as a call went out to all the new students to come to the front of the mess hall for orientation. Weynon did his best to stuff whatever was left on his platter into his mouth before getting up after Dowyr.

The orientation leader was a short, stocky man who looked to be in his thirties. When all the new students had gathered to him, he led them into the hall to speak.

"Alright everyone," he said, "let's start with names, Emogics, and Classes if you know them. I'm Dane, Class 1.9 Puffer and proud."

Dowyr rolled his eyes at the lame joke, but a few students chuckled, and then everyone began giving their names. There were just over a dozen students, most of them young but all of them older than Dowyr. Some didn't know their Class level, but they gave their Emogics, most of them the more common types such as Anger, Fear, Shame, and Worry. The negative Emogics were always overrepresented. When it got to Dowyr's turn, Weynon spoke up for him.

"This is Dowyr. He can't speak, but he's a Class 2.2 Boredom Emogician."

"A mute?" Dane asked. "Can he sign?"

Dowyr nodded vigorously and signed, *yes, and for the love of Hell get me an interpreter!*

Dane looked surprised and took on a stern tone. "You better be careful with what you let those hands of yours say. You can never tell who understands them. I'll let you off the hook this time, but I better not see language like that again."

Dowyr pursed his lips and sullenly signed, *yes sir,* then put his hands behind his back to make a rude comment.

"Good. Alright students, if you'll follow me. You may have heard that the Academy doesn't work like regular schools. There are no semesters, grades, or tests. It's purely lessons and training from the start. Every day new Emogicians arrive needing to be trained to understand what it means to be one and how not to hurt themselves or others with their power. You're here for three months for that purpose alone. I'll walk you through the process of how your first month will go, starting with the classrooms and lecture halls you'll be going to. First up, of course, is the chapel..."

CHAPTER 3

Close Encounters

There was little of the interior of the Academy that interested Dowyr, as somehow it managed to feel even more lifeless than the orphanage. It was pristine, yes, but the soul of mud was far preferable to the soul of a polished and sanctified brick. Dowyr considered whether thinking of it like that was an insult to bricks.

They had not gone beyond the second floor—four in total—as all channeling was done on the top two floors. Only the bottom two had objects infused with Indifference that stopped any attempt at channeling, no matter how powerful the Class. Dane called them voidstones, based on the name used for Indifference Emogicians, Voidspeakers, who were able to block another Emogician's channeling. It was also claimed that, when channeling, they were able to communicate with Hell himself, which was a major turnoff for religious types. Voidstones didn't seem to bother them though. Probably because Hell had nothing to say to inanimate objects. Not that Dowyr believed it was really Hell from The Five Sentinels speaking to Voidspeakers. *Something* spoke to them, but it could easily be the worst versions of themselves.

Dowyr had been momentarily tempted to sneak off to the third floor, but decided against it due to the brawny men that guarded every staircase. If the stairs to the third floor were as long as the ones between first and second floors, he wouldn't have gotten far.

Dreadfully, it was going to be a month before he was allowed to the third floor to start practicing his Emogic. And so his time at the Academy started passing by, most of it being spent on a wagonload of lectures, reading assignments that Dowyr had read years ago, and, of course, mandatory sermon attendance every week. Students weren't allowed to leave the Academy until they had been through three months of training, so there had to be a chapel on the first floor. There was no way they could allow new students to be away from religious indoctrination for so long, or at least that was how Dowyr saw it. He even had to listen to one of Pastor Orson's sermons, the smug bastard. It was an effort to endure, and the only reason he ever managed to get out of bed for the morning services was because Weynon practically dragged him out every time. He didn't begrudge him for it—or at least, not *all* the time. The kid was only trying to help and thought it right. Weynon was never judgmental towards him regardless of his protests, outwardly at least, and so their relationship remained friendly.

To Dowyr's dismay, it was the only relationship that remained friendly. None of the interpreters spoke to him, and the few teachers who could communicate with him did not appear to like him. He did not know why, but the faces they made when he introduced himself as 'Dowyr Mawkin' gave him a suspicion. Mawkin was not really his last name—being an orphan he didn't officially have one—but he had adopted the name as it seemed both befitting and amusing. The reason was because it was a disparaging religious term for orphans, one that had been coined by the Snake Hades. It was used to imply that orphans were Hell's property. Dowyr thought there was a nice ring to it, but of course the teachers disagreed.

The other students around his age also avoided him, although he was used to such treatment from his time at the orphanage. It didn't help that he was unable to communicate with them without something to write on.

Weynon had no issues with making friends. He was the most soft-spoken of those he spent time with and got along with all but the nastiest teens. And somehow, as if by miracle, even the nastiest came to love him and made apologies for their damnable behavior. Weynon forgave them with smiles and handshakes, and seemingly held no resentment. It was the most unusual phenomenon Dowyr had ever witnessed, and he had to wonder whether Weynon's Emogic of Peace played a part, but there was nothing written in any of the library's books about Druids being able to make friends so easily.

Dowyr had initially suspected Weynon to be a holier-than-thou type, but quickly realized he wasn't like that at all. For instance, Weynon stuck to eating with him in the mess hall, which meant just them and an otherwise empty table. Nobody else wanted to sit near Dowyr, even with Weynon there. Perhaps Weynon felt sorry for him, but he did not think it was that. Of all the people in the Academy, perhaps in all the city, Weynon genuinely believed in the Five Sentinels, followed their teachings to the letter, and didn't think himself better than anyone else for it. There was not an ounce of hypocrisy in the boy, and that is what Dowyr liked about him the most. It's what kept him sane through the ridiculous church sermons, knowing that the kid beside him was better than all the pastors and preachers combined. Sometimes he wanted to try asking what Weynon's thoughts were about the more blatant pulled-out-of-the-pastor's-ass type sermons, but he could never bring himself to write out the question. It just seemed like it would be rude.

One evening, Dowyr was leaving his room to go to the mess hall for dinner when another boy, nearly a head taller than him, brushed against him so forcefully that he was knocked to the ground. As Dowyr tried to pick himself up, a foot came down on his back, and suddenly he was surrounded by half a dozen other boys.

"Aw, look at the poor Mawkin," the boy who held him said. "What's the matter? Why don't you cry for help?"

Dowyr recognized the voice of Fenton, a Class 1 Worry Emogician, or Sprinter, who was a suck-up to all the teachers and pastors. Why anyone else liked him was a mystery. Laughs echoed around while Dowyr rolled his eyes and managed to sign, *I can still yell, dumbass.*

"Look at his funny gestures."

"I can wiggle my fingers too."

"Hey, what if he's insulting us?"

"There's an easy way to stop that."

Another boy stepped hard on Dowyr's hands, and he screamed. The other boys jumped back and cursed, even the ones on top of him.

"What in Heaven's name is that noise?"

"That sounds worse than my sister's cat when it was sick!"

"Sounds like a dying dog to me."

Dowyr groaned as they laughed. None of his fingers felt broken, thankfully, and after flexing them he signed, *go to Hell.* And he did *not* sound like a dying dog. He would know.

A new voice came from down the hall. "Hey, I just saw Weynon go in. Come on guys, let's ditch the Hell-loving rodent and get some dinner."

The others bellowed with agreement and strode away. Dowyr pushed himself up and flexed his fingers some more, glad they still bent in the right direction, but they still throbbed with pain at the movement. *Where's a Healer when you need one?* On the third floor, unfortunately. The Academy always kept at least a Class 2 Compassion Emogician on staff to treat injuries, but new students were only allowed onto the third floor to be healed for the most serious cases.

With a sigh, Dowyr continued on to the mess hall, moving slowly in the hopes that the boys would be long gone. When he entered the mess hall, he looked for Weynon and found him sitting at a table with Fenton and the others, who were all innocent smiles and pleasant manners. Dowyr grimaced at them and joined the line. He sat alone at his usual table and stared at Weynon while plucking at his plate and not caring what came up to his mouth or in what order. Weynon smiled apologetically the moment he noticed his stare, but Dowyr just rolled his eyes.

Then, as if out of thin air, a girl walked up to his table and sat down across from him. His jaw dropped, and some food may have rolled out. The girl looked only a couple years older than him, maybe seventeen at the most, and had long strawberry blonde hair with too pretty a face. What intrigued Dowyr most was her clothing; she didn't wear a student's shirt, just an ordinary dress, which meant she either wasn't an Emogician, or she had already completed her training.

"What, have you never seen a girl before?" she asked in a demeaning tone.

Oh, she's a witch, Dowyr thought, snapping his mouth shut. *Well, I'm not talking to her, whoever she is.* He looked past her and saw Weynon and the others looking at them in a mix of surprise and disbelief. *That's just great.*

"Um, hello?" the girl said, leaning towards him and waving a hand. "Are you blind? Blind and deaf? Well, whatever your problem is, I heard you were a Mind Intruder."

Dowyr blinked and looked at her.

"Ah, so you *can* hear me. Well, are you? A Boredom Emogician?"

Dowyr raised an eyebrow and nodded shortly.

"Class 1?"

He shook his head.

"Class 2?"

He nodded.

"Wonderful. Thank you very much, strange little alien!"

She got up and disappeared out the mess hall. Dowyr locked stares with Weynon, who shrugged at him. He shrugged back. *Girls are the aliens,* he thought.

Once finished with his food, he went back to his room and changed into his sleepwear. Weynon came in shortly after.

"Sorry for not sitting with you," Weynon said. "Fenton practically begged me to eat with him and the others."

Dowyr grabbed his journal and charcoal and wrote, *Paradise 5:42?* A verse about doing what others begged of you, so long as it wasn't wrong.

"Yeah."

Dowyr nodded and shrugged, but wrote, *Do you even like hanging out with them? They're just a bunch of jerks.*

"They're not jerks. Fenton is actually pretty smart." Dowyr rolled his eyes. "He knows a lot about history and battle tactics and stuff. His dad's a Colonel. Is there something wrong with your hands? Why are they so red?"

Dowyr had been unconsciously massaging his hands whenever he could. He stopped the moment Weynon mentioned them and resisted the urge to continue. He wrote, *It's nothing. I tripped and landed on them funny earlier.* There was no way he was going to admit he was attacked and couldn't defend himself.

"Oh. Maybe you can get them healed tomorrow if they still hurt."

Dowyr's heart skipped a beat. Had it really been a month already? Quickly comparing the current date to when he had arrived at the Academy, he realized it had.

"Are you nervous about your Emogic lessons?" Weynon asked.

Dowyr shook his head and wrote, *I already know how to use mine, I just need practice. You?*

"A little bit. Being a Druid sounds nice, but understanding plants and animals is kind of freaky. Bird songs are not what you think."

Another time Dowyr would've asked about the birds, but instead he wrote, *Did you recognize that girl who sat down in front of me?*

"No, I've never seen her before. She was really pretty though. What did she say?"

Just asked me if I was a Mind Intruder, that was it.

"Weird. What did you think about her?"

She's trouble. I'll be happy if I never see her again.

"Well if she talked to you once, she'll probably talk to you again. I wonder if she's an Emogician."

Dowyr groaned. That was the last thing he wanted to hear, but instead of complaining about it, he climbed onto his bed with the journal and charcoal and began to sketch. Art was what helped him relax, and so he began outlining a mountain. Landscapes were what he liked to draw the most, especially while stuck inside the Academy. Not a single clear window was to be found. Plenty of stained-glass along the halls and chapel, but it was impossible to see through any of them.

"Do you wanna be an artist when you grow up?" Weynon asked.

Dowyr made a face and shook his head.

"What do you wanna be then?"

Dowyr paused. He hadn't really thought about that, but a smile crept onto his face as something came to mind. Flipping to his writing page, he wrote, *I actually do want to be an artist. A con artist.*

"Oh, that sounds cool. What kind of art is that?"

Dowyr suppressed a laugh. *Religious art.*

"Nice. I think you'd be pretty good at that."

Dowyr faked an appreciative nod, and on the inside was convulsing with laughter. If Weynon had one fault, it was naivety. The kid couldn't be helped, having grown up in a small farm town with his mother and grandmother who didn't have the time or resources to give him a proper education about the world. Yet Dowyr had to remind himself that books limited his own knowledge of the world, and he had never been outside of the city. Even other nations like Kircany or Parasten were only words and descriptions, and everything he'd learned about Arkonia was by word of mouth, as in the books it was barely mentioned enough for anyone to know it even existed. How he longed to go there and get away from all the stifling religious fog that permeated the entirety of Elyssanar. Arkonia might even have better reading material. How much more about the world could he learn from their libraries? It was an exciting prospect.

Dowyr suddenly realized the room was dark. He looked down at his sketch and blinked, barely able to make out the mountain he had outlined. Where had the time gone? He had fantasized about traveling the world from time to time while in the orphanage, but now that it seemed like a possible reality, the idea sucked him in.

Filled with anticipation, he slowly put the journal and charcoal away to not brighten the room's lightstone and tried to calm his mind to fall asleep. Tomorrow couldn't come soon enough.

CHAPTER 4

Empathic Trust Issues

Dowyr stood next to Weynon at the base of the stairs to the third floor, vigorously shaking his hands both from excitement and the minor pain he still felt in them. New students were lined up behind them, as only two were brought up at a time. All of them were wearing new white outfits with insignias sewn onto the shoulders that indicated Emogic type.

"You okay?" Weynon asked.

Nodding quickly, Dowyr hopped in place a few times.

"Yeah, me too."

Dane came down the stairs and focused his attention on them. "Alright you two, let's go meet your Emogic instructors." He turned to Dowyr and signed, *no funny business.*

Cross my eyes, Dowyr signed, doing just that after Dane turned back up the stairs. The brawny guards gave him disapproving looks, which he returned with an innocent smile as he made his way up the stairs with Weynon. At a certain point, it felt like an invisible blanket had been unwrapped from around his body. He could finally channel.

"Weynon, you'll be training with Misses Terson in Room 317," Dane said. "It's just right down that hall on the left."

Weynon took a deep breath. "Okay. Wish me luck, Dowyr."

"Good luck," Dowyr channeled, using the voice of another boy from the orphanage.

Weynon gave a start and looked at him wide-eyed. Dowyr winked and motioned for him to go.

"Don't be nervous now," Dane said. "She'll take good care of you. Go on, you don't want to be late. As for you, Dowyr, you'll be in Room 348. This way, it's a bit of a walk. You're our only Boredom Emogician, so you'll be training with one of our Empaths, Miss Klausgow. It'll be strictly one on one, so you had better be on your best behavior."

One on one? Dowyr thought as Dane led him down a few different halls. He had expected it to be in a full classroom like with everything else he was 'learning' at the Academy. "*Why one on one?*" he channeled to Dane.

Dane missed a step and turned back to him. "Did you just speak?"

Dowyr rolled his eyes. "*No, you just heard me. Why one on one?*"

With a moment of hesitation, Dane replied, "Because it was requested. Are you channeling?"

"*Yes. Requested by who?*"

"By Miss Klausgow. Now you better stop that before you're properly trained; being a Mind Intruder can be dangerous if you don't know what you're doing."

Fine, Dowyr signed despite knowing what he was doing. *Why did she request that?*

"You'll have to ask her. The room is just up here."

Dane led him to a door and opened it, motioning for him to enter. The room inside was just like any other classroom, except all the desks were moved to the back. No one was inside.

Dowyr looked back at Dane questioningly.

"She may be running late," he said. "It's typical of her. Don't worry, she'll be here. Best of luck."

Dane closed the door and signed through the small window, *remember, behave,* before disappearing. Dowyr took a deep breath and let it out through his teeth. That man was aggravating to be around. Being a Puffer probably had something to do with it. *Why is Pride even an Emogic?* he thought, going to a chair against the back wall. Shortly after sitting down, the door burst open to let in the most unpleasant sight Dowyr could have imagined.

"Good morning, my little alien student!" the girl from yesterday said. "I hope you rested well last night. We have a lot to do today, so how about you show me what you got? Come on, channel at me."

Dowyr was in the process of pulling his Emogic out to ask her what on earth she was doing in here, but in a panicked realization he cut himself off. *SHE'S THE EMPATH,* a voice screamed in his head.

"What's the matter? Don't be shy. I'm curious how Boredom tastes."

She is *the Empath,* Dowyr thought. He stared at her, every muscle stiff, and wondered how he could escape. The first problem was that she was bigger than him. The second problem was she'd know if he tried to channel at her. Could he channel to make his channeling disappear from her perspective? He didn't know. If her Class level was low enough it might be possible, but could he take that risk?

Instead of channeling or running, he signed, *do you know signs?*

"You *are* deaf!? Were you—ugh! You have no idea what I'm saying. You only nodded your head yesterday to make me leave, didn't you? I can't believe this."

Dowyr groaned, pointing to his ears and nodding, then to his mouth and shaking his head.

"You're joking. Tell me you're joking."

"*I CAN'T SPEAK, WITCH,*" Dowyr channeled as quickly as he could, though he wondered if he had used the right word. It seemed he had as the girl looked too shocked to react.

"Wwwwow, okay. First of all, I'm an Empath, not a witch. Second of all, then continue to use your Emogic! You spoke with it just now, so clearly you have some understanding of how to use it."

Dowyr vigorously shook his head. There was no way he was letting this girl use his Emogic. The Academy could find someone else to teach him.

The girl sniffed. "Fine, have it your way. Wait right here a moment." She walked out of the classroom and slammed the door behind her.

Dowyr wasted no time in jumping from his chair and finding a spot to hide near the door, which happened to be behind the teacher's desk. How soon would she return? There had to be a window of time in which he could safely leave. After a minute passed he got up and went to the door, creaking it open enough just to pop his head out.

A tower of a man was standing right there, one of the brawny men who always guarded the stairs to the third floor, an unamused expression on his face. Dowyr blinked at him and slowly pulled back into the room and gently closed the door, then dashed back behind the teacher's desk before the door opened again.

"Alright, lad, ye've had yer fun," the man said with a northern accent. "Come on out, I don't want te have te hurt ye."

Dowyr wondered where the girl was. If the man was alone, perhaps channeling at him could ensure escape. Maybe the man didn't even know the girl, and his being here was just happenstance. He could only hear one set of footsteps walking the room.

A voice whispered right next to him, "Why are you hiding?"

For a single moment the teacher's desk seemed like the most insubstantial thing in the world, so it came as a complete surprise when Dowyr smashed right into it and rebounded onto his backside. The ceiling would not stop moving.

"Ouch," the girl said. "This is him, Donnan."

Donnan's head hovered into view, looking concerned, and the girl's head came up on the opposite side.

Dowyr raised his arms and tried to sign, *I can't speak,* though the way he felt his fingers move it probably wasn't anything more than gibberish. He let out a groan.

"I'll get Claire," Donnan sighed.

He disappeared while the girl stayed and stared at Dowyr. He tried to return the look with some contempt, though his facial expression was apparently limited to that of pain. His head was starting to throb.

The girl clicked her tongue. "What am I going to do with you? Look kid, I need you to channel. I can't help you if you refuse. And you could at least be a bit more courteous; this isn't Arkonia. I also hope you realize I can have you sent to the Headmaster."

Dowyr cringed. He had heard about what happened to people who were sent to the Headmaster of the Academy. Endless chore assignments and sermons on proper behavior. Such horrible, horrible things. If there was a time for him to stop being stubborn and rebellious, it was probably now.

"*Fine,*" Dowyr channeled with some effort. "*I'm channeling. Happy? All you can eat buffet of Boredom.*"

He kept the flow of Emogic coming but directed it at the air around him. It was then sucked into her and channeled right back at him in what appeared to be a flood of Emogic. He felt nothing but sudden dread.

Oh...

Oh? Elethe's thought appeared in his mind like it was his own.

What Class are you? Dowyr thought back.

Class 3.9.

Dowyr instantly stopped channeling, cutting her off. *Snakes!* he thought, his whole body somehow becoming even more tense. *Snakes, Snakes, Snakes! That's practically Class 4. Does she know everything about me now? I'm so fu—*

"Your name's Dowyr *Mawkin?*" the girl asked. "Really?"

You got a problem with that? Dowyr signed.

She began to laugh uncontrollably. He tried to scoot away from the alien.

The door opened letting in Donnan followed by a slender middle-aged woman.

"What's so funny?" Donnan asked.

"He's," the girl wheezed, "He's... oh, Heaven help mehehehe."

Donnan moved her aside and motioned the woman, Claire, to attend Dowyr. She came over and knelt by his side.

"I see, just a minor concussion and some bruises on the hands," Claire said. "Not to worry. Have you been healed before?"

Dowyr shook his head.

"Okay, just relax and lie as still as you can. You'll feel a warm, tingling sensation."

Claire appeared to focus on something beyond Dowyr, as though seeing through him. Heat entered his head and hands, though not the unpleasant type. It was more like a blanket hung in the sunlight for a day being wrapped around him on a cold evening. Then it became a strange sizzling sensation, feeling as if his skin had become water just on the verge of boiling. The feeling went from pleasant to the most bizarre thing Dowyr had ever felt, but after a minute or so, all the pain in his head and hands was gone. A faint tingling remained.

"How does that feel?" Claire asked.

Dowyr sat up and signed, *weird.*

"He says 'weird'," the girl said, struggling to suppress a grin.

Dowyr blinked at her. Of course, she understood his signs now.

"Oh, he's a mute?" Claire asked. "I wish that were something that could be healed. Perhaps there is a Class level high enough where it could be healed, but there hasn't been a Healer or an Empath higher than 3.7 in centuries. Well, at least your head and hands should feel better."

Dowyr nodded and smiled gratefully to her before she said her goodbyes and left.

None higher than 3.7? he thought, staring at the girl.

"Now," Donnan said, "Why were ye laughing as if Elysium herself had possessed ye?"

"It's nothing," the girl said. "I just maybe delved too deep into his mind. He channeled while you were away. You're free to go."

Donnan gave her a skeptical look. "If ye say so. Does that mean ye have an answer for Garec?"

"Yes, the answer is yes. For both."

The big man gave a long sigh. "So be it. Best of luck to ye, lad. Don't let her bite ye too hard."

"Hey, I don't bite."

He strode out with a snort, leaving Dowyr staring at the girl.

"What?" she asked. "I can't communicate telepathically unless you're channeling, so if you have something to say do that or use your hands."

You still haven't told me your name, Dowyr signed.

"I'm Elethe Klausgow, your Emogic instructor for the foreseeable future. It seems you've already got lessons one through three down, so congrats on being at the head of the class." She gave a brief round of applause.

Elethe, a common name. Dowyr thought it didn't fit her face, but he couldn't put words to why.

Do I have the rest of the day off then? he signed.

"Not quite. We can just skip to lesson four. If you would channel again, please."

Dowyr stared at her, unmoving from his position on the floor. What was it about her face? And then there was something to do with what she said to the big man. *Answer for what?* he signed. *Who is Garec?*

"My uncle, he runs security here at the Academy. He was just wanting me to confirm yours and someone else's Emogic and Class for his records. Could you please channel, now?"

That did not explain Donnan's unusually somber response. Not to mention, the Academy already should've known his Emogic and Class. And then there was Claire seemingly not knowing Elethe was a Class 3.9 Empath. Was she keeping how powerful she was a secret? What else was she hiding?

Finally it dawned on him why he thought her name didn't fit her face; Elethes were supposed to be trustworthy, and she had a face too pretty to trust, which was all the more evident from what she was obviously hiding. Only trouble could follow a face like that, and Dowyr wanted nothing to do with it. If only he was a Class 2.5, he could channel and search her mind for the truth. Class 2.4 and below were limited to conscious thoughts and subconscious images when using telepathy.

With little else to do, and more regret than he had ever felt before, Dowyr began to channel again.

CHAPTER 5

To Speak With a Druid

The following morning was too soon in coming. Sunlight shone on Dowyr's face through the frosted window, and there was no curtain to shut it out. Weynon was already up and brushing his teeth. He looked over as Dowyr stirred and buried his face in his pillow.

"What's the matter? Aren't you excited for another day of Emogic training?" Weynon asked.

Dowyr grumbled and pulled his blankets over his head. There was nothing to look forward to, not with that girl waiting for him. Granted, yesterday hadn't been *that* bad, but the thought of having to be around that untrustfully-pretty-faced Elethe again sent a chill down his spine. It was also Victorsday, which meant a lengthy religious class after breakfast. At least there were no classes or trainings on Sundays, so tomorrow would be a welcome break. Besides the mandatory church service.

Weynon finished his brushing and came over to pull the blankets off of Dowyr and toss up a change of clothes.

"Come on, you don't want to get a late attendance, do you?"

Dowyr sighed and started changing. It wasn't so much that he cared about his attendance, but Weynon would've stayed with him until he came, and then Weynon would've gotten late attendance too.

"I wonder why your teacher wanted me to join your class today," Weynon said as he put his school slippers on.

Dowyr fumbled his head through his shirt and gave Weynon a confused look. Elethe hadn't told him anything about that. He grabbed his journal to ask Weynon for more details.

"Dane told me that after class yesterday. He didn't say why. But I'm looking forward to seeing what you can do with Boredom."

Dowyr hummed and finished changing. Perhaps Elethe needed another person to have him use his Emogic on to practice more complicated things. At least it'd be a chance to see if he could channel the knowledge of signs directly to Weynon.

They left for breakfast, and Dowyr made sure to stack his plate full. The lunches at the Academy went heavy on the meat, so he had gotten into the habit of stuffing himself to last until dinner to avoid going to lunch altogether. Weynon always saved him some extra bread to help get through the day.

Then came the dreaded religious class. It was always difficult to decide where to sit, as Dowyr wanted to be both closest to the door and furthest from the teacher, but he couldn't have both. Today he opted for closest to the door on the corner of the front row, and Weynon sat next to him.

The teacher arrived shortly after, a young woman with a demeanor that radiated the message *everything is sunshine and divine!* Which, in Dowyr's estimation, were always the worst kind of teachers, because they would usually start with questions like—

"What are the main things we must do to maintain our connection to Heaven?" the teacher asked.

Dowyr nearly laughed. Questions exactly like that, which everybody knew the answer to and yet, somehow, nobody wanted to be the person to blurt out the obvious. So Dowyr gave Weynon a nudge before the silence got too awkward.

Weynon raised his hand and answered, "Pray, read The Five Sentinels, and follow their instructions."

"Good answer, Weynon," the teacher said as though he had spoken something profound. "But pray to who exactly?"

"All of the Sentinels themselves, Heaven, Paradise, Elysium, Valhalla, and Zion."

The teacher took a piece of chalk and began writing the Sentinels' names on the blackboard. "Correct. But we should remember when different prayers should be directed to different Sentinels. You wouldn't pray for a bountiful fall harvest from Zion, would you? And you wouldn't pray and ask Valhalla to help you to do well in a competition."

Dowyr rolled his eyes. That showed what she knew. Valhalla might have been primarily associated with knowledge, but he was also a hunter that competed with his brother Zion all the time.

The lesson continued with the teacher drawing lines between the Sentinels' names and having the class discuss what sort of things one should pray about to which Sentinel. Not that The Five Sentinels ever had anything to say about that. But in the minds of the top religious scholars, it followed that because the Sentinels were all different from each other, prayers ought to be directed at specific ones for specific things.

An hour of torture later the lesson ended, and the dreaded next form of torture loomed around the corner as Dowyr and Weynon made it up to the third floor. The classroom was empty when they arrived, however.

"*It's typical of her to be a bit late,*" Dowyr channeled to Weynon, who gave a start at the sound.

"It sounds weird when you talk like that," he said. "It's like I'm hearing you from inside my head."

"*Sorry. Is it better if I make it so it sounds like it's coming from where I'm standing like this?*"

"Yeah, much better. So do we sit down? All the desks are put away."

Dowyr shrugged and opted to just lay down on the floor and stare at the ceiling. Weynon did the same and winced.

"This isn't very comfortable."

"*Yeah. I just have a thick skull.*"

The door opened and in walked *her*.

"Good morning, my little alien..." Elethe stopped and looked down at them. "What are you two doing?"

"*I call it living in the moment,*" Dowyr channeled to her and Weynon.

"Uh huh. Living in the moment looks rather unsanitary." She came over and lowered a hand towards Weynon to help him stand up. Of course, she didn't lower a hand for Dowyr. "And you must be Weynon, right?"

Weynon gave her a smile. "Yes, nice to meet you, Miss... sorry, I forgot your name."

"You can just call me Elethe."

"Oh, okay. Thanks for inviting me, Elethe."

"Of course! I appreciate you coming." Elethe looked down at Dowyr as if to say, *look at this wonderful example of a nice boy, why can't you be more like him?*

Weynon turned to Dowyr and helped him up, and Dowyr made sure to give Elethe a look that tried to say, *why can't* you *be nice like him and help* me *up too?* Though he had never really been successful with facial communication, for some reason. He had his guesses.

"*So why did you want Weynon to join us today?*" Dowyr channeled.

"To try something I thought of last night that wouldn't work with just me, considering... what I did yesterday. Anyway, I want to see how well you can use telepathy to channel knowledge directly to someone else. In small portions to start."

What had she done yesterday that would make her idea not work? There was no way she had copied his entire brain into her own in that one short go yesterday. Was there? She was still tolerating his existence, and Snakes, even his presence. Sort of. How much did she actually know about him?

"*I can try channeling how to say a sentence with signs,*" Dowyr channeled.

"You can do that?" Weynon asked.

"No idea, but I'll give it a try."

Dowyr shifted his Emogic to telepathy and thought of how to say 'my name is Weynon' with signs, sending the knowledge through the telepathy link in such a way that it seemed firmly planted in Weynon's mind, and... well, that was it.

Weynon's reaction was immediate. He blinked a few times and looked at his hands, then signed, *my name is Weynon.* "Whoa."

"How was it?" Elethe asked. "Do you feel okay?"

Weynon nodded slowly. "Only a tiny bit dizzy."

"Interesting. Well, that's useful to know. I'm curious, before coming to the Academy, did you figure out how to use your Emogic to talk to plants or animals at all?"

"Sort of. Why?"

"Well, I read that—or, I know that it's sort of like telepathy. And I thought, humans are animals too. So shouldn't you be able to communicate with them in a telepathic way like Dowyr can?"

Weynon shook his head. "No, I've tried, and it's like talking to a wall. I think it's because what I do isn't actually telepathy, I don't really get into the mind of whatever I'm channeling to. It just lets us talk. Since I can already do that with other humans, it has no effect."

Dowyr hummed. *"I can't talk. What happens if you try it on me?"*

Weynon made a thoughtful look. "Good question." He turned and focused on Dowyr.

Nothing changed about how Dowyr felt, but then maybe Weynon was only trying to listen. *I am thinking about birds,* Dowyr thought, then channeled, *"Hear anything?"*

Weynon shook his head. "I don't think it's working."

As he spoke, the images of a few hand-signs flashed through Dowyr's mind, making him blink. They meant, more or less, exactly what Weynon had spoken.

"I think it is," Dowyr channeled, then signed, *but differently than expected.*

Weynon gaped. "I just heard... do that again!"

Once more images of signs flashed through Dowyr's mind. It struck him as odd, especially since he could hear and understand normal language just fine. He signed some more.

Talking with my hands, talking with my hands, and you can hear my hands in your head, can't you?

Weynon nodded. "Yeah, that's so weird. I wonder if it won't work when you teach me more signs."

Dowyr winced at the barrage of signs flashing through his mind. *"Okay, stop talking, it's making me see hands in my head and I don't like it."*

"Oh, sorry. I stopped channeling."

Elethe looked between the two of them with an odd smirk. "That's a rather interesting discovery. I'll have to let the Headmaster know what we figured out."

"Does this mean my name will go down in history for helping discover that Druids can talk to mutes?" Dowyr asked.

"Do you think they'd let a kid with a name like Dowyr Mawkin go down in history?"

Dowyr shrugged. *"No, but one can hope."*

"I think he should," Weynon said. "We wouldn't have figured it out without him. But I'd like to learn more signs so we don't have to use our Emogic or paper to communicate."

"You two can stick around and work on that then," Elethe said, walking to the door. "I'm gonna go nap until lunch."

Weynon stared after her. "Aren't you supposed to stay and… teach?"

"Nah, you guys can have fun messing around for a bit. Just don't break anything." She left the room, then her head popped in through the doorway. "Seriously, don't."

And then she was gone.

What an odd creature. Dowyr made his way over to the teacher's desk and climbed on top to lay down and hang his head over the side.

"I guess we can see how much I can teach you by lunch," he channeled.

Weynon nodded, still staring at the door. "I wonder how other animals communicate when I use Peace. It felt different channeling at you compared to birds."

"That's not surprising, most birds are pretty stupid. And plants don't even have brains, but you can still talk to them. What's that like?" The books Dowyr had read about Druids were plentifully detailed of the sort of things plants and animals would communicate, but there was *nothing* about what communicating with them actually felt like.

"It's hard to explain. I haven't channeled to that many plants, so maybe it's different depending on what I channel to, but it was a bit like... music. Like a million voices singing the same thing. Except for potted plants, those were just single voices, and sounded more like untuned instruments, confused about themselves. I think. There's not much they say that I know words for."

Dowyr supposed that made sense. Most Druids became involved with farming or livestock in some way as they were able to understand problems the food or animals were having and what needed to be done to solve them. And with the help of Immortals—Love Emogicians, who were able to make plants grow like it was nothing, among other things—there had almost never been a bad harvest season in the history of Elyssanar.

"Well, that's all fascinating, but let's get you talking using your hands. What do you want to learn first?"

CHAPTER 6

Lightstone Dimming News

Little over a month had passed. Dowyr was laying over the side of his bed listening to Weynon talk about his recent breakthrough in class where he managed to practically put everyone but the teacher to sleep. Peace couldn't force someone asleep, but it could relax them almost to the point of it.

I wish you could do that for me in here, Dowyr signed.

"Yeah," Weynon said. "It would be nice to channel down here, but rules are rules."

Dowyr rolled his eyes. *More like voidstones are voidstones.*

He had been able to teach Weynon all the signs he knew between Emogic lessons, or sometimes even during them as Elethe let him join occasionally. He could only give so much before Weynon became mentally exhausted by the process, so it still took the last few weeks before they could have full conversations through signs. That made Elethe absorbing all his knowledge of them in a single go all the more terrifying to him. The power of Class 4s was hard to imagine. He still wasn't sure how much she had learned about him from that, and was hesitant to ask for fear of what the answer might be. What he didn't know couldn't hurt him.

His own training sessions with Elethe had been strange. Since he had gained full control of his Emogic so quickly, all she had him do was use sensory manipulation on her to produce different kinds of illusions and sensations. In one instance, he made her see a horse enter the room, and when she went to pet it, he made her feel it too. For another session, she had him make her feel varying levels of pain. He thought she was some kind of masochist, but she claimed that it was only to know how real and intense he could make pain feel.

Strangely he felt no satisfaction in hurting her, even if it was only through sensory manipulation, not actual injuries. In some way he thought he'd be glad to make her feel like she'd been slapped in the face, but instead he cringed at every blow he inflicted. Elethe appeared to take it all with high spirits, even managing to say things like, "Wow, that was a good one!" or a strained "Holy Heaven, that stung. Nice job!"

Dowyr could only stare at her with concern. The alien was relentless. What was even more disturbing was the way he caught her staring at him, or through him more often than not. She looked to be stuck in a trance at times, her mind far away before snapping back to the classroom. He could've used telepathy to learn what was going on in her head, but she would've known what he was trying to do, and it wasn't something he was even remotely interested in to begin with. A woman's mind could remain a mystery for all he cared.

Despite his showing that he had complete control, he was still not allowed out of the Academy yet. Other teachers insisted students needed the full three months before they were trained enough to be let out. Elethe had no authority in that regard, so anything she could have said about his progress was futile. At one point she turned to playing board games with him just to use up class time, having run out of ideas for his channeling, but it didn't last long. She rarely won and accused him of cheating once or twice, though she would have known if he was channeling to win. Some days Elethe would spend the entire class period reading a book, bringing an extra for Dowyr. He rather liked those days. She usually brought something interesting to read, and sometimes he talked with her about the highlights, when she was awake anyway. Every few days she would simply fall asleep in her chair. It wasn't a surprise to him; she looked tired every day. If anyone needed Weynon's Emogic, it was her.

"Are you listening?" Weynon asked.

Dowyr blinked at him. *Yes,* he signed with a twitch of his thumb. Had he really gotten so lost in thought about classes with Elethe? No, that was impossible, he didn't like her. The sight of her face filled him with disgust.

"I can tell you're lying, but it's okay. How about we go get dinner?"

Dowyr grunted in agreement and climbed down, but upon entering the hallway, they were met with what looked like the entire school walking briskly in the opposite direction of the mess hall. Dowyr spotted Dane and caught his attention with the wave of his arms, then signed, *???*

Emergency meeting, Dane signed in return without slowing his pace. *Come. Important.*

"What do you think the emergency is?" Weynon asked.

Dowyr shrugged but began following everyone else, Weynon trailing after him. They stayed on the first floor, and eventually the rush of movement slowed as people were cramming their way into the largest auditorium in the building. A good couple minutes passed before Dowyr and Weynon found seats, and almost by luck; the room was packed to overflowing. No one was on stage, which sat below the audience on the far end of the room. The auditorium's seating was geared towards it in a half-circle, each row down a little lower than the last. Lightstones were mounted on poles around the stage and on every few levels of the stairs, glowing bright from all the movement and noise echoing from all directions as people buzzed about what was going on. Dowyr couldn't make out anything specific from what people were saying. He thought Weynon said something, but despite being right next to him, he couldn't hear.

Use signs, Dowyr signed. *Can't hear.*

Loud, Weynon signed.

Dowyr looked at him. *You're kidding.*

I don't like loud.

Me neither.

Dowyr grunted, and for not even being able to hear that, he began to repeatedly sign *shut up!* at everybody, and Weynon joined in by signing *please be quiet.* Not that anyone listened.

Light poured in from the back of the stage as a small procession made its way into view, led first by the Headmaster of the Academy holding a staff with a fist-sized lightstone mounted atop it. Following him was what looked like other important administrators, and at least three men in military uniform. He couldn't make out their faces from this distance.

As soon as the procession stopped in the middle of the stage, the commotion slowly died down until Dowyr could only make out an occasional mumbling. The Headmaster's gaze swept across the audience, and finally he spoke in a low voice.

"I wish we were not here right now. All I can say is for you to listen closely, breathe, and remember your training. There are going to be some extensive changes here at the Academy, and I hope for them to be accepted willingly and courageously. I am immensely proud to have been your Headmaster, but as of today I am humbly stepping down—" That caused some stir, to which the Headmaster—or rather, now former Headmaster—responded with a raised hand until the audience went still. "—and relinquishing my position to Colonel Aggram." He gestured to the most decorated military man. "It has been my pleasure to oversee this fine Academy, and I know it is being placed in good hands. The Colonel will now speak to you."

Weynon leaned over and whispered, "I think that's Fenton's dad."

The former Headmaster went to Aggram and handed over the lightstone-capped staff. Aggram stepped forward and spoke, his voice like a steel hammer.

"There is no way to tell you this except plainly. The reason I am replacing former Headmaster Eldredge is because we are at war." If the audience had been still before, now it was frozen. Nobody breathed.

"The country of Kircany has moved into Parastenian territory and is pushing at our southern neighbors. Our troops are being deployed to secure the border as we speak. All Emogic training is to be reorganized to focus on those of you who may prove to be essential in winning the war. There will be no turning back. Zion's Halberd has been invoked across the nation." A wave of gasps washed across the audience. Dowyr only frowned, but he could feel a bitter pit form in his stomach. Weynon had a sickening expression. There was no channeling Peace in here. Aggram continued without pause. "We will all be gathering in here tomorrow morning to begin assigning new schedules by Emogic and Class. Get some dinner in you and a good night's rest. We have a long day and a longer fight ahead of us. Sentinels be with you. Dismissed."

With the mood in the room, one would have thought he had just sent everyone to their graves. Most of the audience didn't stir for at least a minute after Aggram and the others had disappeared off stage. Noise slowly built as people began speaking with friends and classmates about the news in hushed tones. Weynon was still staring at the stage, unblinking. Dowyr reached over and grabbed his hair, giving it a sharp tug.

"Ow!" Weynon looked at him, shielding his hair. "What was that for?"

Think of hurts now, not later, Dowyr signed. *We won't be recruited until we're old enough anyway.* At least that's what he wanted to believe.

I hope that's true, Weynon signed. He looked around and finally noticed everyone getting up and leaving. "I don't think I'm hungry."

The thought of food made Dowyr realize his mouth had gone dry. *Me neither. Think I'll go straight to bed.*

Weynon nodded, and they both got up and followed everyone out. On the way back to their rooms, Dowyr wondered where Elethe was and if she knew anything more about the war. He hoped that she wouldn't immediately be sent off to fight, though considering she was a Class 3.9 Empath... well, perhaps if she was keeping that fact hidden as he suspected, then maybe...

What if that's the reason she keeps her strength a secret? Dowyr thought. It seemed a bit odd, because why would she have been avoiding being sent into a war for however long she'd been an Emogician? Unless she was just that frightened of the idea. No, that made no sense at all.

Once in bed and the room's lightstone dimmed, Dowyr found sleep difficult to come by. His mind kept spinning, bouncing back and forth between trying to understand why Elethe kept her strength a secret and what was going to happen because of the war. How much was going to change? Would he be separated from Weynon? What sort of training would he receive for the war? Everything felt up in the air, and he couldn't take his own advice of thinking of today's hurts. Tomorrow was a terrifying thing, and perhaps if he didn't sleep, it would be slower in coming.

He remembered long days back at the orphanage, when there was nothing new to read and no one to talk to. Things were simpler back then, but a life without Emogic seemed as fulfilling as eating stale bread.

On the other hand, the prospect of being sent out to war on the front lines with only a weapon or two and his Emogic didn't result in pleasant thoughts. There would be other Emogicians on the field, ones more powerful than him, ones who could cause the air to burst aflame and the earth to tear apart, or worse. Boredom was nothing compared to Rage or Fear. Should he ever cross a hostile Paranoia Emogician it would probably be best to find the quickest way to kill himself. There were reasons such Emogicians were named Apocalypses, Night Stalkers, and Nightmares.

"Are you still awake?" Weynon asked.

Dowyr nearly jumped out of bed at the sound, but he composed himself and hummed in reply.

"I don't think I can sleep. I don't think I want to sleep. Maybe there are people dying right now, and I'm trying to fall asleep. I don't like it."

Dowyr hummed again and climbed down, his movement causing the lightstone to brighten enough to see hand movements. He made sure Weynon was looking at him and signed, *people are always dying.*

"I mean getting killed… you know… fighting. I don't know. I'm a Class 3 Druid, what if I could stop some of it? I could help people. And nature. Animals don't like… you know. I should be able to do something."

You will. Just keep being you.

"What's that supposed to mean?"

Dowyr shrugged. *Hard to explain with signs.* The lightstone was already beginning to dim, so he quickly signed *remember Elysium 8:31* before climbing back into bed. Though he didn't care for The Five Sentinels, he at least hoped reminding Weynon of one of the more encouraging passages could help ease his mind.

As for his own mind, he wasn't sure what to think about to ease it. Zion's Halberd being invoked was what he kept coming back to. He didn't believe in the religious concept, but there were real-world consequences executed by those who did believe in it. At its core it simply meant, no running from the fight. Not a step back. If you ran away and were caught, you were arranged to be killed on a battlefield. If you somehow escaped a second time, you were killed on the spot to await Zion's judgment. You give it your all for the righteous cause or die trying. Dowyr desperately wanted to run away from that. The religious fervor of Zion's Halberd was a bottomless pit.

I'll just trick them, Dowyr thought. *I'll trick them to think I'm dead and escape.*

How he was going to do that, he didn't know.

CHAPTER 7

Flight From the Academy

The time was roughly two hours before dawn, and Elethe was wide awake. Or maybe thin awake? It was a mystery why states of awake-ness were measured by space like that. As odd as her sole student. Although it wasn't as if Dowyr was a mystery to her after the first time she used his Emogic on him. Everything about who he was and why was all there for her to understand. She had laughed at first, given the absurdity of his character, but then she cried herself to sleep that night as the reality of his life sunk in. How did he bring himself to wake up every morning? She could hardly do it herself. And knowing what was going to happen to him soon… it had kept her up a number of nights over the last month.

She had managed to not fall asleep during class today—a small victory to her—but right now, after tossing and turning all night, she wished she had. Colonel Aggram becoming the Headmaster and announcing the war wasn't news to her; she had known about it since the day before, and had known about the war itself for at least two months. Another thing that hadn't helped her sleep. Somehow its official announcement had not lessened her anxiety like she expected, but rather made it worse. That had to be from all the anxiety she was feeling from everyone else. Of all the Emogics voidstones prevented from being channeled, Empathy was not one of them. Or at least, an Empath's ability to sense other people's emotions wasn't. It was constantly there whether Elethe liked it or not. And at a time like this, it was the worst of curses.

She gave a start at her door opening, and the movement of a large person entering and striding towards her made the lightstones brighten enough for her to recognize him. Her uncle Garec, still dressed in the military uniform he wore at the announcement.

"It's time," he said bluntly. "Get your things, we're going right now."

That shot a spike of acid into Elethe's stomach.

"So soon?" she asked breathlessly, getting out of bed and trying to move quickly to put on an extra layer of clothes and grab whatever extras she could pack away in a sack.

"There's no better time. By tomorrow afternoon the Academy will be swarming with soldiers and there'll be an extensive night patrol. I've received orders to send my troops to Fort Calhoun by next week, and I'm not waiting."

"But it hasn't been three months yet, and I thought—"

"Plans changed. Donnan's got a cart of barrels with some gags."

Elethe's mind was spinning, but she had packed all she needed and followed Garec as he marched out of her room and down the empty, dimly-lit hall. The lightstones hardly brightened from their passing. It wasn't cold, but Elethe shivered nonetheless.

"You'll only need... well, no, nevermind." She was going to say he only needed one gag, and it took her a moment to remember Dowyr could still make plenty of noise with his mouth. He just couldn't get it to form words.

Garec gave her a sidelong glance but marched on, his pace nearly causing her to jog. He was a little more than a head taller than her, and she resented inheriting her mother's shortness.

They descended the stairs from second to first floor and met up with Donnan in the student hall. Sitting beside him was a small cart that held two barrels which he watched with a grim look.

"Everything good?" Garec whispered.

"Aye," Donnan grumbled. "Let's get this over with."

They moved down the hall, Donnan pushing the cart slowly to make as little noise as possible. He gave Elethe a worried look as she swayed.

"Did ye get enough sleep?" he asked softly.

"Didn't really get any," Elethe sighed.

He grimaced. "I'm sorry, lass. Need my strength for the cart, otherwise I'd carry ye."

Elethe gave a weak smile. "It's okay, I'll live."

"Here," Garec snapped. "This is the room. Elethe, my wagon is outside the stable. Get the horses ready, we'll be right there."

Elethe nodded and swiftly but silently made her way out of the Academy and to the stable. No guards were around to question her, presumably Garec's work. The stable-boys were awake and conversing quietly about the news, but were glad for the work of saddling horses to take their minds off of it. They asked no questions, and Elethe didn't offer any reasons.

Shortly after the horses were readied, Garec and Donnan appeared with the cart. A colorless aura emanated from Garec as he channeled Indifference towards the barrels. Each Emogic had a different color to Elethe's eyes, but Indifference had none. Instead, it looked like a stream that made anything seen through it look gray and dead. Elethe took a step back from the Emogic, as if it was diseased. She had tried Matching it once, but Indifference tasted horribly bitter and was impossible for her to use.

She looked to Garec as he approached. "How long are we—"

"Until I say," Garec said, cutting her off. "Get the horses hooked up while we load them in."

Elethe grimaced but led the horses to the wagon that sat just outside the stable. It was a simple thing, with room for two at the reins and the back of it covered with a canopy of white canvas. The horses fidgeted somewhat as Elethe got them hooked up to it, but she stroked their snouts and spoke softly to calm them down. She may not have been a Druid, but her father had always said she had a special way with animals. She liked to think she took after her older brother in that regard. If only he could've been here too. He'd have been able to think of something to say to cheer her up.

Two dull *thuds* came from the back of the wagon as the barrels were loaded in. Garec climbed up to the front seat and took the reins, motioning for Elethe to get in the back with Donnan. She did so, putting her sack in first then sitting across from Donnan with a frown for the barrels that sat between them. Garec flicked the reins, and off they went, into the encroaching dawn.

"When can we let them out?" Elethe asked softly.

"Soon," Donnan said, trying to be just as soft, but for him that was like trying to make a stone soft. "When we reach the Company outside the city."

"I wish we didn't have to do this."

"Neither do I," Garec said. "But it may be our only hope. If everything goes according to plan, we'll all return as heroes."

"Aye," Donnan said gravely. "Halberd's stroke or no, I'll not wait around for our enemies te come to me."

Elethe clasped her neck and swallowed. Zion's Halberd had been invoked; there was no turning away, no escape from duty, not one step back. It made her wonder just how bad things were.

"Which is why they'll never suspect us coming," Garec said firmly. "Kircany thinks we're as soft as the Parastenians. They've had ample reason for the last decade. But I'm done with that reputation. We'll deal them a surprise blow even if I have to battle Zion himself."

"I'll pray it doesn't come te that," Donnan said with a short chuckle. "Couldn't think he'd be too happy fighting someone with stubbornness te match Elysium herself."

Despite everything—the cold, the dark, the bumpy wagon, the war, and their destination—despite all of it, Elethe smiled. If her uncle was confident, and Donnan making light of his stubborn will, then things would be okay. Heaven was on their side, and so the war would be won, and they would be the ones who won it.

"Try to get some rest," Garec said. "Any sleep is better than none."

Elethe nodded lethargically and let her head rest back against the canvas. She closed her eyes, but sleep would not come. The jolts and bumps of the wagon were too much, and her mind was filled with the sound of clattering hooves and wheels on cobbled streets mixed with a distant chorus of crickets' chirping. All the city was quiet otherwise.

Time passed, and Elyssanar was left behind.

Traces of light were just appearing on the eastern horizon as the wagon entered a small military camp a short distance off the road. Despite the hour, it was bustling with activity; men taking down tents, putting out fires, packing wagons, and readying horses.

A soldier approached the wagon as it came to a stop and saluted with a hand to his chest. "Welcome back, Sir. We'll be ready to deploy within the hour."

"Good," Garec said, not even a trace of fatigue in his voice. He had maintained channeling the whole way. Not an overly impressive feat, as he was Class 3.1, and likely could channel at only two people for hours without needing to rest. "Our first stop is Hodsun. I want to set a pace that will get us to Fort Mordon by Sunday. Let the other officers know."

"Yes, Sir. We will ride with the blessing of Elysium."

The soldier marched off, and in the same moment Donnan climbed out of the wagon and began to help pack up camp.

"Can we let them out now?" Elethe asked.

"Yes, I need to talk with them," Garec said, hopping over the front seat and standing over the barrels. With a twist of the lid handles he opened them, and two terrified young boys stared up at him.

CHAPTER 8

Conscription Day

Dowyr's heart pounded as he tried to make sense of what was happening. Back at the Academy, he had managed to fall asleep, only for what felt like moments later to be awoken by rough hands grabbing him. By the time he had a mind to fight back, he and Weynon were already bound and getting stuffed into barrels. He had hoped that wherever they were being taken he would be able to channel, but Boredom remained blocked off. Who would be going to such lengths to kidnap them? The only reason he could think of was something to do with the war, but even that made no sense for them to be kidnapped. They'd be sent off to it anyway, wouldn't they?

After being jostled around for what felt like hours, everything stopped. He had heard voices throughout his kidnapping, but muffled and unintelligible. Only now did he hear something loud enough to understand.

"Yes, I need to talk with them."

He heard the lid of the barrel shifting and turned his head up as much as he could. The smallest amount of light spilled in, and two faces stared down at him. He was surprised to recognize one of them. Thick arms reached in and pulled him out of the barrel as if he were as light as a feather and placed him on the side bench of a covered wagon. He stared at Elethe as the man pulled Weynon out and sat him on the opposite side.

Sorry, Elethe signed with a sad but guilty expression.

The man leaned against the front wagon seat and looked between Dowyr and Weynon. "I'm sorry for the rough introduction. I didn't want things to start this way, but I ran out of time. First of all, I'm not your enemy, you don't need to be afraid, but I understand if you feel otherwise. The war scares us all. That's why Zion's Halberd was invoked. Today is Conscription Day in Elyssanar, but for us it's day one of ending the war. I stole you boys from the Academy because I need you. Your records have been scratched, no one in the city knows where you are, and no one will come trying to find you. If you try to run, my men will catch you, but I promise you won't be subjected to the Halberd by my hand. You're too important to me. From here on you are under my complete protection. You may call me Garec or Captain, whichever you prefer. I need to see to some things with my men before we leave, but Elethe will answer any of your questions."

Garec nodded to Elethe then climbed out of the wagon. Dowyr stared after him then looked back at Elethe and she moved to undo Weynon's gag. Dowyr stared daggers at her as she came to undo his. Too pretty a face to trust indeed.

"I'm so sorry about this," Elethe said. "I never wanted to hurt either of you, but it was the only way to… *please* try to understand." Was she crying? "We're trying to help. Garec took you to *save* you. The Academy was going to send all Emogicians with enough training to the war, no matter how young."

Dowyr was still blocked from channeling, and he couldn't respond with signs while his hands were tied behind his back. He moved his arms up and down, and Elethe carefully untied the cords.

After shaking and stretching his hands, he signed, *we're still going to the war, how is this different?*

"My uncle has a plan, and—"

What sort of plan? An escape plan?

Elethe hesitated. "No. I don't know all the details, but our plan is to sneak into Kircany to kill or capture the man leading the war. I know that you two won't be doing any fighting. He just needs your Emogics to help lead us to him."

Dowyr gaped. *How in Hell's name is he going to pull that off without his superiors stopping him? Or was he ordered to do this?*

"No, he wasn't ordered. As for how, those are the details I don't know about."

Dowyr grunted and finally noticed Weynon was still bound and staring off into nothing. Grabbing onto one of the barrels, Dowyr pulled himself up and hopped over to sit next to him and untied his hands, then waved a hand in front of his face to get his attention before signing, *are you okay?*

Weynon nodded shortly.

Now you're the one lying.

Weynon ignored him and looked at Elethe. "Why can't I channel?"

"My uncle Garec is a Voidspeaker," Elethe said. "He'll keep blocking you until he knows you won't channel against us."

"I won't."

"I know, but it's not me you have to convince."

Voidspeaker? Dowyr signed. *What Class?*

"Class 3.1. He's the Captain of Second Assault Company. Donnan is his second-in-command if you remember him."

Dowyr nodded and laid his head back with a sigh. He was still tired, and sleep felt so far away. Trying to adjust into a comfortable position was difficult with his legs still bound, so he signed, *can we untie our legs?*

"I won't stop you," Elethe said softly. "Remember what Garec said? You can run without worrying about the Halberd. But he'll still bring you back."

Dowyr grimaced and untied himself and Weynon. He knew Weynon wouldn't run off no matter what, and Dowyr knew when it was hopeless. There was no running, at least not while he couldn't channel. No, not even if he could channel. He couldn't manage the number of people who might come after him, and he couldn't out-range Garec long enough. There really was no running.

The grim reality made him shiver.

"I can help them," Weynon said, his voice unusually strong. "I can help stop people from fighting."

"That's exactly why ye're here," a new voice said, startling the three of them. Donnan stood outside the wagon, and he took the barrels out to be replaced with crates filled with supplies. "Why we're all here; te stop people from fighting. Not a job for the faint of heart though, ye need to be strong, mighty like Zion, fierce like Elysium. There lay the only way te freedom. Valhalla speaks it true: the weak wail behind the bars of their own working."

"I want to be strong," Weynon said. "I just don't know how."

"Believe first. And pay attention te the Captain; he's the strongest man I know."

"But he's a Voidspeaker."

Donnan barked a cold laugh. "We're more than our Emogics, lad. Ye might want te ask him about his Apex though. There's more to him than meets the eye." He reached down and threw another sack into the wagon. "New clothes for ye both. Ye may want te get changed before we head out, no reason for anyone te think ye're runaway students."

With that he walked off, leaving the two boys looking between the sack and Elethe, who gave an exhausted sigh and climbed out of the wagon and out of sight.

"It's cold," Weynon said as he began to change.

Winter will be here soon, Dowyr signed while looking through the sack to see what might fit him. *At least there are coats.*

"Do you think we'll reach the fighting before it snows?"

Dowyr pulled off his shirt and shrugged. *The border is about 800 kilometers away. It will take a month to get at least that far, maybe longer.*

Weynon finished changing into a plain coat and thick wool britches. "Maybe they have a Jumper."

"Not a Jumper to be found in Elyssanar," a new voice called. The boys looked out of the wagon to find a young man holding a tent bundle. "They're rare. Arkonia might have some low-Class ones. Kircany probably does too, and we can only hope they don't have high class Empaths. This is for you." He set the tent bundle inside the wagon. "The Captain said he'd found the last two boys for his plan. So, what are you? A Seer and Booster to help us avoid problems?"

"I'm a Class 3 Druid," Weynon said. "My friend Dowyr is a Class 2.2 Mind Intruder. He can't speak."

The man looked at them quizzically. "Peace and Boredom, huh? Not sure I understand that when he's got me and the big man. I'm Corporal Henric Dexund by the way. Let me take your Academy clothes, they need to be burned before we leave."

Dowyr had finished changing into the same as Weynon so he bundled up his Academy clothes and tossed them to Henric. He was surprised when they passed right through him and vanished into the ground. Henric looked even more confused, then a look of realization dawned on his face and he turned away with a roar.

"DONNAN!"

A chorus of laughter came in response, and Henric shook his head with his own laugh. "That's the Lieutenant for you. He's a Class 3.4 Ghost. Word of advice: tread lightly with the big man. Ghosts are scary as Hell, so don't piss one off unless you're willing to lose some internal organs."

Dowyr pursed his lips and let his imagination wander for a moment about the things a Ghost could do, and quickly decided to never try upsetting Donnan ever again. Ghosts, which used the Emogic of Yearning, could astral project and phase any physical material, including themselves, in order to move through solid objects. It was widely known to be one of the more dangerous Emogics. One couldn't walk through walls while using it without falling through the ground, so the only way was to jump. Timing was everything.

What sort of Emogician is Henric? Dowyr signed to Weynon, who asked the question after tossing him his clothes.

"Seducer, Class 1.2. Nothing special. One might think poorly of a Lust Emogician, buuuuut... well, let's just say it wasn't your typical Apex of Lust. Garec brought me on board a year back to be his interrogator, though so far my skills of persuasion have gone unused. Who knows, maybe that will change soon. Gotta run now. You boys sit tight."

Dowyr sat down with an impatient sigh. The sun was just on the verge of appearing over the horizon, and the camp was almost completely taken down. He spotted Garec moving about his men, occasionally glancing in his direction.

"When do you think we'll get to have breakfast?" Weynon asked.

Dowyr shrugged, but he still didn't feel hungry. Hopefully his appetite would return at some point.

I'm going for a walk, he signed. Too much was swirling around in his head to feel at ease, and he wanted to stretch his legs after being crammed into a barrel for so long, so he jumped out of the wagon and began to walk around. He didn't get far before Elethe appeared out of thin air at his side.

"Where are you going?" she asked.

Nowhere, Dowyr signed.

"Nowhere no longer exists. Haven't you read The Five Sentinels?"

Dowyr stopped in his tracks to give her the most annoyed look he could manage. The Five Sentinels and its fictional blank land of Nowhere was the last thing on his mind. Elethe wore a slight smirk, but it faded quickly.

"I hope you know that I really am sorry about all this," she said, and even managed to sound genuine. "When I learned that you were a Boredom Emogician, my uncle arranged for me to teach you. I didn't want to, but he was going to be taking you either way. All three of us, you, me, and Weynon. I'm supposed to be his secret weapon, I think." She glanced around and lowered her voice. "Only a handful of people know I'm Class 3.9. Most think I'm Class 2, and it's better that way. My family didn't want the church to find out how powerful I am because they might try to take me away, and we don't want to risk letting our enemies know either. They'd send assassins or something like that. Please promise me you won't say... or sign anything to anyone about this."

Dowyr stared at her in mild shock. *Assassins* were the reason she had been keeping that a secret? It sounded a bit extreme, but he supposed that was understandable in wartime. Worrying about the church finding out was entirely reasonable, of course.

Okay, he signed. *I promise. But only if you convince the Captain to let me and Weynon channel again.*

Elethe sighed with relief. "Sure. Easier signed than done, but I'll do what I can."

She walked off to find Garec, and Dowyr decided his legs felt fine and there was no reason to continue his stroll. Returning to the wagon, he found Weynon still sitting inside, lost in thought staring at the floor. He looked up as Dowyr climbed in.

"That was quick," he said.

I got bored, Dowyr signed with a brief smile. *You good?*

Weynon nodded. "I don't think I like Conscription Day."

Dowyr clicked his tongue. *You mean day one of ending the war.*

"I guess." He leaned back against the wagon and sighed. "I know I might be able to help stop people from fighting, but I wish none of this was happening. Is it wrong to just want to go home?"

Dowyr sat next to him and shrugged. He thought of the orphanage, the only thing that had amounted to a home in his mind. Nothing about it gave him any desire to return. Seeing the world, even one at war, was far more exciting than returning to that life. But he worried what might become of the other orphans with news of the war. Would they be forced into the military? Or be put to working farms, smithies, or mines? Anything seemed likely, especially with Zion's Halberd invoked. Not even children escaped the Halberd. He may not have particularly liked the other children there, but they didn't deserve that. Some of them were so young they wouldn't understand what was happening. Most of them, really. Dowyr had been the oldest, and easily the smartest.

An unexpected rush of guilt overcame him, and he began to cry.

I want to go home too, he signed.

Interlude 1

A Load of Lightstone

Vinsk held loosely to the reins of his wagon's horses as the low rolling hills of Parasten's countryside slowly drifted by. Behind him ran a caravan of more wagons, all of them hauling a load of raw lightstone mined from the western mountains of Elyssanar. Lightstone was always transported raw to major cities, where they had craftsmen, lightsmiths, to do the fine tuning of its shape and reactivity. Some lightstones had to be tuned for public roads, more sensitive and longer lasting, and others for indoor use, shorter or longer lasting depending on room function. Bathroom-tuned ones were such a pain when dealing with troublesome bowel movement as they would dim before one finished doing their business. At least there was never anyone to see you when you flailed your arms about like an idiot to bring the light back.

Such was the world of lightstone. Vinsk had always wanted to be a lightsmith growing up, but he had never managed to develop the proper sleight of hand to do so. Too much roughhousing during his youth had ruined his muscle memory, so he suspected. He was much better at carrying the stone or breaking it into little pieces, which wasn't all that useful for lighting buildings. But he was proud to at least play a small part in its creation.

A little squeak came from the hamster sitting on his right shoulder, busily brushing at furry cheeks with tiny paws.

"It's not much further, Peek," Vinsk said, glancing at the hamster. "We should be coming into view of Irostead soon. Once we drop off the load, it's off to the nicest inn for a good night's rest and treats to boot!"

Peek twitched his nose and laid down in contentment. The fluffy rodent had been his constant companion ever since he began his trade as a caravan master. He had found him alone on the roadside on the very first trip to deliver lightstone, looking rather down on his luck, if a hamster could be said to look such a way. Peek had taken to him quickly after a share of his afternoon snack, and the rest was history.

As for their destination, the Parastenian city of Irostead, Vinsk felt more than a little uneasy, though he tried not to let it show for Peek's sake. And the rest of the caravan, he supposed. Irostead was only a little over a hundred kilometers from the border of Kircany, and news of the war had reached his caravan halfway into their journey. More and more he expected a group of Kircans to come sweeping down on them from the sky or popping up over the next hill, but he hadn't seen a single sign of them. Of course, he was taking a back road, one not well known to any but Parastenians and merchants. So perhaps they were safe. As long as Irostead was still in Parastenian hands, it would be an uneventful trip. But knowing Parastenians and their nonviolent ways...

Well, he pushed it to the back of his mind. This load of lightstone had to be delivered one way or another. It was rare that Parasten's cities ever had lightstone deliveries made to them. They tended to rely on fire for their light, to the point where most villages the caravan passed didn't have a single lightstone. Only the major cities, and even those only for the busiest streets and buildings. But there was a sort of charm to that. Parastenians were a very warm people, and their fires were a signature cultural part of that.

Once again Peek stirred on his shoulder, lifting his head and giving an uneasy chitter.

"What is it, Peek? Smell something?" Vinsk asked.

Peek scurried down his arm and chittered even more nervously. Vinsk took him into his hands and raised him to eye level.

"Slow down, use your words carefully and tell me what the matter is."

Peek looked at him, nose flittering, and gave a squeak before burying his face into Vinsk's palm. Something was wrong.

Carefully setting Peek down on his lap, Vinsk pulled at the reins and called for the caravan to stop. The wrongness became apparent the moment the wagon wheels rolled to a halt; the wagon was still shaking. Horses from the caravan whinnied anxiously.

A rider came up beside the wagon, Vinsk's assistant Dinah. "What's going on?" she asked, giving him a nervous look as she tried to control the dancing of her horse.

"I don't know," Vinsk said, putting Peek into his coat pocket and standing up. "Let me on, I want to see what's over the next hill."

Dinah scooted forward and Vinsk hopped on behind her. Kicking the horse forward at a steady trot, it was only a minute before cresting the hill and seeing what was causing all the ruckus.

Vinsk's heart sank into his stomach.

In the distance was the city of Irostead, and rising out of its center was a colossal earthen pillar, at least three kilometers thick going by the shadow it cast across the city. It rose higher and higher, brightly colored buildings tumbling off the top, stretching ten kilometers tall before stopping as if frozen in place.

And then, it fell like a tree.

The pillar broke apart as it came down, massive chunks of dirt and rock crushing entire neighborhoods and markets. The earth shook, and Vinsk shook with it.

Another spear of earth pierced through the city, just as large as the one before. And another, and another. Mountains began piling up. In some places it looked as though the mouth of Hell opened and began swallowing streets and all who walked them. Vinsk could hear nothing of Dinah's wailing or Peek's chittering, only the rumbling as earth met city.

An eternity seemed to pass before it all came to a stop, and there was no longer any sign of there ever being an Irostead. Just mounds and spikes and crevices of earth beneath a cloud of dust. Dinah was trying to hold back her sobbing, and Vinsk was barely able to manage it himself. All those people, who wouldn't raise a fist to harm another no matter the circumstance, gone. Why? In the names of Heaven, Paradise, and all the Sentinels, *why?*

"You must go back to Elyssanar ahead of the caravan," Vinsk whispered into Dinah's ear. "You *must* tell them. Kircany has a Class 4 Apocalypse. *Swear* to me you will tell them."

Dinah nodded fervently. "I swear on my life and the Halberd."

"Good," Vinsk sighed, then climbed off.

Dinah turned her horse around. "Where should I meet you?"

"The usual," Vinsk said. "Go now."

She hesitated, then kicked her horse into a gallop without looking back. Vinsk stared after her until she disappeared beyond the rolling hills. The caravan started up towards him as she passed.

"Well, Peek..." Vinsk said, taking the hamster out and setting him on his shoulder. "...it looks like we have a new job to do."

The caravan arrived at the top of the hill and everyone took in the view. They had probably seen the pillars rise into the sky, but Vinsk was glad they hadn't seen them crashing down onto the city.

He climbed onto the nearest wagon and stood on its bench, facing towards everyone.

"Unload the lightstone!" he roared. "Cut down every tree in sight and load them in its place. We are going down to Irostead to find all the bodies we can and give them a proper Parastenian pyre burial. If there aren't enough trees, we'll use our wagons. Their fires welcomed us and lit our souls alight, and so we will light our own and let the flames carry their souls to forever rest in the embrace of Paradise!"

Everyone was silent for a moment, then each began unloading a load of lightstone.

CHAPTER 9

Whispers

You're not very talkative, are you? Hell whispered in Garec's mind. *But then, few people are with me. It's a shame. I'm a great conversationalist.*

Garec ignored him, as he always did when channeling. Or rather, he kept his focus on the task in front of him. Easier now than the hours it took to arrive, at least. The Company was almost finished packing, and he was running through the checklists with his officers. Not that he really felt it necessary; his men knew what they were doing, and they always did it well. He'd come to expect nothing less. Some days he felt as though his role as a Captain was just to put on appearances.

I need to be grateful for these times, he thought to himself. *There won't be many of them soon enough.*

Many? I think you mean any, Hell said. *It's all going to fall apart. You'll go out and get everyone killed, and people will wonder what ever happened to you. A great plan, if you ask me. There need to be more men out there like you.*

You are far more annoying than The Five Sentinels makes you out to be, Garec thought.

Why thank you. I do tend to take on the personality that most irks the person I'm speaking with. Frankly I can't help it, it's just part of my nature. The fact I'm even explaining this to you is part of it. But I do love showing off, so maybe that's not the only factor. Actually, that's a lie. Actually, that is too. Everything is a lie. You already knew that. Useless, useless, useless information.

Garec rolled his eyes. He was tempted to stop channeling right then, but he wanted to speak with the boys one more time before doing so. Elethe had appeared at his side asking when he would stop, and he assured her it would be only a few minutes. With another checklist out of the way, he headed back towards his wagon.

You know, just because it takes your Emogic for you to hear me doesn't mean I can't influence others anywhere in the world at any time, Hell said with a sort of smugness. *Your commanding officers, your soldiers, your niece, those boys. I'll tell you what I'll do to them if you ask.*

Garec smiled. *I'll ask if you tell me why you're afraid of Victory.*

That was met with a good deal of expletives. Victory was a strange man in The Five Sentinels that, for no discernable reason, had a small section dedicated to short stories he supposedly told Heaven and the other Sentinels. Hell never responded well when Garec thought of him, though it was a mystery as to why.

Making it to the back of his wagon, he found the two boys sitting next to each other. Dowyr looked at him with caution in his eyes, but Weynon looked almost eager.

If those aren't the faces of kids who will ruin this whole thing, I don't know what are, Hell said.

"I want to know I can trust you two with your Emogics," Garec said. "And I also want you to trust me, however difficult that might be for you. I'm willing to answer any of your questions as honestly as I can to do so."

Dowyr nudged Weynon and signed something to him. Weynon looked back at Garec.

"Why us? What do you need our Emogics for?" he asked.

You don't need them for anything, you vain imbecile, Hell said.

"Information," Garec said. "Being able to gain information through nature, as you can do Weynon, or through enemies we might come across using Dowyr's telepathy and sensory manipulation. Mind reading will be essential."

Dowyr signed to Weynon again.

"Won't your commanding officers try to stop you?" Weynon asked. "How will we escape Elyssanar?"

As stupid as they are, they're not stupid enough to let you succeed, Hell said.

"I'm sure they would, if they knew," Garec said. "I don't intend for them to know. I'm trusting you, and all my men, to keep our plan a secret. As for how… I'm not sure yet, though I imagine with Dowyr's help it should be easy enough."

"Will we get to come back home some day?" Weynon asked.

Nope, Hell said.

"That's what I intend," Garec said.

Hell laughed. *Way to skirt the truth. I approve.*

Dowyr signed to Weynon once again, though Weynon gave him an odd look this time.

"Why do you want to know that?" Weynon asked him.

More signs.

"I guess that makes sense." Weynon turned back to Garec. "What's your favorite animal?"

Garec gave a slight frown, mildly caught off guard at the question. Why *did* Dowyr want to know that?

Snakes, Hell said.

Garec snorted at Hell's answer. "I'd have to say cats. Dogs have never been very fond of me for some reason."

That's a weirdly roundabout way of saying snakes, Hell said.

Garec was about ready to cut his channeling, but there was one last thing he wanted to say. "I won't ask you to do as I say or swear you'll help me, but I hope for the sake of ending this war before it can really start, you'll join me willingly. If you really want to go back to the Academy, I'll let you. But consider that you might be in for a worse fate if you do."

Couldn't have said it more manipulatively myself, Hell said.

"I'm staying," Weynon said without hesitation. He turned to Dowyr. "We need to help."

Dowyr didn't look too pleased, but he gave Garec a serious look for a moment before giving a thumbs-up.

You can't trust them, Hell said. *There's no way these kids want to come with you to get themselves ki—*

Garec cut his channeling and shut the mouth of Hell. "Thank you. I'll do everything in my power to make all this as comfortable as I can for you."

A voice came from Dowyr's direction, though his mouth didn't move. *"I guess I won't ask you to get me a dog. Just as long as I don't have to eat meat, I'll be happy."*

Garec smiled. "That's doable."

That voice must have been Dowyr's channeling. Interesting. It wasn't the sort of voice he expected him to have, but then he could have any voice he wanted. Even Garec's. If he really wanted to, he could probably fool the officers into believing he was allowed to leave.

Garec wanted to trust him, but Elethe would have to keep an eye on him for the time being. A whisper repeated in his mind.

You can't trust them.

We'll see, Garec thought back at it.

*

It was late afternoon when the falling dust and ash touched the hill upon which Royce Tyrden stood. He took long, deep breaths, mildly fatigued from channeling to such a great extent. There was a sort of art to Rage. The energy of it was rabid and indiscriminate, like that of a lightning storm. With it he bent the skies and the earth, the rivers and the lakes. No mountain was too large he could not move, no valley too deep he could not raise. There was not a more fitting name the world could attribute to one who wielded Rage; Royce was the living definition of an Apocalypse. After today, everyone would know him as an avatar of destruction. And what could Heaven or any of the Sentinels do about it? Not even the Snakes would be so feared once Royce was done.

Fear was not what Royce wanted, however. What he wanted, what he *needed*, was vengeance against Heaven and his pathetic world. How was it that Heaven, a being said to be filled with all that was good, could create a place with so much cruelty, injustice, idiocy, and lies? This could not be Heaven's world. It was Hell's. Voidspeakers claimed he said as much himself, and that was all the proof Royce needed. Existence itself must have known something was wrong, and so it had gifted him the power of the Apocalypse. He was the embodiment of Existence's rage against Heaven. With it he would save everyone from this nightmare and restructure the world into the Garden of Paradise it should have been from the beginning.

It was his divine calling.

His brother Roderick stepped up beside him, gazing upon Royce's work with a look of solemn satisfaction. Roderick was much older than him, being thirty-one, twelve years his elder. Roderick had climbed the military ranks quickly, having become a highly respected strategist through a series of successful campaigns against northern rebellions vying for control over the Great Eastern Lakes, and so he was Royce's general.

"Damn Parastenians should have listened," Roderick said, his voice hard. "Perhaps the rest will see reason from now on."

Royce sniffed in disgust. "If they don't, I will give it to them, or they will die."

"There's no need for further examples. Word of this will spread, and the fear of it will shake the nations."

"Existence wills it."

Roderick folded his arms. "Don't get ahead of yourself, Royce. You're the key to winning, but you cannot win alone. We need greater numbers if we are to reach Elyssanar properly, and if the Parastenians do not come willingly, we will simply have to take them."

"Do you think we can hold off Arkonia in the meantime? Their unexpected harrying is a nuisance, and I cannot build a wall across an entire border." Not in one day, at least.

"I'm not concerned about them unless they start to show some real effort. Which wouldn't surprise me after today. But if you can divert the Missionary River to cut down their water supply, we can use that as a bargaining tool for them to leave us alone."

Royce waved a dismissive hand. "Child's play."

Roderick gave a nod. "Good. A new lake south of Florissant would be nice. Prepare to leave tomorrow morning. I'll go find you an escort."

"You're staying behind?"

Roderick turned back down the hill. "I have some things to take care of with the Parastenian capital, but I should return within the week."

Royce was left to admire his work. Before him were the ruins of a city that might as well have never existed. All that remained were towering spikes of earth thrown every which way, kilometer-long mounds burying entire neighborhoods, chasms that swallowed up marketplaces. From afar it appeared as though the skin of the land had been pierced and replaced with a rugged scab. Ash and dust clouds rose above it all, mixing with the echoes of a collective terrorized cry from Irostead's citizens, and slowly fading to mere whispers.

CHAPTER 10

The Silence of Winter

One week had passed since the caravan began its journey, leaving the mountains of Elyssanar far behind. Dry yellow grasslands stretched in all directions to empty horizons, but a sliver of green pierced through it by a narrow, east-flowing river called the Pilgrim. It ran all the way to the border before flowing into the larger Missionary River that led southeast through Parasten, into Kircany, then turning sharply south into Arkonia. The highway road followed the Pilgrim, passing through villages and larger towns alike.

A cold breeze blew against Elethe while she sat on the driver's seat of a wagon next to the only other woman in the Company, Sirona, Donnan's older half-sister; no northern accent, and not nearly of the same stature as him, but surprisingly twice as hard at times. She was a Class 1.6 Healer, the one Compassion Emogician to treat any wounded. For Elethe she was like a strict aunt, but in a good way. Sirona tolerated no nonsense and let you know it, but it was plain that she cared about the wellbeing of those around her.

As if to prove it, she turned to Elethe and asked, "Did you get enough sleep last night?"

"Yes," Elethe lied, and felt guilty for it so she quickly added *something* that was true. "More than usual, thankfully."

"I've noticed you haven't been eating much."

"I'm just not that hungry. Food is… gross."

A mischievous look crossed Sirona's face. "Ah, gross. So, are you absorbing manna from Heaven? Nursing from the breast of Paradise?"

"Okay, ew, why would you give me that mental image? But no." Elethe took a deep breath. "I'm fine, just not hungry."

Sirona nodded. "A lot on your mind. You know what I did when I was your age and things weren't going my way?"

Elethe looked at her expectantly.

"I cried." Sirona looked at her disappointed face and grinned. "It took a long time before I got practiced at holding it in. Took longer to realize it didn't help at all, and *that's* when you really cry."

Elethe shrugged. "I think I'm all out of tears."

"If you ever find some more, I'm sure Donnan is willing to lend a shoulder, cause I'm keeping mine all to myself. Though you should really use your uncles' more than anyone's. Have you talked with him much?"

Elethe winced, as she had not. It wasn't as if she didn't like him. Garec was her favorite uncle of the five she had, but lately she felt disconnected from him, as though an invisible wall had been put up between them. The wall had been there since fleeing the Academy, and she blamed it on the guilt over kidnapping Dowyr and Weynon. They seemed to be doing just fine, but it still stung knowing what she was partially responsible for putting them through.

"You should speak with him when we stop tonight," Sirona continued. "Family is your first line of support. I know things like this can break people apart, but they can also bring them closer together."

"I know," Elethe sighed. "I don't want to feel broken apart. He's just so busy."

"So busy that you can't speak with him? Elethe, do you really know that for truth or did you make it up?"

Elethe cringed and turned away. "I made it up. Sorry."

"It's not me you need to apologize to. Didn't your parents teach you right? You must never lie, to any degree, to others *or* yourself. Lying makes you weak. Consequences cannot be avoided through lies, only delayed, and delayed consequences build interest. When they finally come, you have weakened yourself to the point that they will crush you. Only the truth makes you strong. Only the truth sets you free."

"Okay, okay, I get it Miss Evangelist. You don't need to quote The Five Sentinels at me. I'll talk to him. I just don't know what I'll say."

"You'll say the truth, and will be happier and more fulfilled for it." Sirona lightly slapped her under the chin. "Now stop sulking, your face wasn't made for that."

"Okay, *mom.*" Elethe made an exaggerated grin that didn't touch her eyes.

Sirona laughed. "Do you think I would be a good mother? I have thought about it, but I can't seem to find a good enough man."

Elethe rolled her eyes. "You would inspire fear and admiration in your kids."

"Ah, now that is true. They would be the perfect children who crush the shadow of Hell under their feet."

"What would you name them?"

Sirona leaned back in thought. "I've always liked the name Adorra for a girl. Boy names are always so boring, so if I had a son, I would probably name him Ander, or perhaps Galan, like the heroes from stories of old. No more than two children for me. What about you? Have you given much thought into your future?"

Elethe shrugged. "Not really. I mean, being an Empath I can sort of do whatever I want, but right now I just want to come out of this war alive. I'll have time to think about what to do with my life afterwards."

"No reason you don't have time now. It's still a couple weeks until we reach Fort Calhoun."

"I don't even know if I'm going to get married. Boys are aliens."

"So you've told me, and yet I've noticed you talking to that... mute... quite often."

"You think I'm interested in *him?*" Elethe laughed. "He's the king of aliens. I mean come on, he even *looks* like one. And why do you call him 'that mute'? You know his name is Dowyr."

Sirona shook her head. "He's no king of anything. At best he is a court jester, but no, I know a scoundrel when I see one."

"He's not a scoundrel, he's just an orphan with a free spirit."

"And what better combination is there to produce a scoundrel? For Heaven's sake, he's a *Mind Intruder*. Who knows what he could be up to when careful eyes aren't watching?"

Elethe opened her mouth and heard herself say, "Nothing harmful." Her mouth hadn't moved though.

She abruptly turned around and gave a start when she spotted Dowyr scrambling out the back of the wagon and darting for the one Garec was leading.

"YOU BASTARD," Elethe screamed, ready to leap after him. "HOW LONG WERE YOU LISTENING?"

She heard him make a strange gargling sound, something between an excited giggle and a yell of terror.

"I told you he's a scoundrel," Sirona said with wry amusement.

Elethe turned back with a scowl but said nothing. She would get back at him later... somehow.

*

Dowyr couldn't help but snicker in his own way as he jumped into the back of Garec's wagon. Messing with Elethe had so far been his only means of real entertainment during the journey. His eavesdropping had been largely boring, and he rolled his eyes at Sirona's preaching, but once she started talking about him it was difficult not to cackle maniacally. He stuck out his tongue at her for the scoundrel comment. In a way, he liked Sirona, albeit at a distance. She was somewhat like Weynon; unwavering in her beliefs and not hypocritical in the least, but in a more ferocious manner. He wondered how she ever managed to become a Compassion Emogician.

"Are you starting trouble with Elethe?" Garec asked.

"*No,*" Dowyr channeled, using the voice of a boy from the orphanage that he had decided to stick with as his own. Nik had a nice voice. It was probably being ruined working in the mines. "*Sirona too.*"

Garec freely let him and Weynon channel now, but Dowyr didn't try to push his luck with what he could get away with too much. Weynon talked about listening to the land as they traveled, and how it was growing more and more silent as winter approached. The emotion in it had withdrawn and gone still. Dowyr understood the sentiment towards winter.

"That's worse," Garec said. "Sirona better not be coming after me tonight."

"*Sirona won't, but Elethe will. Not because of me though.*"

"You were spying on them?"

"*Spying is such a strong word. I found a good place for a nap that just happened to be within hearing distance.*"

Garec gave him a sidelong glance. "And that place was the back of their wagon."

"*It looked more comfortable than the rest.*"

"Right. Tonight I want you to start teaching my men the signs you've taught me, starting with the officers. They'll be gathered at the command wagon after dinner."

Dowyr sighed. This is how it was with Garec: he asks if you were making any trouble, says it better not affect him, hints that what you were up to was no good, and then gives you something to do. At least he was more straightforward than the Sisters at the orphanage who fretted over everything.

It was difficult to figure out what to think about him. Being a Class 3 Voidspeaker made him an oddity of sorts; Voidspeakers were treated almost as poorly as heathens in Elyssanar, if not worse. Besides being able to block another Emogician's channeling, they were supposedly able to communicate with Hell himself. To some religious types, they might as well have *been* Hell. But no one in the Company treated him that way, and he always treated his soldiers with consideration and respect. He knew what needed to be done and made sure it happened, and there was nothing Hell could do or say to stop him.

Dowyr didn't believe Voidspeakers could really communicate with Hell though, since there was no way to prove it to his knowledge. The same went for Gratitude Emogicians, or Boosters, the opposite of Voidspeakers that could boost anyone's channeling and supposedly communicate with Heaven. Either were able to communicate with *something*, that was for sure, but for all anyone knew it was just a bizarre side effect of the Emogics. Dowyr liked to think it was aliens. That seemed just as likely as Heaven or Hell.

"You can clean the cookpots instead if you'd like," Garec said, not even a hint of amusement in his voice, just cool matter-of-factness.

"*No, I'll teach them,*" Dowyr channeled. "*Can Elethe help me?*"

"No. As unlikely as it is, I don't want anyone getting suspicious about how powerful she is."

Dowyr hummed and nodded. He and Weynon had been given a stern warning not to give any indication that Elethe was anything other than a Class 2 Empath, and if she accidentally taught the officers signs too quickly, they might grow suspicious. Garec had been rather upset to learn she had revealed her secret to them. It briefly tempted Dowyr to blackmail him into letting Weynon and himself go free, but Weynon was adamant about staying and helping, and Dowyr couldn't just leave him behind. That, and there was probably nowhere they could go and be safe from the Halberd.

That damned Halberd. It was impressive, in a demented sort of way, that Elyssanarans had taken Zion, the paragon of justice and peace, and associated him with unwavering, violent devotion to the country, under penalty of death. It made Dowyr want to tear his hair out. He may not have believed in them, but the Sentinels deserved better than that.

The thought made him wonder what the Kircans believed about them. Did they have some version of the Halberd driving them too? Or maybe something else made them be the aggressors. The clergy in

Elyssanar had said they believed in the Five Sentinels, but followed their teachings incorrectly. He had tried to get details as to how, but most of the examples he'd been given were either irrelevant to the text of The Five Sentinels, or *were* correct ways to follow the teachings, just not according to the interpretation of Elyssanar's religious scholars. Only a small handful of examples sounded like blatant disregard for the sacred text, but he wasn't sure how much he could trust the clergy's word on it.

The world was just too full of liars.

*

Later that evening, the sun just above the horizon, Elethe sat warming her hands at a fire shared by Donnan, Sirona, Dowyr, and Weynon. Dinner had just been finished, and the smell of stew still hung in the air. The convoy was camped outside a small farming town, the Pilgrim River only a stone throw anyway. Elethe hoped the soft rippling sound of it would help her sleep. She always liked sleeping near moving water; it gave a calming sense of peace.

Thinking of peace, she glanced at Weynon. A faint gray glow pierced his head; Dowyr was channeling to him. Boredom looked as she had expected it to, and it tasted about the same when she Matched it. Dry air mixed with flavorless water. There was nothing unpleasant about it, it was just... boring.

She had thought of asking Weynon to use his Emogic on her from time to time, but it felt wrong. After putting him and Dowyr through all this, she didn't deserve to feel at ease ever again.

Garec approached the fire but didn't stop to warm his hands. He locked eyes with Dowyr. "My officers are waiting for you at the command wagon."

Dowyr sighed and got up, signing, *I'm going.*

Garec gave a short nod and walked off. Sirona cleared her throat to get Elethe's attention and motioned to him with a sharp gesture.

Guess I'm going too, Elethe thought sourly.

She followed Garec back to his fire which was surrounded by a dozen empty stools. They passed other groups of soldiers gathered around their own. There was an ambience of soft banter between them, and an occasional burst of laughter. Some were playing cards or a game of Kings on a small portable checkerboard. She still needed to try playing it, especially since she now understood how the game was played, having absorbed that information from Dowyr. The odd tower-looking pieces had always made it look too complicated to try before.

"Dowyr said you would be coming after me tonight," Garec said, sitting on a stool and turning to face her.

"Of course he did," Elethe said coldly. She moved to another stool and sat, holding her hands out to the fire. The sun was close to dropping below the horizon.

"What's the matter?"

Elethe took a deep breath and remembered what Sirona had told her about the truth. She didn't want to say it. It would be easier to just walk away and forget it all. Instead, she opened her mouth and said whatever came to her mind.

"I don't like what we did. What *you* did, and what you made me do. You never said kidnapping them was part of the plan, I thought we were going to wait until they had graduated then recruit them personally." Not knowing what to do with her legs, she stood back up and moved in front of Garec, her back to the fire. "And why did we have to take Weynon? He's *twelve!* We're bringing an innocent, pure-hearted twelve-year-old boy into the mouth of Hell. I want to cry just thinking about it. I feel like this war is putting a wall between us, and I don't know what to do. It feels like the only ones who listen to me are Sirona and the boys. Can't you listen to me too? Or are my problems something you're indifferent towards?"

Garec appeared to listen intently, though his expression didn't alter. Once Elethe had finished, he clasped his hands and exhaled slowly.

"I really wish things could have gone the way we wanted back at the Academy, but we're in wartime. Things had to change. I'm sorry for the hand you had in taking the boys, I hope you can forgive me. You're only sixteen and are already carrying the weight of the world on your shoulders. I know it's not fair. Life can be cruel as Hell. But you're strong enough to fight it and win, perhaps stronger than all the rest of us. Why else would you be an Empath? I need you to be strong. None of this works without you."

"That's the problem, I'm *not* strong enough! I'm not Elysium, I'm a bloody mess forced to feel everything *all the time.* You can't just treat me like I'm some tool to be used. And you can't treat Dowyr and Weynon like that too; we're kids, not soldiers. Did you forget that? Because you didn't used to treat me like this."

He sat still in thought. "What do you want me to do? I can't just make all the problems disappear instantly, and right now there's one taking up all my attention and energy."

"I don't need you to solve my problems! I just want to feel like you're here for me while I'm dealing with them, to feel like you still see *me*, and not just some tool or weapon."

Garec rubbed his eyes and a haggard look came over him. "I'm sorry. I wish I had experience as a father to be a better uncle. If your father knew where I was taking you, he'd likely kill me. I probably deserve it." He took a deep breath and looked her in the eye. "Come talk to me whenever you need. I don't care if it's in the middle of a war meeting or the middle of the night. Just not in the middle of a battle, alright?"

Sitting back down, Elethe let her shoulders relax. "I wouldn't do that to you. But thanks. That's all I needed to hear, and… and you're still hiding something. I know your anxiety has been way up this week. Is it something to do with the plan?"

He grimaced. "Not the plan. I shouldn't have blocked those boys for so long. Maybe it would've been better to knock them unconscious."

She winced. He wouldn't have said it outright, but the message was clear: Hell had been speaking to him that night. How long had he been channeling? Five hours? Six? That was far longer than any believing Voidspeaker would be comfortable.

"He's a liar," she said softly.

Garec sniffed. "Like I don't know, but that doesn't stop him from telling the truth when it's to his advantage. And the truth can be one of the strongest advantages. You want to know something he said?"

Elethe shivered, and not just from the cold. "Not really."

"No, I think you'll get a kick out of this. He said Dowyr serves him and is going to kill you."

He said it so casually that it took Elethe a moment to process the words. "Oh, well, one of those may be true. I'll just have to kill him first, then we'll know for sure which it is." She glanced towards the command wagon's fire a short way off where she saw Dowyr linked to a group of officers with small gray streams of Boredom.

Garec laughed—an actual laugh—and shook his head with a grin. "I don't know, if I had to put money on who wins that battle... well, I'd put it on you, but I think that boy is cleverer than he looks or lets on. Didn't he already know how to use his Emogic when the Academy picked him up?"

"Yes, mainly because he's read all the books about Emogics and channeling you could think of and then everything else in Elyssanar's library. And he remembers every word. I don't know how, but he does. There's something seriously messed up with his brain, which is probably why he's a mute. Or, going by his looks, he could be an actual alien. Being an orphan supports that theory. But unfortunately I also know everything about him, so he's only alien in spirit."

Garec raised an eyebrow at her. "You know everything about him?"

Elethe blushed, remembering the moment. It was rather embarrassing in hindsight. "When I first Matched his channeling, I... dove headfirst. I guess at my Class, Boredom can absorb information like a sponge. Most of his knowledge didn't stick for long, I just can't remember that much pointless information, but anything to do with himself, and signs, yeah. I know it all. It's kind of... uhhh... weird." There were some memories she wished she could get rid of.

He looked in Dowyr's direction with consideration. "Is there anything about him I might need to be aware of?"

She shrugged. "He's a teenage atheist. If you're worried he'll try to run away, or defect, or anything like that, it might cross his mind, but I doubt he'd ever try. He'd never abandon Weynon at least. I don't think his conscience would let him. He doesn't think of himself as such, but deep down he's a good kid."

Garec nodded slowly. "So why does he call himself Mawkin?"

"He thinks it's funny."

"That's it?"

Elethe nodded. "That's literally it."

"Hmph. Teenagers."

"Hey, we're not all bad."

Garec smiled. "I know. What does he think of me?"

"Dunno, but he's still channeling. I can check for you without him knowing what I'm looking for."

"No... no, I have a feeling he'd figure it out and not be very happy about it. Better I learn from him myself, I think."

Elethe rolled her eyes. "If you say so. I think I'm going to get ready for bed now before it gets too dark. Thanks for listening to me though."

Garec waved a dismissive hand. "I'm unworthy of your thanks, just doing as I should. Thank you for coming to talk with me, you're a brave young woman and I'm grateful for your confidence. Sleep well."

Elethe smiled, believing for the first time in a while that she would sleep well.

*

Weynon had made himself ask to sit next to Garec for today's riding, and permission was given. For a good amount of the journey he had watched the Captain, paying attention to how he spoke, whether to his men or to Dowyr and himself. He liked the way he spoke; there was strength in it, but without harshness. Garec was brief in almost everything, yet full of encouragement towards everyone. It reminded him of the way Valhalla spoke in The Five Sentinels. The only thing that made him nervous was his being a Voidspeaker. He could talk to Hell, or at least Hell talked to him personally. That should be enough to give anyone pause. Weynon often had to remind himself of what Donnan had told him, that people are more than their Emogics.

Up until now he had spent most of the journey staying with Dowyr or Donnan, keeping more to himself. It was taking time to adjust to traveling with a couple hundred people. He liked talking with others, but more on the listening side, and crowds had often made him nervous. Donnan was at least a recognizable face from the Academy and would regale him with stories about life up in the wild north, such as his attempts to tame everything from bison and horses to songbirds and foxes. Most were failures, but they made for great stories. Dowyr would talk about his most recent prank on Elethe or what his next one would be, and eventually he branched out to pranking the other soldiers, though subtly with his Emogic.

Watch, Dowyr would sign, staring intently at a soldier sitting by a fire, who would suddenly jerk his head, slap his cheek, and look very confused at his clean hand. Dowyr would make a soft half-cackle, half-grunt sound and explained he made the soldier see and feel a large mosquito land on his face.

"Why?" Weynon asked, genuinely curious.

"Life is too boring to not mess with people a bit," Dowyr channeled.

Weynon didn't exactly understand his need for the pranks, thinking life was more than interesting enough to not need bother people with such things, but at least it made Dowyr happier, and it wasn't like he was doing any real harm.

However, for some reason, he cut his Emogic pranking short when Elethe called him out on it. According to him, she 'spoiled the fun of it', but he just went straight back to pranking her without using his Emogic. On and off, at least. It became more sporadic the closer winter came, which Weynon understood perfectly, now more than ever. Everything slowed down in winter, even the land itself.

Some days it almost made him cry, being able to listen to the land. The sound of it reminded him of a heartbeat, and it was becoming fainter by the day, its beats further apart. Nature was always giving off trace amounts of Emogic, and he could sense it. Winter caused a great deal of Sadness, as though nature believed it was dying and could do nothing to stop the inevitable. Yet deeper down there was a feeling of knowing that this was the way things were, that the cycle of life would begin again and there would be cause for joy. Nature knew that after the end, there was a new beginning, just as was written in The Five Sentinels. Heaven had caused many endings, but always following was another beginning; such was the way of all things, eternally.

Only now the ending of something is what Weynon hoped for. Wars had always been something far away from him, whether by time or distance. They never concerned him except to pray for the souls of those who fought. Now that he was moving straight towards one, he also prayed for his own soul and for the end of the war to come swiftly.

"Was there a specific reason you wanted to sit with me today?" Garec asked.

"Yes," Weynon said slowly, "but I don't know if the question I have is appropriate to ask you."

Garec smiled in amusement. "Just ask, I'll not be offended."

"I've been wanting to ask for a while. What's the story behind your Apex?"

"Ahh, that. There isn't much to it. When I was sixteen my little sister fell in a river, so I jumped in after her without a second thought. I was completely indifferent towards my own life in that moment.

Whatever happened to me didn't matter, I just had to save my sister. I did, and in the middle of it all, I had my Apex."

"That's it?"

"I told you there isn't much to it."

Weynon frowned at nothing. "That must have felt like a curse after doing something so heroic."

"Sometimes it felt that way, but looking back, it was only an occasional scornful look from some pastor or colorful choice of words from a stranger who had heard of me. Most of my family didn't see me any differently, at least the ones who mattered to me. Overall, I've rarely had the burden of needing to use my Emogic."

"So… when you are using it… does he really talk to you?"

"Always."

Weynon shivered. "Did he say anything about me?"

Garec grimaced. "Nothing worth repeating. Best to be content knowing he hates you, which means you're doing something right."

"He hates everyone though."

"Yes, but from what I can tell, you more than most people."

Weynon hesitated. "And… Dowyr?"

"He hates everyone. You know Dowyr is a good kid."

Weynon breathed a sigh of relief. "He is."

There came a distant sound of Elethe shouting from behind, followed by an unholy screech that Weynon guessed was Dowyr.

Garec sighed. "He's going to get himself killed if he keeps doing that."

Weynon smiled. "Probably."

CHAPTER 11

A Game at Fort Calhoun

"I'm soooooooo boooooooooored," Dowyr channeled to Weynon, who sat next to the fireplace reading a copy of The Five Sentinels.

They were in their room at Fort Calhoun, just across from the one Garec and Donnan had been given, while Elethe and Sirona were situated in an entirely different part of the Fort. It was barebones accommodations, with dull wooden floors, cracked gray brick walls, and no windows. Besides the fireplace, two lightstones mounted above the beds helped give the room a warm glow. At least it didn't feel like the prison-cell bunkroom at the Academy, as they were free to roam about and even go outside, though it was far too cold this time of year to want anything to do with the outdoors.

Dowyr lay on his bed, head hanging upside-down over the side so he could stare at the fire. An hour must have gone by since he had begun watching it, and he had shifted into every position imaginable to keep himself comfortable. Being upside down was his favorite, despite how quickly it became uncomfortable.

"So let's play a game," Weynon said, not looking away from his book.

Dowyr sighed heavily and rolled over to be right-side-up. *"Okay. You go first."*

"Not that kind of game. We can play Sentinels versus Snakes. Our room can be my base. We can set the rules of which halls I have to stay in."

"That's too easy, I could just cheat to win."

Weynon closed his book and got up. "But you're not actually a Snake. You won't cheat, and you won't win either. Come on, let's go find the starting spots."

Dowyr rolled off the bed as melodramatically as possible. *"Fine, but if I win, you gotta take care of my laundry for a week."*

"Then you gotta do mine if I win."

Dowyr gave a thumbs-up, and they darted into the halls and began plotting out the boundaries for Weynon's side, and then Dowyr went off into the maze of the Fort's halls and stairs and counted a minute before beginning his attempt at getting past Weynon and back into their room.

Sentinels versus Snakes was typically played on either an open field or a corn maze in a five-on-five matchup. For the longest time it was simply a children's game, but it had slowly grown into a national sport and new variants of the game made it into official rulebooks. The core of it was simple; one team, the Sentinels, guarded a home base, with restrictions on where they were allowed to roam, while the Snakes tried to reach the home base without being tagged out. Dowyr had played it on occasion during his time at the orphanage, always choosing to be one of the Snakes, as that felt like the more fun side to play on. He and Weynon had also played it with the soldiers a few times during their journey to the Fort, and for some reason Weynon's team usually won.

He made his way through the halls as silently as possible, trying to find which way Weynon wasn't guarding. Soldiers occasionally marched past, to which he gave an innocent smile and wave. For the most part they ignored him, though at least one recognized him and signed *safe*, pointing a thumb down the hall he came from. Dowyr responded with a thumbs-up and quickly pressed on, checking around the corners carefully. Down one he spotted Weynon scanning the halls. There was only one other point that gave access to his room that Weynon wouldn't be able to guard at the same time, but it would take a while to make his way back to reach it. By then, he might be checking there already. Timing was everything.

Except Weynon had spotted him, and he was in his territory. The boy made a mad dash towards him, and Dowyr squeaked, practically leaping back down the hall. Weynon was a faster runner though, and Dowyr's territory was too far to reach in time. Somehow he needed to hide.

Turning one corner, he made for the nearest door and as quickly and quietly as he could, pulled it open and darted inside. With it shut, he turned around and found a small group of men standing around a table and staring at him in either surprise or annoyance, Garec among them. The rest looked like older high-ranking officials.

Oh, Hell, Dowyr thought.

In a panic, he channeled and made it seem to them as if he immediately opened the door and ran out, after which it was easy enough to make himself invisible to their eyes. It shouldn't take too long before Weynon left the area.

"That boy is a troublemaker if I ever saw one," one of the older men said.

"I apologize on his behalf, Colonel Aemon," Garec said, "he is my responsibility. I'll make sure it won't happen again."

"See that you do. Continue, Major Ingram."

The man who must've been Ingram cleared his throat. "There's little else to report, Sir. Besides the... new geography around Irostead, all I've gathered is that Kircany is continuing its advance into Parasten while fending off raids from Arkonia."

"I can't believe they've got a damn Class 4 Apocalypse," another man said. "If word of that gets loose, it'll—"

Oh... Hell...

"It's already loose," Colonel Aemon said. "That woman wagged her tongue all the way from Irostead to here. I wouldn't be surprised if it's on the lips of every Elyssanaran by Victorsday. The question is, do we have enough Druids and Cheerleaders to deal with the inevitable morale drop?"

"There'll be enough," Garec said. "And we can do more than just use Druids or Cheerleaders. My men are good at lifting spirits, whatever the circumstances. I'll brief them about the situation before sundown, they'll know what to do as word starts spreading."

"Not through spirits, I hope?"

"Of course not. Fear only works without confidence. We know how dangerous Class 4s are, but they're just as humanly fragile as anyone, without an Immortal anyway. All we need is a reminder that they can be killed."

"Where did this Rage Emogician even come from?" another man asked.

"My sources say he's Roderick's younger brother, Royce," Major Ingram said. "I don't know whether it's true, but I doubt Roderick would use him as bait like that if it weren't."

"Isn't he only nineteen?" Garec asked. "That might be to our advantage."

"Yes, he is still only a naive teenager," Colonel Aemon said. "That is our one saving grace. But him being so close to Roderick is what worries me. Roderick might not be an Emogician, but it's clear he knows war. The General expects an attack once the snows melt. I should be receiving further plans on defensive preparations within the week. We're still waiting for more men to reinforce the border. Captain Klausgow, do you know when the next wave of Emogicians are supposed to be conscripted?"

"It would have been two weeks ago," Garec said. "More will still be training, but you should expect by winter's end to have maximum strength in Emogicians."

"Good. In preparation for them I want all of you to make a list of all your Emogicians and send it to me. I'll be handpicking from them to be specialized Emogic unit leaders. That is all. Dismissed."

Salutes were exchanged, and they began marching towards Dowyr. He moved away from the door and noticed Garec, last to leave, signing in his general direction, *my room, two minutes.*

Oh, HELL.

The door shut behind them and Dowyr cut his channeling, gasping as if he had been holding his breath the entire time. Then, after counting the minutes, he carefully opened the door and investigated the hall. Finding no one, he sprinted out and went straight for Garec's room, not even bothering to slow when he came across a very confused Weynon around one corner.

"YOU WIN, GAME OVER," Dowyr channeled.

"What? Where are you going?!"

There was no reason to answer since Garec's room was only a few more leaps away, and in seconds Dowyr was inside, panting his lungs out. Garec and Donnan were sitting across from each other at a small table, neither looking too pleased. Garec even looked angry, which was a first.

"Sorry," Dowyr channeled. *"I didn't mean to barge in on that, I was—"*

Garec waved a dismissive hand. "I'm not mad at you, and you can barge in on the Colonel bathing for all I care. Handpicking my Emogicians my ass."

"He won't pick anyone ye need," Donnan said.

"Damnit, I need *all* of them, I can't even afford to lose Henric."

"Why?" Dowyr channeled.

"Because we have Elethe, and once… Snakes, Royce is complicating things." Garec slammed a fist on the table and took a deep breath. "Donnan, tell me how this makes sense. We learn Kircany has a *Class 4 Apocalypse,* and our commanders *still* want to just sit on their asses and play Kings all day?"

"It's winter," Donnan said. "They want te keep their arses warm."

"Useless bastards, all of them. If we don't move soon we risk everything."

"We're two weeks from the solstice and ye want us moving already? How's that supposed te fly?"

Garec tapped his fingers on the table sporadically. "It won't. The Halberd would come flying down on our necks. I wish I'd known about Royce before reaching the Fort, I would've turned the Company southeast and gone straight into Parasten. Maybe make a beeline for the capital."

Dowyr looked between them. *"So now what?"*

Garec sighed. "We have to stop the Tyrdens, Royce and Roderick, with Royce being the priority. We can't let someone that powerful roam free, much less alive. The longer he's out there, the more lives it will cost. But there's still the matter of making two hundred soldiers disappear without anyone noticing or being able to do anything about it."

"Why don't you just have Elethe and me help them disappear? We could do it."

"No, you couldn't. Too many eyes to deceive for too long. The moment you stop channeling everyone will know and come after us, and that's it, we'd all be Halberded. We wouldn't be able to get away fast enough."

"We need a Sprinter," Donnan said. "Too bad they're all running messages."

Garec knuckled his chin. "One is due here on Fireday…"

"No, Garec, no, stop. I know what ye're thinking. No more kidnapping."

"We don't need to kidnap one. I could just have Henric—"

"Ye know Lust doesn't work like that at his Class level."

"Elethe can do it."

"Oh, I'm sure she'd *love* that."

Garec tossed his hands. "Fine, then I'm kidnapping the poor bastard! Besides, it'll only be temporary to help us escape. You don't need to be involved. You though," he pointed a finger at Dowyr, "you I could use. Wanna help me nab a Sprinter?"

Donnan sighed heavily and rubbed his forehead.

Dowyr shrugged. "*I didn't like getting kidnapped that much, but with my expertise I think I could make it a more pleasant experience for the poor bastard.*"

"That's what I like to hear. I've got things I need to get done today, so we'll plan it out on Watersday. Donnan, let's go speak with the men."

CHAPTER 12

The Sprinter

A light fog brushed against the ground early Fireday morning, the sun not yet risen above the flat horizon to burn it away. The oppressive gray-blue sky weighed down on Garec as he strode amongst his soldier's tents. They were spaced out evenly in neat rows, immaculately set up and maintained, just as Garec expected of his men. He hid a smile at seeing how it made the other surrounding Companies' tents look pathetic by comparison. It wasn't difficult to hide, as it also reminded him of the general incompetency of Elyssanar's armies. The theocracy was more concerned with its people's faith than the discipline and orderliness of its military. It was one of the reasons he had joined the army years ago. The small things mattered, and in caring for them he had stood out among his peers, helping shoot him up the ranks. He always made sure his men cared about the small things too.

A voice called out as he passed, "Someone in trouble, Sir?"

Garec spared a glance for the Corporal. "Not yet, Henric. Ask me tomorrow."

Henric gave a nod and began walking beside him. "I heard a Sprinter arrived this morning."

"Yes, and?"

"Nothing, I just thought it might be significant. Perhaps some interesting orders will be coming along."

Garec stopped and turned to Henric. "How many know?"

"By now I'd expect the whole Company, Sir."

"Damnit Donnan."

"Fitting nickname."

"Anyone outside the Company?"

Henric smiled. "You know us, Captain, we don't let secrets get outside the Company."

Garec sighed. "I know. How much did he tell you?"

"Just that the last thing you need to get us out of here without risking the Halberd is a Sprinter. I can possibly help with that, if you need, Sir."

"No, that won't be necessary. And whatever he said, we're not kidnapping him, he's coming of his own free will. Now get back to your men and eat your breakfast."

"Yes, Mother. Sir."

Henric turned back and Garec continued on and into the command tent that sat amidst the Company's tents. Inside, his four Lieutenants and their seconds were waiting. It was just spacious enough to fit the nine of them with a table in the middle holding an assortment of maps.

Garec glanced out the tent before starting. "Pardon me for being a bit late. Our little alien friend has done what he can to delay the Colonel from taking our Emogicians." The name for Dowyr had caught on with his men over the course of their journey to the Fort, thanks to Elethe. For whatever reason the boy didn't seem bothered by it, but rather embraced it. Garec had been surprised how well he got along with the soldiers despite his antics, though perhaps it was precisely because of his antics that he got along so well. "But now comes the hard part. We're moving out tomorrow morning, but we have to be precise. I need every man up and ready to disassemble their tents and pack everything onto horseback the second the sun shows its face."

"Sounds easy enough," Boughton said, the leader of the archer platoon and Class 2.8 Happiness Emogician. "What's the hard part?"

"Not getting caught in the process. My hope is that no one will notice we aren't supposed to be leaving until everyone is on horseback, since then it'll be too late. We'll have the Sprinter, and with him we'll be riding hard until I think we need to slow. Hopefully we should be at least fifty kilometers away from here just an hour after sunrise. But if anybody comes asking, we're simply moving to the northern camp to make room for the next batch of Emogicians."

"What Class is the Sprinter? They'd have to be at least Class 3.6 to move the whole Company."

"I don't know." Garec glanced out the tent again and began to sign. *But it doesn't matter. I trust each of you with this secret I've kept, but I won't hesitate to kill any of you should I find out you've violated that trust; Elethe is Class 4. She's the one who'll be getting us out of here with the Sprinter's help, and is the answer to our Apocalypse problem. Beyond anything else your orders are to keep this knowledge guarded with your life. Understood?*

Their reactions varied between restrained surprise and solemn acceptance of reality. *Understood,* they all signed in return.

"Good," Garec said. "And for all the Sprinter will know, we have a handful of Empaths. That is all I have for you. Have the men prepared for tomorrow and I'll see you in the morning."

Garec left the command tent, followed by his officers as they split off in different directions. He himself went back to the Fort, which was roughly half a kilometer away.

The Fort's main defense lines were walls of stone on its north, east, and south sides, though any initial fighting around the Fort would be down at the Missionary River just two kilometers northeast where the bridge stood leading into Parasten, the next closest bridge being fifty kilometers south. High towers were positioned sporadically around the bridge and Fort for high Class Emogicians to channel and attack from. Come Spring, Colonel Aemon would have everyone digging in on the east side of the river, or else have the bridges destroyed if Kircany comes marching sooner than expected. Garec doubted it would matter to a nation with a Class 4 Apocalypse. At this point, having any defensive positions where large groups of soldiers congregated was just asking to have a mountain dropped on them. Higher command was convinced Royce wouldn't expose himself on the front line and would only pose a threat if Elyssanar went on the offensive. Garec failed to understand their reasoning given how Irostead now had a mountain sitting on top of it. They were happily saying to Hell with Parasten as a whole.

That pissed him off, to put it mildly.

There was a sharp scent of smoke as he marched past soldiers huddled around fires and cookpots, talking quietly amongst themselves. Days earlier they were loud and animated with playful banter and jokes that kept their hearts warm, but after the recent news of Royce, the camps grew quiet. His own men had done what they could, going from fire to fire to tell and reenact stories from The Five Sentinels that encouraged bravery in the face of Hell, which no doubt they were all facing. From what Garec could tell, what helped most were the short, simple stories about Heaven and his friends, particularly about Paradise and her acts of kindness. Paradise was the icon of kindness and compassion, and she was like a surrogate mother watching over them. When soldiers fought, they shouted war cries for Zion or Elysium, who among the Sentinels were most renowned for their feats in battle, but it was to Paradise they prayed.

Yet no amount of praying on Garec's part rid him of Hell's incessant voice whenever he channeled, nor the memories of what he had said. The only thing that helped him escape the voice echoing in his head was keeping busy, whether through going over his plan and devising strategies with his men, the occasional game of Kings with Donnan, or speaking with Elethe and the boys.

Weynon had taken more of his attention than he expected, visiting his room and striking up conversations about the Sentinels and his thoughts on them, particularly the passages of Paradise's wisdom regarding behavior.

"I want to be strong," Weynon told him, "but I've always thought wisdom is what makes someone strong."

Garec nodded. "That is a good way to think, but it also depends on what having wisdom means. You can know what is wise to do in a given situation, but if you do not do it, are you really wise?"

"I guess not. Is that why Heaven says Victory was the wisest man he ever met? Because his wisdom is stories of people doing things?"

"I suppose so."

Weynon looked lost in thought for a moment. He was such an earnest boy, always taking everything seriously. "What... does Hell think about Victory? Has he said anything about him?"

"No. Well, not by name, but I remember one time... for most of my life I didn't believe Victory was a real person—something about him just struck me as unrealistic—but one time when I was channeling, I thought about Victory and his stories, and all of a sudden there was this intense hatred coming from Hell, more than I've ever felt coming from him for anyone. And with it I could also sense fear... not strongly, but it was there. Since then, I've believed Victory was a real person, and that's the only time I can remember sensing Hell being afraid."

"I wonder why, since it's not like he's one of the Sentinels. I wish Heaven had told us more about him."

"I think it's better he remains a mystery, otherwise his stories might lose their intrigue. If anything, it gives me hope that a such a plain, normal man had such an impact so as to make it into The Five Sentinels. Perhaps it means a man like myself can come up with a plan that will save our country."

It will fail, Hell had said, voice echoing as Garec continued on to the Fort. *Donnan will betray you, your men will abandon you, the boys will be captured, Elethe will be killed, you will live to see a burning, conquered Elyssanar.*

"Freeze over," Garec muttered.

During Garec's training at the Academy, keeping emotions under control was one of the first and most important things learned so that he could maintain channeling, especially as a Voidspeaker. If only he had learned to also keep his thoughts in check so the voice didn't haunt him even when not channeling. It made him grind his teeth in frustration.

Once inside the Fort he went to Dowyr's room and found the boy staring at the ceiling from the hard floor. Weynon sat on his bed reading The Five Sentinels.

Dowyr looked at him and jumped up, and Garec heard his voice come from nowhere at all saying, "*Party time?*"

"You're already awake?" Garec asked. "Did you eat breakfast?"

"Not yet," Weynon said. "I don't think Dowyr slept much either."

Dowyr briefly glared at his friend. "*Not hungry, not tired.*"

Garec snorted. "Then let's get it done. The Sprinter is upstairs. You know the plan."

He nodded and went to put on his boots. Weynon closed his book and walked to the writing desk that sat in the corner of the room and picked up a letter.

"A soldier told me to give this to you since you were gone," he said, handing the letter over.

Garec turned the letter over and narrowed his eyes. "From Elyssanar?" He opened it and began to read.

"What's it say?"

Garec quickly scanned the letter, hesitated, then read it again, then once more, and finally a fourth time before stuffing it into his coat pocket and clearing his throat. "It's from my sister," he lied. "Just an update from home is all. Nothing to be concerned about. Let's go, Dowyr. Time's wasting."

"*Right behind you.*"

They marched out into the halls and made their way to the Fort's upper-level bunkrooms where mail-carriers and other unimportant temporary guests stayed. Garec went in while Dowyr stayed hidden out in the hall. There was only one person in the room, a woman who looked roughly around his age, resting on one of the bunks. She lifted her head to look at him as he approached.

"Can I help you, Captain?" she asked.

"I'm looking for the Sprinter."

She sat up. "You've found her. Class 1.7 Sprinter Clarine Gowens, Sir."

Garec's heart skipped a beat. "You...?" He cleared his throat and composed himself. "Colonel Aemon wants to see you, Gowens."

*

Dowyr was only waiting in the hall for a few moments before Garec strode out, discreetly signing the name *Gowens,* and a tall woman following behind him. That didn't seem right, but before she could spot Dowyr, he channeled and made himself disappear from her perception, then followed behind. Garec led them down to his room where no one would disturb them, and Dowyr split his channeling to make sure Colonel Aemon was waiting for them both inside.

"How are you, Gowens?" Aemon asked as Garec went to stand by him.

"As well as ever, Sir," Clarine said, hesitantly looking between them. "And yourself?"

"Just the same. I'll cut straight to the point: I'm having you transferred to Captain Klausgow's Second Assault Company." Garec handed her a letter of transfer that was sitting on the table next to the Colonel. Forged, of course.

Clarine glanced at the letter and looked back at him in confusion. "I don't understand... I'm just a mail-carrier, not even Class 2... I mean, I'm a mother, I have a family waiting for me, I was told I wouldn't be sent to fight."

While she was distracted Garec signed *off script,* a stone-hard look in his eyes.

"You won't be," Aemon said. "Second Assault Company is—"

"It's only a temporary transfer for a simple patrol mission," Garec interjected. "We're only going a short distance into Parasten. The Colonel decided to take some extra precautions by having a Sprinter for the Company's Empaths to make use of. Naturally, being our only option, you were selected for the job. We're moving out early tomorrow morning."

Clarine still shifted uncomfortably. "What about the Kircans? How close are they to the border?"

"Our scouts haven't spotted any, so it's doubtful they're anywhere nearby. We don't expect to encounter a fight."

Clarine nodded as if to herself then gave a salute, right hand over the heart. "I understand, Sir. I'll do what I can."

"Good." Garec returned the salute. "Find one of my officers down in the southern camp, they should be around the blue command tent. They'll brief you on tomorrow morning's plan. Dismissed."

Clarine walked out, looking a touch dazed, and Dowyr cut his channeling. Garec gave a heavy sigh and sagged a little.

"*That wasn't the poor bastard I expected,*" Dowyr channeled.

"Snakes and ashes," Garec muttered, giving no reaction to Dowyr's comment. "Snakes and *bloody* ashes. She's a mother. Tell me we're doing the right thing."

"*Why? I mean we're just using her to get out of here alive, right? Doesn't seem like a big deal.*"

Garec was silent for a moment. "Maybe. I just hope she doesn't suspect anything with what we're doing. I don't want her running off to get the Halberd chasing after."

"*I'd just run away from this whole war altogether if I were that fast.*"

Garec shook his head and sat down at the table. "I suppose I can't fault you for that. Where would you go, if I might ask?"

"*Arkonia, where it's warm.*" Dowyr hated the cold almost as much as he hated hypocrites.

Garec smiled briefly. "That's fair. Thank you for not running, though, and for your help. We wouldn't have this chance at all without you."

Dowyr shrugged. *"You got a plan to kill the bad guys while everybody else sits on their ass. Maybe we all die to do it, but, eh... gotta be worth it to save more."*

He had been thinking about the Captain's crazy plan, and he didn't like the idea of going deep into enemy territory towards someone who could literally bring a mountain down on top of them, but with Elethe and the other Emogicians, he thought there was at least a chance of success. Garec seemed like a good leader. Good, though Dowyr wasn't sure how intelligent. Not that he himself knew how to command a small army. He had read books about strategy, but they consistently warned that reading never made you a good strategist. It was too much like life; complicated and unpredictable.

As much as Dowyr wanted to get as far away from the war as possible, he had to admit to himself the worthlessness of his own life. He was an ugly, mute orphan. Nobody wanted or cared about him. Yes, he was a Boredom Emogician now too, and that seemed useful enough for Garec's purposes, but there was no real value he would offer to a world at peace. Going to war was the best place he could be. The Five Sentinels stated every individual had worth, no matter who they were, yet it still lauded personal sacrifice for the good of the world. Dowyr thought that should've just been common sense for any decent person.

"It will be worth it," Garec said, though he shifted uneasily in his chair. "Well, anyway, I should check on Elethe, let her know what's going on. Have you spoken with her recently?"

No, Dowyr signed. Channeling was starting to drain him. It was always better to do it in small amounts at a time to recover from each use. *She's not talking to me.*

"What'd you do this time?"

Nothing at all. He had channeled at her while she wasn't looking, and when she turned back claiming to know what he was doing, she saw a huge monster. Her scream had attracted at least a dozen soldiers, who weren't too pleased with him, but her reaction had been so worth it.

"We'll pretend I believe you for now. I need you to… if you'll… no, no, there's nothing I need you to do." Garec gave an exhausted sigh. "Why don't you go find Weynon? Get some breakfast."

Dowyr hesitated, wondering what had sucked all the energy out of Garec. He had looked fine when he first came to Dowyr's room, except maybe after reading that letter, but he wasn't sure.

Spurred by his grumbling stomach, he left. Whatever the Captain was dealing with this morning, he would probably get over it. Garec was strong.

*

Elethe sat still while Sirona cut her hair, and she was taking her sweet time with it. During their time at the Fort, Elethe had been real busy doing nothing at all. And yet, somehow, everything still felt like a chore. Walking was a chore. It was too cold to do it outside, and walking through the Fort's halls was so unbearably boring that watching paint dry would have been more entertaining. So she had spent a good deal of her time pacing in her room which she shared with Sirona. When not driving the other woman mad with it, she tried to read—often not getting far—or search out Dowyr or Weynon to play a game of Kings with, the only board game one could find in a Fort. She played Garec a couple times, but she could never beat him and got too frustrated to play more.

"You've been awfully quiet since Garec stopped by," Sirona said. "Does his plan bother you?"

"Of course it does," Elethe said. "We're either going to end up heroes, dead heroes, or just dead, probably with a higher chance of dead.

I thought we'd be going after some Emogicless old man when he first told me about his plan, and now it's this Class 4 dude who's only a few years older than me. Plus I hate riding in winter. But that's not why I'm upset."

"That mute bothering you again?"

"No," Elethe said sharply. "Well… yes, but no, and Snakes, stop calling him that. No, it's Garec. I sensed a spike of anxiety and regret from someone earlier this morning, but I never imagined it would've been from him. He was being overwhelmed with it, and being the stubborn uncle he is, he wouldn't tell me what happened."

"Maybe it's just nerves about tomorrow morning. If anything goes wrong… well, I'd rather not think about that."

"He's not nervous though, and when he told us the plan there was nothing but confidence. The anxiety and regret are from something else. Maybe Dowyr knows."

Sirona sniffed. "You believe that boy would tell you if he did?"

"If he channels I have a way to know for sure. Ow."

"Hold still. So you'd invade your own uncle's mind to pry out whatever information you want?"

"Light of Heaven, you make it sound worse than it is."

"I'm telling you exactly what it is. If Garec does not want to tell you, then you must let him bear his burden, whatever it is."

Elethe gripped her shift and grumbled. "He shouldn't have to bear it alone."

"You're right, he shouldn't, but I'll tell you now, many men choose to bear pain alone because they want to protect others from its burden. They feel responsible. They are stubborn mules, but it is their way of being strong. Or perhaps giving themselves the illusion of strength. I am not sure."

Elethe was silent at that. She hadn't thought that perhaps it was Garec trying to protect her from something. Though if that were the case, then something terrible must have happened. A death in the family? Snakes, if he was holding back about something like that…

Anxiety and regret, that's what he was feeling. Had it been her mother? Her father?

A bitter pit formed in her stomach as her imagination lingered on the possibilities. Now she would have to ask him just to make sure, and hope, desperately, that it wasn't the case.

CHAPTER 13

Leavetakings

It was just before dawn, the first hints of light barely noticeable through the overcast sky. Garec breathed deeply, getting a fill of crisp, chill air. His heart was pounding as he stood in the center of his camp. There was movement all around him as his men prepared and ate breakfast or woke their fellow soldiers, but it was quiet, no shouts or bustle, just slow, calculated motion and whispers. Underneath it all Garec could sense a frenzy; the way his soldiers held their shoulders, shifted their eyes, and turned their heads gave it away. The sun would not be making an appearance to mark when camp was to be disassembled, and so the men waited, tense.

Donnan came up beside him, a solemn look on his face as he regarded the men. "I wish we were here under better circumstances."

"Such as there not being a war?" Garec asked.

"Certainly that, but I meant not needing te resort te this sort of task apart from higher command. Or this method of escape. It's too much like leaving without saying goodbye."

"We'll be back." Garec fingered the pocket where he kept his letter. "Besides, it's easier to make a surprise greeting than a surprise goodbye."

Donnan gave a nod. "I do look forward to seeing the look on people's faces when we make our triumphant return."

Garec smiled and took a deep breath. "Sentinels be with us."

"Sentinels be with us."

Garec could almost hear the voice of Hell whisper, *and I'll be here too.* A foolish thing to imagine what he would say. Garec had to remind himself that Hell was never anywhere, and would continue to stay that way for the foreseeable future.

"Are the boys and Elethe ready?" he asked.

"They're helping prep the horses with Sirona," Donnan said.

"Good. Well—" Garec scanned the camp, noting that his men had doused their fires and were waiting for him to give the signal. "—that's it then. Time to ride."

He gave a nod then began to march to the stables with Donnan. The men came alive, packing up supplies, and disassembling their tents. They did it with practiced precision, making as little noise or fuss as possible. By the time Garec had reached the edge of the camp, every tent had been packed away, and now the men were forming up behind him. At the back of the line should've been his Lieutenants along with the Sprinter, Clarine. If she ran now, it would all be over.

But no, she would not run. Donnan and his men would stay by his side, the boys would be safe from capture, Elethe would live, and Elyssanar would remain free. Nothing would stop them.

"They finished quick," Donnan said, nodding to the line of horses already saddled.

"It's a sign," Garec said.

"Aye. We'll ride with the speed of Elysium."

Garec climbed atop his horse Fletcher, a strong war stallion, and prodded him towards the road. Donnan soon came up beside him on his own horse along with Elethe. She looked tired and uneasy, but it had been an early start; she liked sleeping in. Garec heard the sounds of his men mounting and riding up from behind.

"Are you ready?" he asked Elethe.

"It's only two hundred soldiers and their horses," she said casually. "I should be able to manage for an hour."

"Good. As soon as you sense Clarine channeling, hit us with all you've got."

*

Elethe was never sure how to explain what it was like to sense another Emogician's channeling. It was like hearing a noise and knowing exactly where it was coming from, only she didn't hear anything. Or maybe it was like being able to feel a ray of sunshine hitting something far away while standing in the shade, and for whatever reason the sun had different flavors.

No, that's stupid, she thought, right as she sensed Worry being channeled far behind her. It was no issue reaching out and Matching the Emogic; all Class 4s could channel to at least ten kilometers away. At Class 3.9, she was limited to only eight kilometers, but that was still nothing to scoff at.

Worry had a strange taste that rapidly switched between sour and spicy, and the energy was awkward to control, wanting to jump around and zig-zag sporadically. She reigned it in without effort and channeled it, splitting the energy into strands that pierced all the soldiers and horses. Once confident she had everyone, she poured all her strength into the Emogic and shifted it for speed, then nodded to Garec.

At his command, the Company began to move, trotting horses through the snow. It was hardly deep, and it was the dry sort that blew everywhere, but Elethe was fascinated by the way it moved with their passing. Nothing about the way the soldiers or horses moved indicated that they were really being affected by Elethe's channeling, except the snow tossed by the horses looked as if it was floating in place. Many others appeared entranced by it as well.

"Not something ye see every day," Donnan said, his voice weirdly warped and muffled. "Whoa, listen te that. Is that my voice? Heheheheh."

"Heeelloooooooo," Garec said, and the two men laughed. Elethe got caught up in the ridiculousness of its sound and laughed along.

Soon all the men were talking and laughing at their own voices. A few even fell off their horses because of it, amplifying the laughter all the more.

"Never thought we'd be leaving like this," Garec said, grinning. "I wonder what all this might sound like to everybody else."

"Screeching," Donnan said with a chuckle. "Very high-pitched screeching, if they can hear it at all. That's how a Sprinter I met a few years ago sounded like when he gave a speech while channeling. Ye'd think the poor man was dying, and he rather looked like he was too."

Garec snorted. "Well let's just hope we don't wake the entire Fort. Not that I'm worried. How you holding up, Elethe?"

"Just fine," Elethe said. "This really isn't that hard. Like I said, I could probably manage for an hour."

"And you didn't leave Dowyr behind?"

"Of course not."

She saw a gray tendril shoot towards Garec, and he nodded. Dowyr was only a short way back with Weynon and Sirona. They had done a surprisingly good job at saddling the horses. Weynon said he had done it a few times before, and Dowyr had seen it done from enough angles to do it himself.

They rode on for a time, the soldiers chatting between each other amicably. The bridge into Parasten was guarded, but only lightly, and there were no barriers on it. It must have been a complete surprise to those on guard when an entire Company passed over in the blink of an eye. Likely by the time they would manage to report it, the Company would be at least thirty kilometers into the country.

Strangely, once past the bridge, Elethe sensed Garec's anxiety spike. He didn't show it on the outside—something he had mastered—but Elethe was sure there was something wrong. She couldn't remember ever feeling so much negative emotion coming from him before news of the war came, and even afterwards it was never that much. It just wasn't like him. He was always determined and solid, never letting anything get him down. But how was she supposed to confront him about it? There was no way to tell how it might have to do with her family. Could it be something else?

"Uncle Garec, what do we do if we run into Kircan soldiers?" she asked.

"Run," he said, with no change of emotion. "You, Sirona, and the boys at least. The rest of us fight."

"What if they have Emogicians? Shouldn't I counter them?"

"Only if you can tell they're Class 4. Otherwise let me handle it. Weynon!"

Elethe frowned as Weynon moved his horse closer to Garec. So he wasn't anxious about encountering Kircans. What then? Did it have to do with the Sprinter? That didn't make sense, he was letting her go once far away enough from the border.

"What is it?" Weynon asked.

"When you listen to the land, can it tell you where there are people?"

"I don't know, I can ask though."

Elethe saw the Emogic of Peace pour out of Weynon, like a stream of sky blue that flowed smoothly through the air and laid gently over the ground like a giant blanket. Weynon focused on the earth for a few moments, as though seeing something beyond it, and blinked as he let go of the energy.

"It knows we're here," Weynon said.

"What about elsewhere?" Garec asked.

"I don't know, I tried to ask but... I don't think it understands the question. It just knows that we're where we are. I asked, 'are there more people far away?', and it just said, 'you are here, now there, moving swiftly'. The land doesn't understand distance. Maybe a bird would know."

"Ask if it understands direction."

Weynon looked back at the earth and channeled again. After a moment he made a confused look and stopped. "It... sort of does. It refers to the sun like a compass, but there's also some sort of energy that comes from 'the core' that's like another compass, but I don't know what the core is or what kind of energy it means. It's not an Emogic."

Garec shook his head. "Keep trying to learn what it knows. If there's any useful information the land can give us, we need it. And how are the horses? They're not freaked out, are they?"

Weynon channeled once again, this time moving the energy to a few different horses around him including his own. "They're fine, and some would like to go faster. It's cold and they want to run."

"Good, I want to put some distance between us and the Fort."

"Fletcher also hopes for a snack."

Garec smiled and patted his horse. "Soon."

Elethe sensed another wave of anxiety from him as he called for the Company to ride harder. She let her horse fall behind until she rode next to Sirona, who was keeping a hard eye on Dowyr. He didn't look entirely comfortable with riding despite claiming to have read all he needed to know on the subject.

"I'm worried about Garec," Elethe said to Sirona, though her voice hardly carried with the way sound behaved.

"What was that?" Sirona asked, and Elethe mentally slapped herself.

"I'm *worried* about *Garec.* There's something wrong, I just know it."

"So ask him, fool girl."

"Aren't you worried too?"

"Plentifully worried, and I suspect it's because you're channeling it. The Captain won't say anything to me anyways, I already spoke with him last night, so stop trying to get me to do your dirty work."

Elethe glanced back at the source of Worry she drew from. She couldn't see the woman, but it sent a chill down her spine knowing that Garec had been willing to trick her into coming.

It's only until we're far enough from the Fort, she told herself again.

Is that what was causing his anxiety? Having to let her go? She couldn't believe that, he wouldn't go back on his word. But if he was thinking about it, having any sort of temptation could explain his emotions.

Elethe decided to wait and see, and tried to tell herself it wasn't for fear of the truth.

There was little talk now, and after about half an hour—to her perception anyway; it had probably only been a couple minutes to the rest of the world—the Company slowed its pace, and she was beginning to feel channeling fatigue. It was faint, but as she expected it meant she had roughly twenty minutes left before channeling would become too difficult to continue. She wasn't worried about the Sprinter; simply drawing the Emogic out took about as much energy as keeping your eyes open.

Suddenly Garec called the Company to a halt, and everyone began pulling at their reins. Elethe urged her horse to the front, and she finally saw what had caused them to stop. A small pack of wolves was a short distance ahead of them, though they looked almost frozen in place. She could barely make out their heads turning towards them.

"Weynon," Garec called. "I want you to talk to them."

CHAPTER 14

The Boy Who Spoke Wolf

Weynon stared at the wolves ahead, his heart thumping. He had never run across any creatures more dangerous than a street dog, and just the idea of talking to wolves was terrifying. They were hardly moving, and at least a stone throw away, but he couldn't help himself from wanting to turn his horse and run. Even the horses looked agitated at the sight of the wolves, though not Fletcher.

"I won't be able to hear them going this fast," Weynon managed to say, hoping Garec wouldn't risk the wolves being able to chase with their usual speed.

"Elethe, stop channeling once you see Weynon make a connection," Garec said.

Weynon clenched his reins. There had to be another excuse to get out of talking to them, but he couldn't think of one.

Dowyr rode up beside him and channeled, *"Are you seriously scared of talking to wolves?"*

He nodded and, not wanting Garec to hear him, signed, *big scary teeth.*

"But they're like the coolest animals! Come on, you can do it."

"Don't worry, Weynon," Elethe called. "If anything goes wrong, Donnan and I can take care of it."

Weynon took a deep breath and nodded, then channeled, first reaching out to the horses and calming them, then reaching out to the pack of wolves. He felt and heard nothing at first, but then the wolves were suddenly moving normally, and they stopped abruptly to turn towards the Company, a spike of alarm coming from them at the sight of everyone.

Hello, Weynon sent. *Don't be afraid, we won't hurt you. I'm Weynon.*

A long series of images flashed through Weynon's mind, which was common when communicating with animals, but he also received scents and feelings. It all translated in his mind into understandable language.

A two legs that speaks wolf? Curiosity.

He who speaks wolf, but is not a wolf. Wonder, and something else… nostalgia?

Earthbrother. Awe.

Another swarm of images flashed in Weynon's mind, and he understood them to be the names of all the wolves. Short Snout, Prancer, Raindrop, Smellerbug, and Farsight, the pack leader.

Weynon sent his name to them again.

We do not know two legs' names, Farsight sent. *We will call you Little Rider.*

"Well?" Garec asked.

"I'm talking to them," Weynon said. "What do you want me to ask?"

"Ask if they know where there might be enemy camps."

Weynon did so, and the wolves' responses came quickly.

Two legs are all the same to us, and we do not go near them, Farsight sent. *But we have smelled many packs wandering from morning to evening sun.*

How far? Weynon asked.

What they returned was confusing to him, making him wonder whether they understood the question. He saw the sun move across the sky, as though it would take that long to reach the two legs at a wolf's pace, but had no clue how far that meant.

Your horses move like lightning, Raindrop sent. *We did not smell you coming.*

Do you hunt other two legs? Prancer sent.

Just two very dangerous ones, Weynon sent. *Thank you for your help.*

How dangerous? Farsight sent before Weynon cut his channeling.

One leads big armies, the other moves mountains and changes rivers.

The wolves snarled in response, sending a mix of fear and hatred. Some of the nearby archers stirred, watching the wolves and fiddling with their arrows.

We know this Earth Slayer, Short Snout sent. *He has killed many of our brothers and sisters.*

Weynon's eyes widened and he turned to Garec. "They know Royce."

Garec's face hardened. "Could they lead us to him?"

Weynon asked the question, and the wolves looked between each other as if discussing their answer.

We do not hunt for two legs, Farsight sent. *Nor do we have Earth Slayer's scent, but we will share your name and scent, Little Rider, so our brothers and sisters will know you are an Earthbrother friend and give you guidance.*

Be wary, young pup, Smellerbug sent. *The final hunt is long away, but Shadowwalker stirs.*

The wolves all looked towards Garec, then dashed off into the brush.

"What was that?" Garec asked. "Do they want us to follow?"

Weynon shook his head. "They don't know where Royce is, but they're gonna tell other wolves about me, ones who might know where he is and can lead us to him. I think." He did not like the idea of who knows how many other wolves knowing about him. What Smellerbug had sent also sounded ominous, and vaguely familiar, though he couldn't think of why. "Dowyr, would you know what or who 'Shadowwalker' is?"

Dowyr looked surprised. *"That's an obscure name for Hell. It only appears once in The Five Sentinels, in the book of the Blind Poet. Why?"*

"One of them said that he stirs, and that's when they looked at Garec."

Garec idly tugged at his riding gloves. "Interesting. They must be able to sense Voidspeakers. Maybe that's why dogs have always avoided me since my Apex. Was there anything else?"

Weynon nodded. "They said there are groups of two leg—I mean, humans moving from morning to evening sun. East to west, I guess. I don't know how many or how far exactly. Probably an hour or two away by horse, I'm not sure. Wolves speak very strangely."

"Better than nothing. We'll move north for now. Elethe, are you okay to continue?"

Elethe looked like she was falling asleep in her saddle, but she shook herself and nodded. "Just need some food and water. Had a light breakfast, so if I can rest a bit, I should be able to channel for another forty minutes, probably."

"We should be safe enough for that." He raised his voice and began riding to the back of the Company. "Everyone, ten-minute break."

Weynon climbed out of his saddle, glad the snow was barely covering the ground, and put a feedbag on his horse as the rest of the soldiers did. He helped Dowyr put it on for his horse, as he struggled just to stay standing.

I can't feel my legs, Dowyr signed.

Weynon smiled. "You'll get used to it."

Can your Emogic bring peace to muscles?

Weynon laughed and shook his head. "Why don't you ask Sirona for healing?"

Dowyr gave him a look of utter horror and channeled, "*You really think she'd willingly make me feel* better? *No sir! I will happily suffer instead.*"

Weynon nodded and took a small notebook and charcoal out of his pack, then made a checkmark. "That's willingly enduring suffering off the list."

"Hey, hey, hey, what's that? Are you trying to see if I'm following teachings from The Five Sentinels?"

Weynon grinned. "Somebody's got to keep track."

"Oh yeah?" Dowyr marched up to Weynon and punched him in the gut. He folded with a gasp and dropped the notebook. *"Willingly endure that, you—"*

Dowyr noticed the notebook and picked it up. He would've found no such list, just a checkmark on a blank page. Weynon held his stomach, laughing and wheezing.

"You... damn you. You're a real bastard. Get up." Dowyr reached down and pulled Weynon to his feet as he began coughing. *"Light, I didn't mean to hit that hard. Are you made of paper or something? Go see Sirona."*

"I'm fine," Weynon wheezed, smiling. "She kinda scares me too. Got you real good, though."

Dowyr shook his head, though he couldn't help but smile too. *"Yeah, you did."* He smacked him on the forehead with the notebook. *"Don't do it again, or you're gonna start seeing why Hell was named Shadowwalker, kay?"*

Weynon took back the notebook then looked towards where the wolves had been. "Why do you think wolves are cool?"

Dowyr shrugged. *"Because... they're smart. I read a couple books about them, and they're a lot more sophisticated than most people think. In a lot of ways, they're like us. They hunt together, protect each other, and they make sure everyone knows who's in charge without killing each other. Well, maybe not like us there."*

"In all the books you've read, have you ever found something called the final hunt?"

Dowyr looked thoughtful. *"No, I don't think so. What is it?"*

"I don't know, just something one of them mentioned. I think it's related to Hell somehow."

Dowyr was motionless for a moment, then narrowed his eyes at Weynon. *"Have you read all of The Five Sentinels? Beginning to end?"*

"No, not yet. I'm not old enough to read the last three books. Why?"

For as long as Weynon could remember, it was taught that The Five Sentinels could only be read up to a certain point depending on your age. Any child, no matter the age, could read the first few books, roughly a quarter of The Five Sentinels. They were full of simple stories and doctrines, many even a four-year-old could understand. At the age of eleven, all but the last three books became available, adding more in-depth books like The Wisdoms of Paradise, Zion & The Halberd, and Three Sages' Parables. The last three books were not to be opened until the age of seventeen, said to contain the most complex truths and mysteries.

Dowyr made a funny laugh. "*Of course, you wouldn't secretly read ahead like everyone else. Well, what that wolf said could have to do with something mentioned in the last book.*"

"What's that?"

Dowyr gave him a skeptical look. "*You really want to know?*"

Weynon shrugged. "Nothing says I can't listen to you tell me about it."

"*Fair enough. Well... the last book references the first, restating that Heaven will come to Earth someday, but there's more context as to why. He's supposed to come because Hell will break free, and so there'll be one final battle. Completely ridiculous, but maybe that's what the wolf was referring to.*"

Weynon silently thought about that. A final battle between Heaven and Hell? A final hunt related to Hell? They certainly sounded similar enough to be related, but how could that be true? Hell was meant to stay imprisoned for the rest of time. What did it mean that he could escape? Perhaps the answers would come when he was old enough to read the last books of The Five Sentinels. And at least the wolf made it sound like the final hunt wasn't any time soon, so he tried to not worry.

"Mount up!" Garec called, and Weynon and Dowyr began scrambling to ready their horses and climb back on with the rest of the soldiers. "Let's get moving again. Elethe, how long do you have left?"

"Ehh… I'm going to say half an hour," Elethe said.

"I'll take it. Whenever you're ready."

Weynon took a moment to channel at Elethe and sent a wave of calmness to her. She looked at him with mild surprise.

I want to help, he signed with a smile.

She grimaced and signed, *Thanks, but please don't. I don't deserve your help.*

Weynon's smile faded, but he set his jaw and channeled another wave to her. *Says who?* he signed. *You get it anyway.*

Elethe didn't look pleased with that, but at least the tension in her shoulders melted away for the moment. That was good enough for him.

The Company began to ride north at a steady pace, and there was little to speak of. The land rolled gently by in mild snow-covered slopes with a sparse gathering of bare trees and bushes. Weynon felt terribly exposed from all sides, not only to human eyes but also wolves. Who could ever feel comfortable knowing wolves were spreading your name amongst themselves, intending to find you again? Even knowing they were trying to help him, it sent a shiver down his spine.

CHAPTER 15

A Need For Worry

Dowyr was getting real tired of horses. They didn't always do what he wanted, the ride was terribly bumpy, and it was such a hassle to take care of them. The worst of it was that he wanted to think, and he found it unbelievably hard to concentrate on anything other than staying upright and in control. At least the beast wasn't intentionally trying to throw him off. Yet.

Relief finally came as Garec called the Company to a halt near a stream for a break. They were still out in the open, though they hadn't found a trace of any Kircan soldiers. Donnan found a dry stone to sit on and began to meditate, or so it looked, but it was less than a minute before his eyes opened and he came up to Garec.

"Nobody but us from here te the horizon far as I can tell," he said. "The stream continues northward for maybe another three kilometers, and another directly east that looks like it goes on much further. It's got a road alongside it, though I couldn't make out a bridge anywhere. Maybe four meters across at the narrowest point."

"How far do you think we've gone?" Garec asked.

"Anywhere from thirty-five te forty kilometers I'd guess."

Garec turned to Dowyr, signing, *link.*

Uh oh, Dowyr thought, but channeled and made a telepathy link with Garec.

She's going to become suspicious if we go much further, Garec thought, and Dowyr had no need for him to say who *she* was. The image of Clarine came with the thought.

So? We're letting her go, no big deal. We've got Elethe.

But think of the lives we'd save with access to a Sprinter. It could mean stopping the Tyrdens weeks sooner than we would otherwise, and they'd never see us coming. Without her, we'd need to go slow and plan every step of the way. That might mean months before we have a chance at them. We'd have to hide through the winter.

Dowyr shifted uncomfortably. Garec had a point, but something didn't feel right. *I guess. But what can we do? It's not like I can just make her want to stay.*

I have an idea. Go talk with her, read her mind and learn what her children look like.

Dowyr narrowed his eyes. Talk with her? Learn what her kids looked like? What, was he supposed to make them suddenly appear and somehow maintain the illusion until—

You want me to show her kids being held captive by Kircans, Dowyr thought matter-of-factly.

Garec's face remained passive. *It's the only thing that can convince her to stay and help us. Go; wasted seconds cost lives.*

Dowyr was so startled from the sheer weight and force of Garec's thoughts that he cut the link and started for the officers in search of Clarine. His mind scrambled for words, but everything sounded so fake. Memories sprung up of times back at the orphanage when he listened to the other boys and girls talking with potential mothers and fathers while he sat in a corner, ignored. Why was he remembering *that*? He hated those days, not able to go outside or be alone, just being out with the rest of the orphans and adults, most of which couldn't understand him. Eventually he understood he had gotten too old for anyone to want him, and those who approached him and understood signs were usually church clergy that took pity on him, and he didn't need some stuck-up pastor lording it over him, so he usually met them with blasphemy of some sort. He had eventually become infamous in religious circles, and soon pastors or other clergy were coming in trying to convert him or demonstrate some sort of intellectual superiority like it was a competition. That lasted maybe two months. At the time, it was amusing that even though they believed Heaven never gave up on anyone, they gave up on him. Now it was just pathetic.

All crap memories. What was he doing again?

"Something wrong, alien?" a voice asked.

Dowyr shook himself and saw one of Garec's officers giving him a wave.

Looking for Clarine, Dowyr signed.

The officer pointed behind himself. "With her horse, just a bit further."

Thanks.

Dowyr walked past the officer and spotted Clarine brushing down her horse. A thought occurred to him: if he spoke with her through channeling, she'd know he was a Boredom Emogician, which might make her suspicious of anything she saw from then on, perhaps including seeing her children captive.

I'll make it look like I'm not mute, Dowyr thought. *Just in case.*

He began channeling at her, part sensory manipulation, part one-way telepathy link so he could sense the words and images going through her head, though he only focused on any images. Now to figure out what to say...

"*Hi, I haven't met you yet,*" he 'said', using what he thought sounded like childish curiosity. Really it sounded unbelievably stupid.

Clarine turned to him and her eyes widened. She got down on one knee to be at eye-level. "Where did you come from? You can't be one of the soldiers."

"*Oh, no, I'm just—*" Dowyr felt a flood of panic as he realized he had no excuse for his being with Garec. *What Emogic am I?* he thought. *Why would Garec need me?* His mind ran through the list of Emogics, and halfway through the answer came. *"Just one of the Boosters for our Empaths, helping out however I can."*

"But you don't look any older than thirteen, why in Heaven's name would you be in with the army?"

Dowyr tried to imitate Weynon's innocent smile. *"I'm fourteen. I told Heaven I want to help, and he said to do whatever I can that my bravery allows, and I'm very brave. I met the Captain back at the Academy; I liked him and asked if I could help him, so he took me and promised to keep me safe. My name's Dowyr, what's yours?"*

What complete *idiocy*. Clarine was eating it all up at least.

"It's nice to meet you, Dowyr. I'm Clarine, just a Sprinter here to help with our patrol mission. It certainly is very brave of you to be here, but what about your parents? Aren't they worried sick about you?"

Dowyr shook his head. At least with this he could be honest. *"I'm an orphan, I never knew my parents. You wouldn't happen to be looking to adopt, would you?"*

Clarine gave a pained smile. "I'm afraid my hands are already full with two little monsters to take care of." And there they were, a boy and a girl floating through her mind, though they didn't look like monsters. That was easier than expected. "Is the Captain the one taking care of you?"

"Yes, but I can take care of myself too," Dowyr 'said'. *"He's busy enough being the leader. I'm just happy to help. I have to go do something for him now, but it's nice to meet you, Clarine!"*

"It's lovely to meet you as well, Dowyr. Heaven bless you."

Dowyr turned and ran off, heart pounding. He felt drained, unusually so considering how little he'd been channeling. That was the first time he'd ever lied in such a way. He'd lied plenty of times before, but they were always little ones, and he didn't consider using his Emogic to prank others lying. What he made them see *was* real, in a matter of speaking. So if Clarine really did see her children held captive, that would be the reality, because she'd act as if that were the reality.

Except he knew it wouldn't be. But it had to be worth it if it meant stopping the war early. Anything had to be worth that; he remembered reading historical accounts of past wars, and going by them, there couldn't be anything worse than letting a war go on. Even the wars in The Five Sentinels were brutal. The earlier it ended, the better. It couldn't be any other way.

Dowyr found Garec at the front of the company. *I have them,* he signed once he got the Captain's attention.

Garec nodded, then crashed to the ground as though a boulder had smashed into his side. Dowyr was knocked over in the same way, and he heard the soldiers and horses begin screaming. He barely caught a glimpse of the entire Company being knocked off their feet or horses. In the midst of the calamity, he heard Elethe's strained voice shouting.

"CLASS 3 PUFFER!"

*

It was a short-lived battle, but chaotic nonetheless, as battles tend to be when Emogics are involved. The first of which in retaliation came from Elethe Matching the Pride that had knocked them down and directing it back to its source, striking at the small force of Kircan soldiers and giving time for the Company to gather its bearings. Elethe wasn't sure what else to do as she sensed people start channeling from all around. A Class 4 had to be careful or they risked collateral damage.

Garec cried out, "Dowyr! Link!" as he scrambled to his feet, though it took Dowyr a moment to figure out which way was up as adrenaline rushed through his system and a hundred things seemed to be happening at once. He managed to establish the link, and in the time it took to do so, Garec spotted Clarine at the back of the Company and channeled Indifference at her, barely stopping an attempt to speed away and hide before the fighting escalated. She still panicked and ran as the soldiers realized where their attackers were coming from and began grabbing weapons.

Oh, looks like my plan's coming together, Hell said in Garec's mind, though he hardly noticed it as he prepared more streams of Indifference to channel at enemy Kircans. Which direction were they? East?

Dowyr crouched low to the ground as Boughton and his platoon of archers launched into the sky and began raining arrows down on the Kircans who were struggling to retreat after being knocked down by Elethe. It had only taken their Puffer realizing Elethe was near Class 4 to convince them to run. The smart ones knew the futility of running and dropped to the ground with their arms raised, but the raining arrows didn't discriminate. Dowyr covered his ears, focusing only on maintaining his link with Garec.

What do I do, what do I do? he asked, though the Captain was preoccupied with running up the hill to see what was happening.

Weynon was channeling to calm both himself and the horses so they wouldn't run off and trample anyone, while Sirona was darting to any soldiers who'd been seriously hurt when thrown to the ground. The rest of the Company was in full assault of the fleeing Kircans, sparing none. Arrows and violent Emogics took most of them out, with mounted spears finishing off the rest.

Now's the time, Garec finally sent through the link. *Make Clarine stay with us.*

Dowyr's heart pounded as he whipped his head around in search for Clarine. He didn't want to be here, he didn't want to be doing this, but those were less important thoughts. Lives were at stake, even if they were ones he'd never know. Running away from the battle, he cut his link to Garec and spotted Clarine, still fleeing for her life.

He began channeling the deception. The screams of her children, a handful of enemy Kircans hauling them on horseback, and a Jumper teleporting them away. He made sure she was watching, made sure she understood. And it worked. The woman went berserk, though Garec still blocked her channeling. Once the fighting had come to a halt, quite abruptly as the Company had easily crushed what little resistance there was, Garec cut his channeling. Clarine zipped towards where she had seen her children vanish, a trail of snow bursting outward from her passing, and a cry of anguish that reached everyone's ears. Their hearts raced at the sound, some from battle adrenaline readying them for more, but others as if they had been struck with guilt of a terrible crime, which Dowyr felt most of all. Garec went to where Clarine knelt. The eyes of the Company followed him for but a moment before turning to their post-battle responsibilities; retrieving arrows, cleaning weapons, checking on comrades. But Dowyr watched him, frozen in place as he waited for her sobbing to subside.

"We're going after them," he said, his voice loud and clear. "We'll get them back."

Had Elethe not been so consumed by the torrents of emotion coursing through everyone, she might have wondered what he was talking about. Weynon was occupied talking to the horses that had been left behind by the archer platoon. But Dowyr was listening, hearing over the beating of his own heart.

Clarine breathed for a moment, then her voice rang like ice. "I'm coming with you."

A chill ran down Garec's back. *Forgive me, Heaven,* he thought, *because I don't think this woman ever will.*

CHAPTER 16

The First Torments

Dowyr's heart dropped into his stomach at the first sight of the body. He'd seen paintings and illustrations of the dead, but something about those always seemed unreal and distant. Out here, in the freezing cold and surrounded by soldiers, it was altogether different. Patches of snow were painted dark red around the body. The arrows that pierced it—no, him—had already been removed and cleaned. Here was a man, just a man, who once had a whole life ahead of him, probably with family and friends who loved him. Now he was gone forever, and it was almost certain they'd never learn what happened to him. Dowyr couldn't see his face, buried in the snow as it was. A part of him wondered what it looked like, but he shuddered at the thought of turning him over to see.

Weynon approached and stopped next to him to also stare at the body.

"*We should at least bury them,*" Dowyr channeled.

"No," Weynon said with no hint of emotion. "The snow will bury them, then nature will take care of the rest when Spring comes."

Dowyr gaped at his friend, too stunned for words. Weynon didn't seem to notice as he turned back to the Company. Dowyr's stare followed him for a moment, then he looked back at the body one more time before going to find his horse. On the way back he spotted Elethe alone by her horse, crying inconsolably. He turned away, worried that the sight would end up with him in roughly the same state. Sirona was still helping some of the soldiers who'd been injured when knocked off their horses. There were amazingly no casualties on their side.

He passed Garec and Donnan and overheard some of their conversation.

"How did they ambush us like that?" Garec asked. "You said there was no one in sight."

Donnan hefted his shoulders with a deep frown. "I said I couldn't tell if there was anyone but us. They must've had a Deadbeat."

That would have explained how they had ambushed them out of nowhere. Deadbeats, or Depression Emogicians, could conceal people from a Ghost's astral projection sight as well as the channeling of Emogics. An essential Emogician for surprise attacks.

Garec scanned the soldiers. "We're alive, at least. I want you to bury them and get rid of any trace there was a fight here."

"Aye, I'm glad I can do that much. I didn't see any escape but you should double-check with Boughton."

"Right. We'll get a move on as soon as you're done."

"Won't take but a moment."

Donnan walked off and Garec caught Dowyr's eye and approached, glancing around warily.

"What did she see?" he asked.

Jumper teleported her kids and a couple Kircans away, Dowyr signed.

Garec gave a nod. "Well done. I'll let my officers know what happened. With luck, this will all be over before any more cities get buried. Mount up, we need to get moving."

Dowyr hummed and continued on toward his horse. The beast seemed entirely oblivious to the battle's aftermath. He wished he could have that same luxury. As he struggled to get on, it occurred to him that he needed to be careful not to use signs if Clarine was in sight, or at the very least move his mouth when talking to someone else. That would be annoying.

More annoying than believing your children have been kidnapped? He winced at the thought.

A Sunray flew overhead—Boughton, the Class 2.8 Happiness Emogician that led the platoon of archers which killed most of the fleeing Kircans—and landed next to Garec. Dowyr initially questioned why Garec didn't just use someone like that to fly a small team of assassins straight into Kircany, but he realized that there could be a few different complications. Kircany would at least have Emogicians dedicated to detecting and stopping anything like that. A small Company of soldiers was probably the best way of going about it, especially considering Elethe. Anything too powerful coming at them could be fired right back, or Garec could cut off their channeling, or Donnan could bury them instantly.

An hour later they were on the move. Elethe was too tired to help speed up the Company for the time being, so Garec kept them at a steady pace. Dowyr rode next to Weynon near the front of the column. Everyone was silent, a stark contrast to how they started out this morning.

Dowyr made sure Clarine was out of sight before channeling to Weynon. *"Are you okay?"*

Weynon shrugged. "I'm fine. You?"

Dowyr stared ahead, unsure how to respond. *"Didn't the battle... bother you?"*

"They were the enemy, and we didn't lose anyone. I'd rather we didn't have to fight at all, but it's our responsibility to deal with our enemies, and they attacked us first. Did the battle bother you? I can help with that."

Dowyr shook his head. *"No, no... I'm fine. Just wanted to make sure you were okay."*

Weynon smiled. "Thanks. Maybe you should check on Elethe too."

Dowyr looked back to Elethe. She rode a short way from everyone else, though perhaps unaware of it. Her head was cast down, and her arms dangled while holding her horse's reins as if she didn't care where the beast went.

"Okay."

He let his horse fall back, but not all the way to Elethe. For some reason he couldn't bring himself to talk to her. Well, it wasn't like she would want to talk to him of all people after what happened. Who would? What could the ugly mute twerp do or say to make anything better? All he'd been good for so far was mentally kidnapping a young woman's children.

Why did I say I was a Booster? He thought, turning his eyes to his saddle's pommel. It was easier to stare at that than meet anyone else's gaze. *I can't pretend Heaven talks to me; Heaven's not even real.*

He grumbled at himself for not thinking of something better, then gave a start as he realized Elethe had brought her horse right next to his and was looking straight at him. He shifted uneasily, only managing short glances at her.

What? he signed, making a point not to channel, then quickly glanced around to make sure Clarine was nowhere in sight.

Elethe spoke softly, only loud enough for him to hear. "You did something during the fight that makes you feel terrible. What was it?"

I didn't do anything. He was glad signs didn't have the issue of tone of voice which sometimes gave away when someone was lying.

"I know your thumb twitches when you're lying."

Bloody Hell. She knew that too? Just how much did she know about him? He would've asked right then if he hadn't thought she'd lie about it.

I don't want to talk about it, he signed, still not looking at her. *What about you? What did you do during all that?*

Elethe grimaced and looked away. "Are you afraid of me?" she asked, almost too softly for him to hear.

She didn't look back at him to see an answer, but he didn't give one. Instead, he leaned over and slapped her arm. It didn't quite have the effect he wanted with her coat's padding, yet it was enough to get her to glare at him.

Wouldn't do that if I was, he signed.

Elethe rolled her eyes. "You're still not channeling to say that."

"I'm tired, give me a break," he channeled.

In truth, he was afraid of her in a way. Elethe was perhaps the most powerful person on Earth. All she needed was a small handful of Class 1 Emogicians to become unstoppable, and that terrified him. But then, she was only a teenage girl a couple years older than him, and without someone else channeling, she couldn't do much except sense others' emotions. In that sense, she was only scary because she was a girl.

He continued to channel at her and decided to finally ask about what had been bugging him for months. *"If you want a real answer, tell me how much you learned about me when you first used Boredom back at the Academy."*

As he channeled, he added telepathy to listen in on Elethe's thoughts in case she tried to lie. Her answer immediately made itself clear to his mind.

Everything.

That made him cut his channeling, but then she answered with her voice.

"Everything."

Dowyr stared at her in shock, half for telling the truth, and half for the answer itself. She had used his own Emogic against him, learned everything there was to know about him, and still hadn't killed him?

Snakes, she knows everything about me, he thought, his face reddening.

He supposed she could always kill him later.

"Sorry," Elethe said. "I didn't mean to. I was… tired. You don't have to channel or give me an answer if you don't want."

He snorted. *"Don't tell me what I don't have to do. Yeah, I'm not afraid of you. You think I'd prank a Class 4 Empath as much as I have if I was?"*

She gave him an annoyed look. "I feel like you've done it so much precisely because I'm… what I am… and you know you can get away with it."

"Nah, you're just the most fun to prank."

He thought he caught the briefest glimpse of a smile from her, but he could've just been seeing things. They rode on in silence for a time, and his mind drifted back to the battle. He was grateful he hadn't seen all that much of it, but he never wanted to experience other people within shouting distance deliberately trying to kill him ever again.

"How many Emogicians did they have?" he asked, curiosity getting the better of him.

Elethe shook her head. "I don't know, there was so much going on at once. At least two. If I hadn't been so exhausted from channeling, I might've felt their presence earlier."

"Donnan thought they had a Deadbeat, so it's not your fault. At least we didn't lose anyone." Except Clarine's fake children.

Elethe narrowed her eyes at him. "That felt like a lie."

"What? I wasn't l—"

He noticed his Emogic surge into Elethe and rush back at him, and he barely managed to cut his channeling as it touched him. It was too late, however, as Elethe gasped in shock.

"You made her see...?" Her eyes filled with understanding as she looked back at where Clarine would be, then narrowed again as they darted to Garec up ahead. "And he told you to..."

A blaze of determination sparked in her eyes, and she kicked her horse forward.

Dowyr made a strangled yelp and flung his arm at Elethe's reins, seizing them and pulling her horse back. She shot him a dangerous look, which he answered with an exaggerated shaking of his head.

"You can't say or do anything," he channeled.

Elethe scowled. "Why not? I won't let my uncle bully you and Clarine into doing this."

Dowyr gave her the most serious look he had probably ever given anyone in his life. *"He didn't bully me to do anything. I did this. It's my burden, not yours. We need Clarine. If we lose her, we'll probably die, and so would a lot of other people. I don't want the lives of thousands of people on my conscience. I can deal with tricking one woman into thinking her kids are in danger. Besides, think of the happy ending: we kill the Tyrdens, end the war, Clarine gets to know her children were safe all along, and we all go home as heroes."*

Elethe stared at him without expression, but her eyes began to glisten with tears. "I hate what this happy ending is making us do. Especially someone like you."

A shiver ran down Dowyr's spine. Before today, he had never seriously thought of killing anyone. Some part of him had clung to the hope that someone else would put a stop to Royce and Roderick before the Company did. He still wanted to hope that could happen, but the reality of what they were doing had sunk in. Of what they *had* to do. He could taste bile rising in his throat and forced it down.

It's just me and Weynon, he thought. *Me and...*

He took a deep breath and channeled, *"Will you promise me something?"*

Elethe frowned. "What?"

"If something goes wrong with all this, and we're in danger... save Weynon. If you can."

She sniffed. "Chances are I could save you both."

He shook his head. *"If for whatever reason you couldn't, and you had to choose, pick Weynon. Promise."*

She grimaced and looked away. "Alright. I promise."

He gave an appreciative nod. More than anything he wanted to make sure Weynon came out of this alive, and with Elethe knowing everything about him, he figured she would understand and agree. Not that he hoped such a scenario would ever come up.

The rest of the day's travels went with little else said. Elethe regained enough strength to channel Clarine's Emogic to speed them along one more time, and by the day's end, they were nearing the Parastenian town of Leife.

CHAPTER 17

Leife

Weynon leaned against a tree, arms folded and shivering. It had gotten horribly cold once the sun dipped beyond the horizon, and no one was getting a fire started. There was still light in the sky, quickly fading, allowing him to make out Garec who stood nearby, watching Donnan sitting on the ground with his eyes closed and head drooped. A minute later, his eyes opened and he stood up.

"Possibly a full platoon of Kircans, hard te tell," Donnan said. "Got spooked thinking one of em sensed me, might've been an Empath. Class 1 if he was, otherwise I'd have been discovered for sure."

"And the townsfolk?" Garec asked.

"Didn't see many of their men about, but otherwise acting as ye'd expect of Parastenians."

"Lovely. Well, we can't just sit here and expect them to help themselves. Boughton! Alann! You're with us."

The two men came running up. Weynon had played Sentinels versus Snakes with them both. Boughton even made a few games more interesting by channeling to let everyone fly. Alann was a Class 1.7 Fear Emogician who always played on the side of the Snakes and was the only soldier Weynon hadn't been able to tag out. Maybe that was because the others had gone easy on him, but he wanted to believe he was just that good and Alann was simply better.

"What's the plan, Sir?" Boughton asked.

"We're flying in and taking out the Kircans. Quietly. Alann, you'll give us cover on our approach, and if you spot any officers, paralyze them. We want any who might know something about the Tyrdens alive. Donnan will land just outside the town and take care of any problems."

The two soldiers gave a "Yes, Sir," and within a moment, darkness enshrouded the four of them before they launched into the sky, vanishing.

Weynon remembered why Fear Emogicians were called Night Stalkers and shivered all the more. He looked around to the other officers left behind. "What are we supposed to do?"

"Wait until he gives word," one of them said. "Shouldn't be long."

Dowyr came walking over, keeping his hands squished under his armpits. "*More fighting ahead?*" he channeled.

Weynon shrugged. "Not for us."

"*Good. You know something funny? I can make other people's hands feel warm, but not my own. I thought I should be able to because I can make myself see things, but I guess I can't make myself feel things. So unfair.*"

"Maybe it's a good thing. Like how would you know if you were getting frostbite if you couldn't feel it?"

Some of the soldiers gave a brief look of confusion at Weynon before noticing Dowyr. It was always weird to be having a conversation with someone no one else could hear, unless he specifically meant them to.

"*I guess, but I still hate it. I hope whatever they're doing out there will mean we get to sleep indoors.*"

Weynon nodded. Sleeping outside most of the way to Fort Calhoun hadn't been too terrible, but it had gotten much colder since. They had no Emogicians that could create shelters from the cold, only a Dragon—a Frustration Emogician—for starting fires, who was currently lighting some torches before they were in pitch darkness. No moon shone, but the sky was clear and the stars were out in full. Weynon tried to focus on them instead of the surrounding darkness.

A part of him was scared he'd see a pair of wolf eyes out there, ridiculous as it was. He doubted the wolves would find him again the same day, but that hadn't stopped him from shifting around in his saddle and keeping an eye on all sides of the Company.

Perhaps half an hour later, though it had felt like an eternity, Boughton landed from out of nowhere and gave the all-clear. The Company began moving into Leife.

Leife was a decently sized town, with fields and farms aplenty surrounding it, and the layout curved alongside the river. A large stone bridge wide enough for a carriage was built across the river in the middle of the town, though why anyone would want to travel further north was a mystery to Weynon. There were few towns this far north as it was.

He noticed an odd lack of any lightstones anywhere, which most towns in Elyssanar used to light the streets. Instead, large torches mounted on poles gave enough light to see the way, and they also illuminated a garish array of colors painted on the houses. Weynon wondered why anyone would want their home to look so sickening, though maybe they looked better in daylight. There was another thing about the houses that was peculiar; each had at least one fabric cone sitting on the roof. Sticks poked out from their tips, creating small openings from which smoke drifted upwards. Each cone had a different pattern with colors to match the houses.

Dowyr noticed him staring and pointed at one of the cones. "*Chimney covers so the Snakes can't sneak into their homes through the chimney. Parastenians also have a strange belief that making everything look bright, fun, and silly helps ward away Hell and prevent violence. I wish it worked. Gotta respect them for sticking to it though.*"

Weynon frowned. "My mom told me about them, how they wouldn't fight back even if Heaven told them to."

"*They don't believe Heaven would ever tell them to.*"

"Then they shouldn't name themselves after Paradise, because she's wise enough to know that if people won't fight when Hell comes against them, Hell wins."

"Unless nobody fights. Hell only comes against people through people. That's their point. There's a reason they say you can't change a Parastenian's mind about violence any more than you can turn a chicken into a cow."

Weynon scoffed. "It's a stupid point."

Dowyr made a noncommittal sound and looked around with a curious expression. *"I wonder why there are piles of clothes all over the pla—"*

Dowyr gasped and buried his face in his horse's mane. Weynon looked around, wondering what had frightened him, but there were just the odd piles of clothes, all similar looking, and a disturbing lack of people. He caught glimpses of eyes peeking out from windows or doors, but they vanished almost as he saw them.

The clothes, Dowyr signed. *Those were Kircans.*

Weynon finally realized what he meant. Donnan had phased the enemy soldiers out of their clothes and straight into the ground. Weynon shivered and channeled to calm Dowyr. A terrible way to go, but perhaps painless, done in an instant. Merciful. Yes, it was good to at least give their enemies a merciful end.

They reached the center of the village, a small open field in front of a large inn. Near the inn stood Garec and Donnan talking to a middle-aged man dressed in a bright green sleeping gown, who looked none too pleased, especially at the sight of the rest of the Company as they approached.

"You are welcome to our fires," the man said, "but I must ask you and your men leave all weapons with your horses."

Garec gave a slight bow. "Your fires warm my soul, and it will be done as you say." He looked at the approaching Company and called the order. The officers began repeating it down the line.

"How long do you mean to stay?" the man asked.

"One night," Garec said. "I intend to see this war over before it really begins, and that demands we keep on the move."

The man grunted. "And how to you plan to do that? More killing?" He shook his head. "Whatever you might think, a few dead men don't end wars."

"Haven't ye heard news of Irostead?" Donnan asked.

The man grimaced. "A day to make Paradise weep twice over, once for the city and its people, and again for the man so consumed by rage and violence."

Garec nodded. "If anything, I aim to prevent another city from suffering the same fate. No man alone should have such power."

"Hmm. Except to build up something greater than himself. I suppose we should get your men situated for the night. Cold, much too cold for this talk." He turned to the Company and gasped upon spotting Weynon, then again for Dowyr. "What madness," he breathed, eyes beginning to glisten. "What madness has taken you for there to be *children* in your ranks?"

Weynon frowned. "I'm here because I want to be."

The man blinked at him and shook his head, then walked to the inn with Donnan following. Garec gave Dowyr a meaningful look and signed, *get Elethe, need you both.*

Dowyr turned his horse away and rode back through the Company while Weynon started looking for a place to leave his horse. An officer came up to him and offered to take care of it. He thanked him, took his blankets, and made his way into the inn.

Two fires burned in the large common room, filling the space with a refreshing warmth that enveloped Weynon as he entered. There was an odd lack of anyone else from the town inside. He'd expected at least some young men playing dice or Kings at the tables, but there was only the green-robed man and Donnan, who busied himself moving tables and chairs to make room for sleeping mats. The green-robed man turned to Weynon when he entered.

"I cannot express how deeply the sight of you breaks my heart," he said. "What's your name?"

Weynon shifted uncomfortably, refusing to meet his eyes. "Weynon."

"You are welcome to our fires, Weynon. I am Elan, mayor of Leife. Forgive my forwardness, but, if I may ask… how did you come to be in such company?"

"The will of Heaven." Weynon hadn't meant for it to come out so coldly, but there it was. "He needs me to help stop Hell from using the Kircans to destroy us."

Garec, Dowyr, and Elethe entered and moved towards a staircase at the far end of the room.

"—don't know if I can channel any more without passing out," Elethe was saying, and she certainly looked on the verge of falling over right there.

"It will only be for a moment," Garec said. "You should be able to learn what we need in seconds."

Elethe sighed and nodded. Garec began leading them up the stairs, and Weynon caught Dowyr's eye long enough to sign, *?*

Mind-read interrogation, Dowyr signed back.

Elan watched them go up the stairs with narrowed eyes. "Mind-read? So all you children must be Emogicians."

"I'm a Druid," Weynon said, making himself stand a little taller. "Even the animals are helping us stop the Kircans. Why won't you?"

Elan sniffed. "I doubt Heaven's creatures care for one side over the other. We do not fight because it is not the way of Paradise. If the Kircans occupy our lands and take away our young men, so be it, they are welcome to our fires, just as all are. But we nor the men they take will bow to their demands."

"What if they decide to hurt you? Like Irostead?"

"Then we run."

Weynon scowled. "That's not what Heaven would do."

"We are not Heaven. It is arrogance to presume we can do what he can."

Weynon shook his head and moved past him to start helping Don-nan with the tables and chairs. Elan frowned and went back outside.

"Best te leave it be," Donnan said to him. "They're not the type to be reasoned with."

"They mock Heaven," Weynon said coldly. "They let fear tell them what to do."

"Not fear, no. That is a misreading. It is courage, and perhaps a stubbornness tougher than steel. Do they flee in the face of pointless death? Perhaps, but that can be said of all men. But when it comes te certain death, where there is no hope of running, they stare it in the face, side by side. It may frighten them, but they face it anyway. That takes courage, and it has always been their strength. It's what attracts people te them. That, and I suppose their beautiful women, which is a rather unfair advantage."

Weynon supposed he could see that courage, but it still seemed misplaced to him. The whole point that The Five Sentinels makes is that evil will always exist and rise up, and good must rise up against it. He would never be able to understand how the Parastenians might believe their way would put an end to evil.

The only right way was to fight back. That was the end of it.

*

Dowyr yawned as he followed Garec up the stairs. It wasn't nec-essarily late, but from the day's traveling, the battle, and the amount of channeling he'd done, exhaustion was setting into his bones. Elethe looked in even worse condition, mostly due to her channeling near her limit for long periods of time.

They entered a room with four men, one of them being Alann. He was focused on the other three, who stood stiff as a bone. Only their eyes moved, and wildly. Dowyr shivered at the sight.

"I just need you to read them," Garec said. "I'll ask questions if it'll help. It should only take a minute."

The men's eyes widened and began darting between Dowyr and Elethe. It made his skin crawl.

Elethe shrunk back but nodded. "Questions should help."

She looked to Dowyr. With a deep breath, he channeled his Emogic out, not sending it anywhere, and he saw it rush into Elethe and back out at the three men.

"Ready," Elethe mumbled.

Garec gave the men a hard look and began asking questions, pausing for a moment between each one. "Where's Royce? Where's Roderick? Do you know someone who would know where they are? Where can I find them? Are there any more Kircans scheduled to come here?" He turned to Elethe and was barely quick enough to catch her as she fainted. "Snakes! Dowyr, what—?"

She's fine, I think, Dowyr signed. *Too tired. Probably got the information we need though.*

Garec shook his head. "I need the information *now*. Can you get it?"

Dowyr bit his lip. "*I'll try. One at a time.*" He channeled a telepathy link to the first Kircan.

I'm gonna die, I'm gonna die, I'm gonna die, I'm gonna d-

He cut the link and nearly heaved up what was left inside his stomach.

"Are you ready?" Garec asked.

Dowyr shook his head and held up one finger. He cleared his throat and channeled to the next Kircan, trying to fuzz out all but the subconscious thoughts that crossed his mind. He gave Garec a thumbs-up.

"Where's Royce?"

Doesn't know, Dowyr signed.

"Do you know someone who would know where they are?"

Doesn't know, next man does. Dowyr shifted his channeling to the last Kircan. *Ready.*

"Where can I find someone who knows the location of the Tyrdens?"

Dowyr clenched his jaw as he tried to concentrate on the thoughts streaming through the Kircan's mind. He was putting up a mental fight, only bits and pieces coming through, but it was enough to get a solid answer despite his defensive efforts. *The City of Norwood, roughly 160 kilometers east and a bit south of here. A Colonel is stationed there. He knows.*

The Kircan hadn't known the distance, but Dowyr remembered all the maps he'd ever looked at and was confident the information was correct.

"Are there any more Kircans scheduled to come here?"

In two days.

Garec grimaced. "That's good enough, you can stop Dowyr. Go downstairs and get some rest."

Dowyr hesitated and looked between the frozen Kircans. *What are you going to do to them?* he signed.

"Nothing you need to worry about. Come on." Garec picked up Elethe, limp in his arms, and turned to the door.

Dowyr followed him down and wondered what the Kircans' names were.

CHAPTER 18

What's Hidden in the Fog

Weynon awoke to the sound of sniffling. As he looked around the common room he realized he'd slept longer than everyone else, as all the rest of the soldiers that had set up their mats on the floor were already gone, their things packed up. He could hear them outside though, so at least he hadn't been left behind. Dowyr and Garec wouldn't let that happen, of course.

Crouching near one of the fireplaces was Elethe, the source of the sniffling. Her back was to him, and she didn't seem to hear him as he got up. He thought of channeling to help her, but ever since he had done it without her asking, it felt wrong. Still, he couldn't let himself do nothing, so he walked over and crouched beside her, holding his hands out to the fire.

The only problem was he had no idea what to say. He couldn't think of anything comforting or profoundly meaningful. Not even a passage from The Five Sentinels that might bolster her spirits.

"Are you alright?" Was the best he could manage.

Elethe wiped away a tear. "I'm tired," she sighed. "Even after all that sleep."

Weynon nodded. One of the first things he'd learned back at the Academy was that if you exhausted yourself by channeling to the point of passing out, all the time spent unconscious hardly counted as proper sleep.

"No one knows what it's like being a Class 4 Empath," Elethe continued. "I can feel everything, all the time. I try to block it out, but sometimes… it gets so intense. Last night, every Kircan that got…" She made a sharp downwards gesture. "Two seconds of sheer terror, then nothing. Blip, blip, blip. And I have to pretend it doesn't affect me. I can't stand it. And now Garec is… I can't even bring myself to face him. I thought things got better on the way to the Fort, but now… hah… I shouldn't be telling you this. You're too young, you're probably having a worse time of it than I am."

Weynon frowned. "It's okay. No one's expecting you to be invincible."

Elethe sniffed. "Aren't they? I'm supposed to be the one who wins this for us."

"But you're not doing it alone. You shouldn't pretend that you are. You can let me help."

"I don't want your help," she snapped, then she stood and turned away, shoulders slumping. "I'm sorry. Please don't help me like that. It feels like cheating, and I only feel guilty."

He stood up and turned to her. "I won't do it unless you ask, or if it seems like an emergency."

"…Thank you." She turned back. "I'm sorry."

"You don't need to say sorry. I want to help, however and whenever I can."

Elethe gave a weak smile. "You're a good kid. I don't even need my Emogic to tell that you mean it."

"I always mean what I say."

"I know. And if I think of anything, I will ask."

Weynon nodded. "Whatever is in my power to do, I'll do it. And… I also have something I need to ask you."

She hesitated. "What is it?"

He took a deep breath. "I know that Heaven watches over our path, and that with him by our side we'll see victory, but just in case there's a fight and maybe Dowyr and I are both in danger… and, for whatever reason, only one of us could be saved… if it's in your power, save Dowyr."

Elethe only stared at him. He stared back, resolute.

"Why?" she finally asked.

"Because my soul is at peace with my fate. Promise me you'll protect Dowyr if I can't."

Elethe grimaced but nodded. "Alright… I promise."

"Thank you."

She nodded again then turned and went outside, slamming the door behind her. A moment later she stormed back in and went to the back room, vigorously rubbing her hands together.

"Coat, coat, coat," she muttered.

Weynon decided to get dressed as well. When he finished, he opened the door outside to be greeted by a thick wall of fog. He could only make out an occasional shape moving around in it.

"In or out, bud," Elethe said from behind, making him jump.

He walked out, looking around for familiar faces. Elethe followed close behind, then she grabbed his shoulder and turned him down another street.

"Dowyr is over here," she said. "One nice thing about being an Empath, it's easy to figure out where certain people are in all this soup."

She led him around, occasionally having to dodge Parastenians appearing out of nowhere in their colorful coats giving warm greetings and commenting on the morning weather. There was music coming from all around, and paired with the fog, it gave off an almost ethereal feeling. Weynon recognized the tones of cedar flutes, buffalo hide drums, and lutes, all of which were played back in his home village on special occasions. How strange to hear a bit of home in a place so far away.

Eventually they came upon Dowyr, shivering his arms off and watching as a couple soldiers saddled his horse.

"*What took you so long?*" he channeled.

"Well…" Weynon turned to the fog and gestured broadly.

"Was everyone waiting for us?" Elethe asked.

"Like I'd know. I just wanna get out of here."

Weynon smiled. He was glad Dowyr let him in on anything he was saying to other people. It helped make things less confusing.

"Do you know where we're going next?" Weynon asked.

"No one told you? We're going to set an ambush for the next group of Kircans on their way here. Garec doesn't want them to realize we came through and alert others. He's also thinking of using enemy uniforms to sneak into Norwood and needs more." Dowyr shivered. *"Not looking forward to all of this."*

Weynon pat his friend on the shoulder. "Don't worry, we'll be fine."

"Ah, there ye are," Donnan said, appearing out of the fog like a looming mountain. "Garec is looking for ye three. We'll be on the move soon. Come, and stay close. Did ye eat breakfast yet? Air's a bit thick this morning."

"I just woke up," Weynon said, the three of them now following Donnan.

"Overslept? Well, can't blame ye. I'll let Sirona know and she'll bring some hot soup."

"Are we going to ambush the Kircans outside of town?" Dowyr channeled.

"A bit further than just outside town, the mayor is quite firm after last night that there'll be no fightin' between his people's doors. But they've arranged for a little farewell party, as is their custom for guests."

"What sort of party?" Weynon asked.

"Oh, just singin' and dancin', good food, what they can spare anyways. Lift the men's spirits, and their own I suppose, after what they've been through. Plenty of dance partners to go around after so many of their men have been taken. I hope we'll be successful soon enough after we leave that they'll be troubled no more."

They soon began to hear singing and clapping. Weynon caught glimpses of groups dancing in the fog and those who watched with smiles and laughter. He smiled and felt the urge to join, especially when handfuls of young boys and girls came along and beckoned them to a warm fire, but Donnan shooed them off with a lighthearted word, and if that didn't work, an imposing glare to chill their bones.

They met up with Garec as he was addressing a couple of officers, and only a moment later he turned his attention to them.

"Good morning," he said, giving a dismissive nod to Donnan. "How are you guys doing?"

"Good," Weynon said.

"Fine," Elethe said.

Cold, Dowyr signed.

"You'll be feeling warm soon enough," Garec said. "When we move out, I want you boys staying at the back. I don't expect the Kircans to get the jump on us again, but just in case, I want you away from any danger. Elethe, you'll stay behind me. We're not having you channel today, just keeping a feel out for any foreign Emogic. If all goes to plan, we'll ambush the next group of Kircans tomorrow and not lose anyone."

"Do you want us to help fight?" Weynon asked.

Garec's eyes widened. "Light, no! I don't want you anywhere near the ambush. You'll be with Sirona as far away I think necessary."

Weynon nodded, though a feeling of uselessness seeped in. At least in the battle before he'd been able to calm the horses down.

"What about me?" Elethe asked.

"I'll have you staying back too. You're too valuable to be near danger. Instead, I might have you try using Dowyr's Emogic to link with me and the other officers to coordinate the ambush. With you being able to sense what the enemy is channeling you can communicate what's going on to us. We'll practice early tomorrow morning to work out any problems."

Sirona came over with bowls of steaming soup on a tray for Weynon and Elethe. She gave an accusatory look to Dowyr, who returned an innocent smile.

"What did he do this time?" Garec asked her.

"Nothing," Sirona said with a sniff. "At least, that I know of, *yet.*"

She turned away, and on her back was a piece of parchment with a drawing of some sort of wild-eyed, gaping wolf. Then she vanished into the fog.

Dowyr glanced at Garec, still maintaining his innocent smile, and signed, *she's nice.*

"Better hope someone takes it off for her before she finds out," Garec said quietly.

Elethe rolled her eyes and got to eating her soup.

"Is that everything you wanted to tell us?" Weynon asked.

Garec gave a nod. "Yes, go ahead and find a nice fire to sit by. Someone will come for you when it's time to go."

They made their way through the fog and followed the sound of soldiers chatting to find a nearby fire to sit at. The soldiers hardly paid them mind, and some got pulled away from the fire for a dance with the Parastenian women for a time. Music continued to ring from all around, as if out of nowhere with the fog hiding its source. Weynon ate his soup quietly, enjoying the sounds of home. Dowyr sat by him, holding his hands to the fire and tapping a foot to the beat. Elethe sat across from them, bobbing her head to the music. A handful of young boys tried to pull her away for a dance, but she politely turned them down. Some of the teenage girls even tried to get Weynon to dance with them, but he'd never been able to dance properly with others, so he too declined.

"Why don't you go to dance?" Weynon asked Dowyr.

Dowyr blinked at him. "*I don't know if you noticed, but no one's asking me to dance with them.*"

"So?"

"*So, I'd rather not embarrass myself.*"

"I bet you're a better dancer than me."

"He is," Elethe said. "He's watched people dancing in public perfor-mances then practiced himself when no one was watching."

Dowyr gave her a flat, dangerous look, when a girl in a bright yellow and blue jacket came up to him and asked him if he'd like to dance. All the soldiers around the fire turned their attention to him. Weynon grinned, and Elethe looked like she was trying to suppress a laugh.

The girl was rather pretty. Maybe a year older than Dowyr, but Weynon could never tell how old people were. She looked confused at everyone's sudden attention for a moment, but still kept a smile on, awaiting Dowyr's answer.

Dowyr looked at her with a blank face and signed, *I can't speak.*

Weynon sighed inwardly. This boy was hopeless.

"Oh!" the girl exclaimed. "Are you deaf? I've learned a little bit of signs. Hold on…" She began signing, *dance... want to... with me?* "I hope I got that right."

Dowyr pursed his lips and channeled, "*Weynon, what should I do?*"

"You got it right, he's just a bit slow and needs some encourage-ment," Weynon said, nudging Dowyr.

"*Shadowwalker's gonna pay you a visit.*"

The girl smiled and offered her hand to Dowyr, and he took it. He followed her into the fog, looking back at Weynon with eyes like dag-gers before disappearing.

"*A long visit.*"

"He's happy," Elethe said. "Sort of."

"Course he is," one of the soldiers said. "A dance with a girl like that would make any alien happy."

"I'm just glad he accepted," Weynon said.

"What about you?" Elethe asked. "Why don't you go and dance?"

"I'm… a really bad dancer. And I don't like it, really. Listening to the music is good enough for me."

A couple soldiers muttered they were of the same mind, and their companions bantered back about their lack of spine. Weynon finished his soup and a passing Parastenian took the bowl away. He stared at the fire, drumming his hands on his legs in time with the music. A few minutes later, Dowyr stalked back and sat down, his face blank. All eyes once again turned to him, expectant. He refused to look at anyone.

"That's not going to work on me," Elethe said. "Nuh-uh, even if you try hiding it, I can still feel it, and you can't do anything about that."

Weynon looked between her and Dowyr, confused. Then suddenly Dowyr was no longer sitting next to him, as if he had never been. Weynon's head whipped around, searching, but wherever Dowyr was, the fog hid him.

"What's going on?" Weynon asked.

"He tried to make us think he came back like nothing happened. I saw him sit next to you, but he wasn't really there. I think he's gone back to the inn."

"Why?"

Elethe shrugged. "I don't know, he's an alien!"

Weynon got up. "I'll go make sure he's okay."

"He's fine."

"Maybe, but you can only read feelings, not minds."

"That's… fair enough. Can you find your way back?"

"Probably."

It took him a few minutes, and some help from a passing Parastenian, but he got back to the inn and went inside. A couple soldiers were packing up his sleeping mat and blankets. Garec always made sure they were taken care of, but he felt bad the soldiers had to clean up after him, despite their assurances that it wasn't a big deal.

Dowyr was sitting next to the fire, just where Elethe had been when Weynon awoke.

I don't want to talk, Dowyr signed.

Weynon sat down next to him. "I thought you couldn't talk."

Dowyr gave him a dour look. It was hard to suppress a grin. "Sorry."

Weynon contented himself to enjoy the heat of the fire and dance of the flames as he sat by his best friend. There might be less than an hour before they'd be back in the saddle, hoping for clear skies and a sun to give them some semblance of warmth. He wondered if the wolves would come find him today. Perhaps he'd find a bird willing to keep an eye out for them in exchange for something to eat, though most birds he'd encountered so far didn't seem to be intelligent enough. Perhaps he'd be lucky enough to spot a crow, though a cardinal would probably work well enough too.

"She said I was a good dancer and kissed my cheek," Dowyr channeled.

Weynon nodded. "She was pretty. Is Shadowwalker still going to pay me a visit?"

Dowyr's face reddened slightly. *"No. Sorry."*

"I know you didn't mean it."

Dowyr pursed his lips. *"I kinda did. Maybe not literally. I don't know."*

"It's okay. I shouldn't have made you go dance. I could tell you didn't want to."

"It's not that I didn't want to. I guess... I don't want to get attached to anybody."

Weynon winced. Did that include himself? "Why not?"

"Because it hurts less when they leave. Everyone eventually realizes I'm not what they first thought and leave, or they find... someone better, nicer, more cute or handsome, whatever. It's easier to just not bother. Less painful."

Weynon wasn't sure how to respond. He wished Elethe had come too, she would've known what to say, would've understood what Dowyr was feeling.

"I won't leave," Weynon finally said.

Dowyr smiled briefly. *"You're the exception, since you cheat."*

Weynon frowned. "Cheat?" He had never cheated at anything in his whole life, as far as he could remember.

"*Yep, because you can't leave. I don't mean literally, I mean in here.*" Dowyr touched Weynon's chest. "*I think it's impossible for you. You cheated, somehow.*"

Weynon laughed, partially relieved that he wasn't talking about cheating for real. "I'd never leave any of my friends. I still think about the ones I made back at the Academy and keep them in my prayers."

Dowyr nodded. "*Me too. Except, no prayers, you know. Just thoughts.*"

"I think that's good enough."

"*I guess. But I hope we succeed out here for their sake.*"

One of the soldiers entered and hollered at them to get to their horses and be ready to ride. Weynon jumped up, not quite happy to leave the warmth of the fire, but glad to be on the move again. Every inch forward gave him hope, and he was ready to do his part in ending the war. They *would* succeed.

CHAPTER 19

Ambush

Dowyr squinted at the sun high in the southern sky as it shone down on the rolling hills and floodplains of Parasten. It felt surprisingly warm, and the snow had melted enough to see the muddy ground in sparse patches. Despite that, a shiver ran down his spine as he thought of what was going to happen soon, what he and everyone else was waiting for. How nice it must be for Regret Emogicians, who could channel to see the future, to always know how things would turn out.

Garec and the archer platoon were far ahead, lying in wait for the contingent of Kircans heading for Leife. Donnan had been keeping an eye out for them through the morning's travels with his astral projection and had spotted them about an hour prior. Now it was simply a matter of time.

The rest of the Company was with them, tending to the horses mostly. Few talked, and those who did were merely giving soft-spoken positioning orders. Elethe stood near, looking in the direction of the ambush. Dowyr could see a long stream of transparent gray coming out of her as she channeled his Emogic to Garec and those with him. Dowyr wasn't part of the telepathic link, though he supposed he could have channeled at Elethe and gotten some idea of what was going on, but he thought better of it.

Weynon came up to him and handed him some bread and cheese. He took it and ate more out of politeness than hunger. His appetite had vanished when Donnan announced the location of the approaching Kircans. It was hard to think of anything else, except perhaps Aiyana.

That was the name of the girl who'd asked him to dance the day before. Her face kept popping into his head, annoying him to no end. She had danced surprisingly well and was unusually polite. At least, in his experience. It made him immediately suspicious. When they danced, he tried to be subtle about looking around for other teenagers who were waiting for a prank to land, but he never saw any, and one never came.

There was no ulterior motive, no trick being played. Like Weynon, everything she'd said and done was genuine, and when he watched the rest of the Parastenians dancing and interacting with each other or the soldiers, he realized they were all like that. It was nothing like how he expected people to act in Elyssanar. The fact buried itself deep in his mind, and he wasn't sure how to react, except to ignore it as much as he could. He and the rest of the Company were leaving them, after all, and if other Kircans came, there wasn't anything they could do about it. The Parastenians could easily be killed, and it seemed likely if the Kircans found out they had accommodated their enemies.

No, no, put it out of your mind, Dowyr thought.

"Are you alright?" Elethe asked, glancing worriedly at him.

Dowyr nodded and gave her a thumbs-up. He knew Elethe probably didn't buy it, but he couldn't care less. These were his emotions and problems and he didn't need some snobbish girl involving herself. He could handle it.

"I didn't ask for you to lie."

I didn't ask you to ask, Dowyr signed.

Elethe frowned. "I'm just trying to help. It's better to talk about it."

Dowyr rolled his eyes. *I can't talk though.*

"Oh my Heaven, you know what I mean you twerp."

Weynon came to his side and whispered, "You could just say you don't want to talk about it."

Dowyr gave him a level look. *I don't think she'd listen.*

Weynon shrugged and gave Elethe a look that seemed to say, *kinda pointless, don't you think?*

Elethe sighed and turned her attention back towards the ambush. "I think they're about to attack, I'm not s—oh no." She turned back to the rest of the Company and screamed "They need help!" before dashing off towards the ambush.

Dowyr's head darted around in confusion as the Company mobilized and followed Elethe. Weynon grasped his shoulder and gave him an assured look.

"Let's see if we can help."

Dowyr shook his head and channeled, *"We shouldn't get involved, we can't fight."*

"No, but we should do what we can. But if you want to stay behind, that's okay. I'm going."

Weynon ran off with the rest of the soldiers. Dowyr stared after him, his heart racing. Something must be very wrong if Garec needed help, but if that was the case, he didn't want to be anywhere near trouble. Yet Weynon was getting further and further away, heading towards an unknown threat.

To Hell with it, Dowyr thought, and charged forward.

*

The Kircans had expected the ambush; their own Ghost sensed Donnan when he spotted them. There was usually no telling what the opponent's side would have in store once open combat erupted. If an unexpected Emogic sprang up at a high enough Class, any hope of tactical advantage was thrown out the window. The general rule of combat with Emogicians was prioritizing out-ranging or surrounding the enemy. Most Emogicians were too low-Class to be effective outside of close-quarter combat.

This group of Kircans, however, had a special advantage: a Class 3.2 Immortal, an Emogician that channels Love, widely considered one of the most powerful Emogics besides Empathy. Not for offensive purposes, but defensive. It could cancel out most negative Emogics or create an Emogic shield around someone to deflect any weapons or harmful Emogics from affecting them.

And so, when Donnan began channeling to start dropping the Kircans into the ground, nothing happened.

They have an Immortal! Donnan sent through the telepathic link.

A sharp alertness flooded the link. Boughton and the archer platoon took to the sky and began raining arrows, hoping that some among the Kircans were not protected. They found none. Arrows were fired back, striking soldiers out of the sky. Plumes of fire burst from one of the Kircans, and lightning struck from nowhere by the channeling of another. Garec began to channel, but stopped himself short, remembering another important detail about Immortals. Void-speakers couldn't channel at them, nor any they were protecting.

He began to run.

Everyone retreat! Garec sent through the link. *Elethe, Match the Immortal and save who you can. Donnan, use the ground!*

What about the uniforms? Donnan sent.

They don't matter!

The archer platoon began retreating, their numbers cut in half before Elethe could protect any of them, and not a scratch on the Kircans. Their advance slowed as the Immortal spread word that they were up against an Empath more powerful than himself.

We're coming, Elethe sent.

Garec halted in his tracks. *No, stay back!*

ABSOLUTELY NOT.

Following the thought came a massive ball of fire from Elethe's direction, haphazardly aimed, but its sheer size scattered the Kircans despite not injuring them. That was enough to convince them. They called their own retreat, hoping that with two invulnerable forces it would create a stalemate.

Elethe and the rest of the Company reached Garec, but he called them to hold until they could be sure of their offense. The archers regrouped, the mounted spears lined up, and they watched as Kircans began dropping with the ground under their feet one-by-one. Dowyr and Weynon finally caught up and were confused at the lack of anyone being engaged in battle, until they noticed what was happening to the Kircans.

Can't you go faster, Donnan? Garec sent.

I can't bloody well phase the whole continent! Donnan sent.

That one's the Immortal, Elethe sent, telepathically pointing out who she meant. Donnan immediately focused his attention on him and dropped a hundred feet of earth beneath his feet. What arrows and Emogics couldn't accomplish against an Immortal's shield, gravity and blunt force impact could.

The loss of the Immortal broke the Kircans' morale, and they began scrambling away as fast as their feet would carry them. Garec channeled at them and called for the archers to reengage from a safe distance. They took to the skies and began to rain arrows down once again. There was no retaliation, no Emogics fired back, just death. It was a sorry sight. They cried out as arrows struck them.

"Heaven save us!"

"Mercy!"

"Paradise forgive me!"

Dowyr turned away from the slaughter and covered his ears, ready to sick up. Weynon looked on, and hearing their cries he began trembling as though a hammer had struck him. Dowyr noticed and wondered whether the cold was getting to him.

Elethe turned to them, sensing something that screamed *wrong*. "Weynon?" She darted over to him and cried out in a panic. "Weynon!"

You know, I have a love-hate relationship with war, Hell said in Garec's mind as all this was happening. *It causes so much wonderful suffering, and stops so much at the same time. And it has this nasty habit once it's over where people will—*

It was not Garec ceasing his channeling that cut Hell off, but Weynon with a gut-wrenching scream.

"STOOOOOOP!"

Elethe fell back as an explosion of Emogic came out of him, aimed at everyone and everything, pulling all of nature's emotion that he could find; fear, sadness, the expression of winter. The earth itself lent him its power, and in obedience to his command, all things stopped.

For a moment, he held everything; for a moment, silence.

And then he collapsed.

The rest of the Kircans followed.

CHAPTER 20

The Second Torments

Dowyr stared at Weynon who laid unconscious across his saddle, only sparing a glance for Elethe who rode next to him. She stared just as intently at the boy.

"I know Sirona said he's fine, but…" She shook her head. "He's not. I felt it; before he froze everyone, something inside him broke. Went berserk. I've never felt anything like it."

Dowyr shifted uncomfortably. *"Is it why he passed out?"*

"No, he channeled so much so quickly it burned him out in an instant. When I turned to see what he was doing, it looked like he was trying to channel as much as a Class 4 could. He wasn't just channeling Peace. There was Sadness and Fear in it too. Just enough to stop everyone in their tracks. Everything he could take from nature."

Dowyr grimaced, wondering what had caused his friend to lash out like that. Weynon had been so cold towards fighting before. Had seeing the ambush struck him differently?

"Do you think we should get a copy of The Five Sentinels to wave in front of his nose?" Elethe asked, almost half-serious by her tone.

Dowyr grunted. *"Not really a good time for a joke. That also wasn't very funny."*

She pursed her lips. "Sorry… Just wanted to try lightening the mood. Obviously not very good at it. I'll just go."

He stared after her as she prompted her horse forward. That had been unusual of her, even for how strange she'd been back at the

Academy. What was her deal trying to make a joke like that at a time like this?

Dismissing it as a bizarre mood swing, he looked around at the other soldiers, who weren't in the best of spirits. They'd lost friends today. Sirona had been able to save a couple archers, but the platoon's numbers had been cut in half. A crippling blow. Some of the dead had even played a few games of Kings with Dowyr.

Don't get attached, he thought to himself. *Don't remember their faces.*

After the battle had finished, they gave everyone a proper burial and ceremony, even the Kircans. They left nothing to mark their graves. Garec wanted to leave no trace of their passing, and even had Donnan do what he could to collapse the holes he had phased into the earth.

There still weren't enough Kircan uniforms for the whole Company to infiltrate Norwood, but Garec decided there was no need for everyone to enter Norwood. A small group would have to be enough while the rest of the Company hid nearby.

He came riding up and stopped beside Dowyr, giving Weynon a worried look.

"I feel like I've been neglecting you boys too much," Garec said. "I could have prevented this."

"He'll be okay," Dowyr channeled, hoping he sounded confident.

"Physically, yes, but… I've heard people scream like that before. Immediately come tell me the second he wakes up."

Dowyr nodded.

"Good. Are you doing alright?"

He shrugged. *"I'm fine."*

Garec gave him a skeptical look. "You're free to speak your mind with me, you know. This isn't the orphanage or the Academy where you had to suck it up and guard your words. I can't be as much help if you keep things from me, even things you think I don't want to hear."

"I don't want you to worry about me, I can take care of myself."

Garec placed a hand on Dowyr's shoulder, making him flinch. "You can, and you also can't. Perhaps you think you know it all, and, to your credit, you probably do know more than I ever will. But all the books on Earth can never prepare you for the real world. Words on parchment can be beautiful, full of ideas, wisdom, and knowledge, but they inhabit a world purely in here." Garec touched his forehead. "They are not a replacement for the real thing. A painting of a rose is lovely to look at; a real rose has thorns."

Dowyr nodded irritably. "*I know that. You can spare me the lecture. I've seen enough of the world to understand its realness. I don't like it, and never want to. The only thing I care about is helping to end the war and making sure Weynon comes out alive, even if it means I don't. So don't worry about me.*"

"I intend for you both to come out alive. For all of us, if I can help it. From here on, we're avoiding fights as much as possible. I'll need you for that. With your talents, we can trick enemy officers into believing anything. But I need you in your right head. Whatever you need, tell me, or Donnan. I don't want to figure it out by what Elethe might tell me."

Dowyr sighed. "*Okay. I will.*"

Garec gave a nod. "Good. Don't forget to tell me when he wakes up." He kicked his horse forward and blended back into the Company.

Dowyr scanned the horizon looking for something else to occupy his mind and spotted a group of wolves in the distance. They appeared to be following the Company, watching them. Watching *him*, it seemed. Weynon. They must have felt him during the battle, or perhaps they had something to tell him.

Wolves are cool, but please stay away until Weynon wakes up, he thought at them.

He and other soldiers noticed the wolves through the day's travels, and thankfully they kept their distance. Garec looked more and more anxious for Weynon to wake up and often checked on him.

"I need to know if they have something important to tell us," he muttered.

Weynon remained unconscious for the rest of the day, however. When it was time to set up camp, Donnan came to help bring Weynon over to a sleeping mat beside a warm fire. Dowyr sat on a folding stool close by to warm his hands and keep an eye on him.

"I'm worried he won't wake up," Dowyr channeled.

"He will," Donnan said, starting to set up Weynon's tent. "Always hard te tell how long with burnouts. Perhaps not tonight, but he will. Be sure te get him something te eat and drink when he does, he'll need it."

Dowyr nodded and took his sketchbook and charcoal out of his saddlebag. He let his hand wander, drawing whatever came to mind. It had become something of an evening ritual, something that could help take his mind off the day's events. Most of his sketches were trees or the western mountain range, an occasional flower. Things that reminded him of living in Elyssanar. Tonight he decided to try sketching some people. The Sisters at the orphanage, the other orphans, street vendors he often passed by, the old geezers he used to play Kings with. They came easily, line after line. He began a new sketch of someone, not knowing who. His mind meandered, visiting the few memories he was fond of. Watching birds by the river, reading a gripping tale at the library, good days at the Academy, exercising his Emogic on Elethe.

"Watcha drawing?" a voice asked, making him jump.

Dowyr glanced back at Elethe, who stood looking over his shoulder with a curious expression. He finally noticed that he'd been sketching a picture of her sitting on a desk at the Academy and quickly turned the page.

"I didn't know you drew people so well."

"Haven't tried to before," he channeled.

Elethe brought a stool over and sat next to him. "Can I see?"

Dowyr reluctantly handed her the sketchbook. It wasn't like there was anything he could hide from her unless he decided to forego channeling completely.

She flipped back to the sketch of her and gave it an appraising look, then went through the other pages. "I like them. People from the orphanage, right?"

Dowyr nodded.

"They all look rather sad."

"It was a rather sad place."

"Yeah. I imagine most orphanages are. You must've been glad to end up at the Academy."

"I suppose. I think I got lucky with having Weynon as a roommate. Don't know how I'd have endured it otherwise."

"I'm surprised you get along so well. And at the same time, I'm not, if that makes sense."

Dowyr gave her a curious look. *"Why would you be surprised?"*

"Well, you're like polar opposites, religiously speaking, and obviously that's never gone over well for you."

"Why does that have to be the basis for me getting along with someone? Weynon's my friend because he cares about me as I am instead of trying to make me change like everyone else does."

"Hey, I haven't tried to do that either."

"What, helping kidnap me doesn't count?"

Elethe grimaced. "It… that's not the same."

"That's fair. I guess you haven't really tried to change me, even knowing… what you know. Thanks."

"Don't mention it. Seriously." Elethe cleared her throat and handed back the sketchbook. "Thank you for sharing."

She stood up and walked away. Donnan finished putting up Weynon's tent and came to warm his hands at the fire.

"Won't ever get used te people talking to themselves around ye," he said.

Dowyr snorted. *"It's exhausting to channel to everyone within hearing distance."*

"I know. Best te keep up yer strength. Anyway, I'm going te put Weynon inside. Ye having yer tent put up here too?"

He nodded and put his sketchpad away. *"I'll go get it."*

*

Weynon awoke to something brushing against his cheek. He tried swatting it away, but his hand touched nothing. Something in the darkness snorted. He opened his eyes and sat up to find the silhouette of a wolf standing at the entrance of his tent, eyes glowing a faint yellow.

He wanted to yell, to jump up and run, but the wolf's gaze had frozen him in place. The wolf tilted its head and sat down, as if waiting.

Calm down, calm down, Weynon thought. *It's not going to hurt me. Why do I feel so exhausted? What happened?*

He tried his best to ignore the wolf and thought back to the last thing he remembered. The ambush, the screaming Kircans, then nothing. Had they all been killed?

No... no, no, no, no. They were running away, they were calling out...

He froze again as the wolf stirred. It moved closer and licked his hand, then looked at him. He took a deep breath and channeled a small stream of his Emogic out. Something felt unusual with his channeling, for so little Emogic. He directed it to the wolf.

Hello, Weynon sent.

Little Rider, the wolf sent. *I am Thunder. I and my pack have followed you two legs since we heard your call, but you did not call again.*

I don't remember calling you.

Thunder sent back confusion. *But you did, a call of distress. Are you not distressed?*

I... think I am. I don't know. You should leave. If the others see you, they might think you're attacking me.

But you are an Earthbrother, and my pack was seen by the other two legs. They did not attack, and we did not smell intent to kill. You hunt Earth Slayer. Is he what causes you distress?

Weynon was unsure how to respond. Words weren't coming to him, so he sent a mix of feelings instead. Worry about the people Royce was hurting and the need to stop him, but focusing more on the pain and regret of the slain Kircans that were fleeing the ambush.

Thunder had sat back down while he was piecing together what he felt. *You are distressed by killing your prey?*

Weynon shook his head. *They weren't my prey.*

Then they were your predators, and yet you live, and they do not. That is good.

"No!" Weynon said, and he jumped at the sound of his voice.

He heard rustling from nearby tents and the sound of someone running over.

Dowyr's voice rang in his head, *are you awake, Weynon?*

Weynon could tell it was a telepathy link and sent back, *yes, I'm fine.*

There's a wolf in your head.

Thunder looked to one side of the tent. *There is another two legs voice in your head. Is it a predator?*

What in Hell's name was that? Dowyr sent.

Weynon was starting to get dizzy, unsure which voice to respond to. *You need to go back to your pack now,* he sent to Thunder. *I'll make sure no one attacks you.*

He could hear Dowyr getting up and decided to go out as well. *Wait here until I say,* he sent to Thunder, then stepped outside his tent and into dim firelight. As he did, both Dowyr and two soldiers appeared, all worried looks.

"I'm fine," Weynon said softly. "There's a wolf in my tent, but he's a... friend. He only wanted to make sure I was okay."

Dowyr took a step back from the tent, while the soldiers gave it a sharp look. More soldiers were coming out of their tents. Elethe and Garec both appeared, the latter walking directly up to him.

Before he said anything, Weynon heard Thunder make a low growl. All eyes went to the tent, and everyone became tense.

"He won't hurt anyone," Weynon said. "Just let him go back to his pack safely."

"Did he tell you anything about Royce?" Garec asked.

"No... I don't think they know where he is yet."

Garec nodded and waved away his men, who all returned to their tents. Dowyr and Elethe remained.

"You can let your friend return."

Weynon channeled to Thunder and sent, *you can come out and go now.*

Thunder came out of the tent slowly, looking between all of them, but Garec most of all. Dowyr and Elethe backed away a few steps, gaping at the wolf. Weynon finally realized how big he was and took a step back himself.

Shadowwalker stirs, Thunder sent. *Be wary, Little Rider.*

Then he ran off into the night.

Weynon released his channeling and let out a yawn.

"Are you alright?" Garec asked.

"I'm okay," Weynon said. "Tired. Head feels heavy. Hard to think."

"Do you remember what happened yesterday?"

Weynon grimaced. "Yes. I don't want to think about it."

Garec nodded. "Yes, not right now. Best we all get back to sleep. Another long day ahead of us."

"I understand what you're going through," Elethe said. "We're all here for you. It gets better, somewhat."

Weynon nodded lethargically. "Anything is possible with Heaven. Goodnight."

Before Weynon was able to enter his tent, Dowyr walked up and grabbed his shoulder.

"If you need anything, wake me up. Whatever it is."

Weynon gave him a thumbs-up and went inside his tent. He shivered as he climbed back into his blankets that had already gotten cold. Settling himself into a comfortable position, or at least as comfortable as he could get on the lumpy ground, he closed his eyes. Then the screams of dying Kircans began to ring in his ears.

They wouldn't stop.

CHAPTER 21

A Change of Plans

It seemed to Elethe that everyone's emotions were going haywire. There was so much going on it was hard to focus on anything, or even think rationally. Sleep was nearly impossible. The cold certainly didn't help, and every day it grew colder. Garec's men were handling things as expected of soldiers, though plenty had lost good friends in the fight. They put on stoic faces and kept moving. It shocked Elethe how easily they were able to hide their emotions, as though shoving them as far away from their conscious minds as possible. Of course, they'd been through rigorous training to do just that, but it was still an impressive and yet sad sight to behold. No one even approached Weynon for help to calm their nerves, though that was no surprise. Everyone wanted to put as little pressure on him as possible.

One benefit of the battle—if she could call it a benefit—was that there were fewer men and horses to channel Clarine's Emogic to, letting them speed along for at least two hours before she needed to take a break. The odd effect it had on sound didn't lift anyone's spirits anymore; having to speak as loudly and clearly as possible to understand one another had become a nuisance.

Even Sirona's spirits had dampened, with her usual vigor and bluntness turned to uncertainty. It struck Elethe harder than she expected, especially after a short conversation during a rest break.

"I'm worried about the boy," Sirona said to her. "Both of them, really, but mostly him."

Elethe was silent for a moment, partially stunned that Sirona said such a thing to her in the first place.

"I don't know what I can do," Elethe said. "I feel like I'm intruding if I try to talk to Weynon about what happened. He doesn't seem to want to talk about it."

Sirona sighed. "I cannot blame him. He's been terribly shaken but wants to stay focused on the bigger picture. So much courage in such a young boy. Though, when I look at him… I wish there were more things Compassion could heal than the body." She deflated in her saddle a little. "Even being able to heal the body I could only save three. I should have been there when it began."

Elethe could feel the guilt and shame oozing from her. She searched for words that might help, but everything that came to her sounded childish.

Why can't I ever think of the right thing to say? she thought. *I'm an Empath, I know exactly what everyone goes through, I should know what to say to help them!*

Garec was the only one who ever knew what needed to be said to get people on their feet. He spoke to Weynon first thing in the morning. Elethe didn't hear what he said, but whatever it was, it made something about Weynon's emotions and countenance harden.

Even still, she could sense that Garec was dealing with spikes of anxiety. Any time he looked at her, or the boys, it was there. How much doubt did he have for their mission? Or was there none, and he was merely overwhelmed with concern for her and the boys' survival?

What she'd give to be a Mind Intruder instead of an Empath. She could ask Dowyr to channel for her, and there were plenty opportunities to just use it without asking, though he might cut her off if she spontaneously Matched it. But she was afraid of what she might learn, and so never tried.

All of these thoughts and emotions were simply a distraction from what her mind kept coming back to.

Why did they both ask me to save the other?

At least Weynon had told her his reason, and she could understand it to a degree. She wished she had his same confidence for the fate of her own soul. But Dowyr didn't say anything about his reasons, and part of her didn't want to ask. Knowing him as well as she did, she doubted it had anything to do with selflessness. Unless he was simply that loyal to Weynon, which she could believe. He almost never left his side now and looked more concerned about him than anyone, which made it difficult to ask for his reason privately without Matching his Emogic, something she didn't want to do.

As the day dragged along, however, the question burned in her mind more and more. She needed to know his reason, perhaps just so she could decide whose was more noble, or sensible, if the time ever came that she had to keep one promise or the other.

Keeping both was the only acceptable answer regardless. But... if something did go wrong...

She had to know.

An opportunity came as Dowyr channeled to Weynon. She reached out and pulled his Emogic into her and Matched it, sending it back and channeling sensory manipulation. He hardly had time to react.

"I need to ask you something, privately," she channeled.

He didn't cut her off, surprisingly, but she didn't Match his Emogic for long. A minute later he awkwardly brought his horse up to her and glanced around warily.

"Whatever it is, I didn't do it," Dowyr channeled.

"Whatever it was, you probably did," Elethe said. "This isn't about that though. It's about my... promise."

He gave her a cautious look. *"What about it?"*

She took a deep breath. "Why did you ask me to make it?"

Dowyr went rigid in his saddle. She couldn't sense much emotion from him, however. If anything, he felt mildly embarrassed. Why would he be embarrassed?

"Because if one of us had to die, it's better that it was me."

"Why is it better?"

He looked away. For a long moment he didn't answer, and Elethe almost thought he was going to leave, but then he channeled again.

"Because he's better. A better person, a better, more powerful Emogician. He's worth saving."

Elethe wanted to retch from heartbreak at the words. How could he say that, and while feeling nothing, as if it was a matter of fact? She tried to stay unphased on the outside.

"And you're not?"

"Exactly. So, now you know. Happy day."

He began to turn his horse away.

"Weynon made me promise to save you."

He stopped and looked at her, face blank. *"When?"*

"Does it make a difference?"

"It does if you promised me first. I don't tolerate takebacks."

Elethe scoffed and shook her head in frustration. "What are you gonna do if I take back my promise? It's not like I can control every-thing. Either of you could die without me being able to do anything about it."

"Your promise isn't about what you can't prevent. It's simple: if you can only save one of us, save Weynon. And if something happens where you save me when you could've saved him... I don't know what I'd do. But I doubt I'd survive the rest of the war."

Elethe couldn't take it anymore and screamed. "Maybe I'll let you *both* die!"

She kicked her horse into a gallop and rushed ahead of the Com-pany. Garec's voice rang out from behind, calling her name, but she didn't slow for him. She had to get away from all the noise, all the emotions.

But there was no getting away.

*

Dowyr watched as Garec chased after Elethe. Despite how flat the horizon looked, the land rolled enough for them both to disappear. Donnan kept the Company moving without pause.

Elethe's sudden outburst had surprised him. One moment she seemed completely collected, and the next...

Mood swings, he thought, remembering something he'd once read about women. *Just a teenage girl and her weird mood swings, that's all it is.*

Though now he couldn't be sure if she would keep her promise. He at least hoped she liked Weynon more than him and kept the promise just by preference. Not that she liked him at all, and best to keep it that way.

With all the thoughts of promises, he wondered what he would do after the war if they were successful and survived. He liked having some sort of plan for the future, but he'd hardly thought of it beyond the war. There were too many things that could go wrong for him to think there was any point. Still, he tried to entertain the thought that nothing would go wrong from here, and once the war was over, he'd be lauded as a hero, instrumental in ending the war. That's why Garec had taken him. Surely at the end of it all he'd be given the money and freedom to go wherever and do whatever he wanted.

An orphanage. He'd go to Arkonia and open an orphanage and do a better job at it than the churches in Elyssanar. He could teach the children signs and be able to know what they were thinking if it seemed like they might be getting into mischief. None would have to feel left out and alone. Yes, that's what he'd do. It would at least offer some relief for his conscience. Maybe.

He let his horse fall back to Weynon, who looked to be staring off into the distance, perhaps channeling and communicating with the Earth or some far-off animal.

"Seen any more wolves?" Dowyr channeled.

Weynon shook his head, keeping his fixed stare.

He'd been far less talkative since last night, which was worrying. What was going on in his head? Dowyr could get some idea, if he wanted, but he'd decided to use telepathy as sparingly as possible, judging the morality of using it on friends to be questionable, if not flat-out wrong. Weynon would tell him what he wanted to tell, and that was that.

Garec and Elethe then reappeared, the latter appearing lost in thought as she found her way back to Sirona's side. Garec came straight to Dowyr with a face hard enough to crack stone.

"You've made her quite upset," he said, then turned to Weynon. "Weynon, I would like to speak to Dowyr alone, please. This is only for him to hear."

Weynon gave Dowyr a questioning look but nodded and prodded his horse towards Donnan at the head of the Company.

Garec sighed. "How do you intend to resolve this?"

"*Resolve?*" Dowyr channeled, glancing towards Elethe. "*I don't understand. What did she tell you?*"

Garec spoke softly, but Dowyr's heart began racing all the same. "That is none of your concern. What's clear is that you've caused her nothing but trouble, by means which I'm sure you're keenly aware of, and I won't tolerate it any longer. So, I ask again, how do you intend to resolve this?"

Garec sat there, awaiting an answer. For the first bit, Dowyr could only shake his head in confusion.

"*I don't know, I don't... I never meant to cause her trouble, not seriously. If it's my stupid pranks, then I'll stop! But if I don't know how she's been troubled by me, how am I supposed to know what to do about it? Without knowing it even makes apologizing pointless.*"

"Not pointless. A start. It's your job to figure out what's wrong, not mine to tell you."

"*Elethe never tells me anything.*"

"Have you asked her yet?"

Dowyr grimaced. There was no getting out of this. *"I'll talk to her."* He glanced at Garec's hard stare and quickly added, *"And apologize."*

Garec gave a nod of acceptance. "Go do it now, please."

Dowyr grunted and urged his horse forward, awkwardly steering between the other soldiers towards Elethe. He wasn't even remotely sure of what to say, even for an apology.

Sirona spotted him coming first and touched Elethe's shoulder, gesturing to him then falling back. Oddly she didn't even give him the usual sour look. If anything, she looked shockingly *sympathetic.*

He came up beside Elethe but couldn't make himself look at her. *"Sorry,"* he channeled. It was a start.

Elethe said nothing, merely staring ahead.

Dowyr still wasn't sure what exactly he was sorry about. He had meant what he said, and there was nothing that would change his mind about the promise he had her make. It wasn't as if he hoped she would have to keep it. Even if she did, there was no reason for her to hesitate. She *had* to hate him, if not for his roguish behavior along the road, then for everything else she knew about him since delving into his mind way back at the Academy. He didn't care how well she'd been pretending to tolerate his existence.

"I don't mean to cause you so much trouble," he continued, remembering Garec's words. *"If there's something I need to do or stop doing to help, tell me. I don't care that you hate me, whatever you need me to do, I'll do it."*

"You've got it all wrong," Elethe said softly. "I don't hate you. Not even a little, much as I'd like to."

Dowyr sniffed. *"Didn't Sirona teach you not to lie?"*

"I'm not lying," Elethe snapped. "And who are you to say anything about lying? You lie all the time about how you're feeling, even to me when you know I can tell it's a lie. Everybody does it, like saying it makes it true!"

"Well what else do you want me to say? That I'm not, in fact, having the time of my life? That I'm terrified for my life and Weynon's? Is there really a reason for me to spell it out? I already know how I—" Dowyr stopped, re-

alizing he'd been pulled into a pointless argument. He took a calming breath. *"I hate this. We have enough enemies to worry about. I don't care what you think about me, just leave me alone and I'll leave you alone."*

He turned his horse away and headed back to Weynon, who had drifted a short distance away from everyone else.

That might not have been how Garec wanted things resolved, but then he did not think there really was a way to resolve Elethe's problem. The best he could think of was leaving her alone from now on. And he would; there wasn't a reason to bother her in the first place. It would have to do.

Weynon looked to be staring off into space again. Dowyr sighed and channeled, *"See something out there?"*

Weynon jumped in his saddle. "No. Just… thinking."

"Want to tell me?"

Weynon remained silent for a moment, then nodded. "Back when Garec took us from the Academy, I had so much hope that I could help stop people from fighting, help stop the war. When we heard about Irostead, I thought… it's so horrible, Heaven would want us to fight, because Hell must be behind what the Kircans are doing. But then, at the ambush, when I heard their cries for Heaven… I realized it's not their fault. They must want to be on Heaven's side as much as we do. I can't fight them, and I don't want to let us fight them. But they won't stop fighting us. I don't know what to do."

Dowyr grimaced, unsure how to respond. He had some suspicions about why Weynon had reacted the way he did during the ambush, but this? Weynon had seen the Kircans as absolute enemies on the side of Hell, and now that illusion was breaking. How did one find the strength to keep fighting if you didn't see the other side as your enemy? Dowyr almost felt guilty not having that issue. He didn't like fighting and killing, but the Kircans were their enemies whether they liked it or not.

Wanting to help Weynon sort out his thoughts, an unusual idea came to him.

"I want to show you a scene from The Five Sentinels," he channeled.

Weynon looked at him in surprise. "Which one?"

"The battle of the Three Kingdoms, when Heaven first renewed the world. Can I show you?"

Weynon hesitated, understandably. It was an intense moment in The Five Sentinels.

"Okay."

Dowyr took a deep breath. *"Brace yourself."*

*

Weynon held his reins tight, waiting for something to happen. For the longest moment, there was only the endless plains of Parasten, but in the blink of an eye it became something entirely different. The chill air became thick and heavy with the scent of smoke, and the sudden heat came near to suffocating. Weynon still sat on his horse with Dowyr beside him, and they were atop a small hill. Pockets of raging fires surrounded them, around which armies fought against each other amidst villages scattered across the land. There were no Emogicians evident among them. It was a time before Emogic, before Hell was sealed away, before the world as Weynon knew it existed at all. Three cities burned in the distance, and beyond them towered Whitewall, the great mountain, a tinge of red in its pale face.

Weynon was only vaguely familiar with the story. The passages regarding it were difficult to understand, and teachers rarely went over it in detail. It was a simple story, in principle. Hell had roused three kingdom cities against one another, then Heaven stopped it and renewed the world.

But this... this did not look like a war being stopped. He could hear the death cries and rallying shouts of men all around. Volleys of arrows were firing every which way, and catapults launched pots of oil that were then ignited by a flaming arrow. Unholy screams followed. He saw people fleeing their homes as they became engulfed in flames, only to be cut down. Women, children, none were spared by any side. There was so much chaos that parts of the armies even turned on themselves.

"Where is Heaven?" Weynon asked, squinting to hold back tears.

Dowyr glanced at him. *"He's watching from the top of Whitewall."*

A dark voice boomed out of the ashen sky, shaking the ground and reverberating in Weynon's head.

DO YOU UNDERSTAND, NOW? THEY WILL NOT LISTEN TO YOU.

The armies didn't even notice the voice, so consumed by the rage of war. Another voice rang out from above, a cry of agony.

I WON'T LET YOU DO THIS. That must have been Heaven.

Hell's voice rang with a laugh that made Weynon wince. *IT IS ALREADY DONE. THEY DIE FOR ME.*

I WON'T LET THEM. I WON'T LET ANYONE.

HOW? FOOLISH BOY. THIS IS THE ETERNAL FATE OF YOUR CREATION. YOU WOULD HAVE TO STOP YOURSELF.

NO. NOOOO!

A bright light pierced the sky from the top of Whitewall, beaming upwards then expanding out, enveloping everything, washing it all away until it became nothing, became Nowhere; a realm of endless white in all directions. Weynon looked around, standing on his own feet now, his horse nor Dowyr anywhere to be seen. There only sat a boy in white, arms hugging his legs to his chest, and another boy in black standing over him, glowering. The boy in black turned his head ever so slightly in Weynon's direction, striking him with the gaze of a single eye. His heart skipped a beat, and then he was back in his saddle, the chill of winter once again seeping into his bones.

"Why?" Weynon breathed. "Why did you show me *that*? Heaven didn't even renew the world."

"Yes he did. That's what happens every time the book mentions him renewing the world. He wipes it away, returning everything to Nowhere before starting over with the world. I showed it to you because it shows even in The

Five Sentinels, with Heaven right there, that's what war is, always has been, and always will be. It's a reality we have to accept so we know how important it is to stop it. That was hardly the worst of what's in The Five Sentinels."

Weynon stared ahead at nothing. He didn't want to accept that. Heaven had won in the end, after all. One story about Hell causing that much pain and suffering didn't mean anything. It couldn't. Heaven knew how to deal with it now, and he was dealing with it, through himself and Garec and the rest of the Company. He had to be.

"At least the war will be over soon," Weynon said.

Dowyr nodded slowly. *"What will you do after we win?"*

That was an easy question. "Go home and help my grandma with her garden."

Dowyr looked at him curiously. *"That's it?"*

Weynon shrugged. "I don't know. She's getting old and needs more help with it, and I like spending time with her." Though perhaps that was more to do with how many treats she baked for him. "What about you?"

*

Garec kept a sharp eye on his surroundings as he rode beside Donnan, despite the lieutenant being able to scout the land from an aerial view. As with the rest of Parasten, there was little to see. A mass of low rolling hills, scattered shrubs and barren trees, and dozens of shallow rivers, streams, and ponds, most of which had frozen. The days were only getting colder. It worried him. There was little time left to find the Tyrdens and kill them before winter would halt the Company in its tracks. Perhaps they could hide among the Parastenians until Spring came, but that was not a risk he was willing to take.

Why did I bring us out here?

That nagging thought came back again. It had plagued him since leaving Fort Calhoun, and there was no getting rid of it. Not a thought from anything Hell had said to him while channeling, but the bastard certainly fed it. This was no place for his troubled niece, or two children. At the time, it seemed expedient to move into Parasten even with winter just beginning. There weren't any reports of Kircan activity near the front, so Parastenian villages should've been completely vacant of any soldiers. Had Elyssanar even been paying attention to what was happening to the Parastenians outside of the events in Irostead?

No, no use thinking over how things had gone. Even despite encountering fights, they were still on the right track, and that's all that mattered. If worst came to worst, he would at least ensure that the children and as many of his men as possible would survive.

A memory of Hell's voice came. *You won't ever get to see your child.*
SHUT UP, he told it.

Hell couldn't speak to him without channeling, but his voice still rang in his mind as if he could. It was enough to drive a man mad. Many people believed that the mere fact Hell spoke to people who channeled Indifference meant they were destined to turn evil. How could one not, when so directly influenced by evil incarnate? Yet those who knew Garec before his Apex wouldn't believe such a thing possible for himself. Nor many of those who came to know him after his Apex, primarily Donnan and the rest of the Company. To them, they served a good Captain and a friend, nothing more. He was proud to be their Captain, but a growing sense of isolation festered in the back of his mind.

Why did I bring us out here?

Shaking his head, he turned to Donnan. "Can you see Norwood yet?"

Donnan closed his eyes and went still. A moment later he shook his head. "Not yet. Probably won't until tomorrow afternoon, I suspect, assuming the lad was right about the distance. Plenty of Parastenian villages though."

"We're not risking more villages than necessary."

"Never said we should. Are ye alright, Garec? Ye've been more tense in the shoulders since we left the Fort."

"I'm fine," Garec lied.

"Well just holler should ye be needing a good shoulder massage, aye?"

"I'll keep it in mind."

Garec looked back at Dowyr and Weynon. He was glad Weynon looked to be doing better. His talk with the boy had been short, perhaps too short, but there were only so many words for what he had to say, and he liked it simple. Weynon seemed to take them to heart. It would help.

Dowyr, on the other hand, worried him more than he expected. Particularly in the case of his relationship with Elethe. Garec knew it wasn't his fault, really. The battles, the cold, their whole situation, it understandably put a massive amount of pressure on Elethe. As long as Dowyr apologized and kept from adding more pressure onto her, things should be okay. If not, he considered keeping them forced apart. At least for now it seemed unnecessary. He would wait and see. Elethe wouldn't do anything rash without provocation. But how little provocation was needed? Maybe it was too big of a risk to wait and see.

This is absurd, he thought, scowling at himself. There was no point in mulling it over. Elethe was becoming a grown woman. She could deal with it on her own. Perhaps Sirona would keep her in line anyway.

The woman herself appeared by his side as if the thought of her name had summoned her. She wore a grim face, or at least grimmer than usual. Sirona always seemed grim to Garec, even when she was in a pleasant mood. It was such an odd contrast to her half-brother Donnan, who she now glared at as though to dismiss him. Whatever she had to say, it must have only concerned Garec himself, so he waved a dismissive hand at him. The big man huffed and let his horse fall back.

Sirona waited until well after Donnan had gone out of hearing range. She almost looked nervous. That couldn't have been good, if true. Garec decided it must be something else; frogs would grow wings before Sirona was ever nervous.

"What did you say to the girl?" Sirona asked as if making idle conversation.

Garec gave her a sidelong glance. "Why do you want to know?"

"To understand how to fix whatever you've mucked up. Elethe obviously isn't any better for it. She needs real help."

Anger flared up inside him. Elethe was *his* niece, not Sirona's. She had no business in the matter, and to blatantly imply his help was worthless to his face! Yet he made himself shove the anger down and pull back from the situation. If there was anything he'd learned as a leader, it was to listen to those who brought problems to his attention and to take them seriously. This was one such time to do so. He turned to Sirona, keeping his face straight.

"I told Elethe to ask herself if it was worth it, and that I would deal with Dowyr."

Sirona waited as if there would be more to the answer, but in all truth there wasn't. Elethe had tried to argue, but he had only repeated himself until she gave up.

"The poor girl is in love," Sirona said.

Garec's eyes widened. "*What?*"

Sirona gave an exasperated sigh. "I don't know how it could be more obvious. You said you'd deal with Dowyr? Wonderful, except there's nothing you can do short of leaving him behind. And on top of that Elethe is suffering through this war and all the emotions it entails. What did you think would happen? She doesn't need a pep talk. She needs someone who loves her, and that boy is obviously in no condition to be that someone."

Garec stared at her in bewilderment. Elethe was in love with *Dowyr?* When had that happened? It seemed to him that she had only been frustrated and annoyed by him. Although, in his own experience, such feelings did not exclude love from the mix. But he had thought whatever positive interactions they had was simply the existence of an odd, if strained, friendship, especially considering what Elethe knew about the boy.

He shook himself, remembering the last thing Sirona had said. Now it was clear what her intentions were in bringing this up, and he had to admit to himself that she was in the right.

"I really have mucked it up," he muttered. He half expected Sirona to make a self-satisfied look, but if anything, her face had a touch of sympathy in it.

"I can't give her the help she needs either," she said softly.

Garec nodded, and without a word, prodded his horse back into the Company's ranks to find Elethe.

He found her all the way at the rear, lagging behind the rest of the soldiers. One of his officers appeared to be keeping an eye on her in case she tried running off again. The officer gave a nod to Garec, which he returned before stopping in front of Elethe. Her eyes were downcast, and it took her a moment before realizing he was even there. Once she did, he dismounted.

"What?" she demanded with a frown.

"Come down," he said.

Her frown deepened, but she swung off the saddle and gave her horse an assuring pat on the neck before walking up to him.

"Is something—?"

Before she could finish the question, Garec stepped forward and embraced her gently. "I understand what you're going through."

That was all he said. For a few short seconds, Elethe stood as stiff as a board, then melted in his arms. He softly brushed her hair as she began to shake and sob into his chest. There was no telling how much time passed until Elethe spoke.

"I hate this," she said.

Garec sighed. "I know."

"I'm so tired. I didn't want to believe or accept how I felt. I thought it would go away. I wanted it to, but it only got worse. And all he thinks is that I hate him. I wish I could." Elethe looked up at him. "How much longer do I have to feel like this?"

"I don't know. We can never choose how we feel or for how long. But we can choose what to do about it." He felt at the letter in his coat pocket. "If you want to go home... I can have Boughton fly you back."

Elethe pulled away, wide-eyed. "You'd let me go?"

"You'd be safe. Away from all this and from him."

Garec felt a stab of anxiety as Elethe appeared to think on the offer. He didn't want to let her go. Clarine would stop being of any use, and without the two of them, there was a much higher chance that his mission would fail. Yet he shoved the emotion down, not wanting her to sense it and let it influence her decision. It was hers to make.

"No," she said, then shook her head. "No, I said I would come with you, and I'm not going back on that. I want this war over. I just wish it wasn't so hard."

Garec restrained himself from sighing with relief. "So do I. And I promise that if you ever change your mind, I'll let you go. But thank you. I hope to make it as easy as possible from here on. No more fighting. We can't afford it."

"What do you plan to do?"

"I've been thinking that maybe having the whole Company with us is a mistake. We can be faster with fewer people, so I think I'll send them back to Leife. Everyone except the essential Emogicians. It's safer than returning home or coming with us, at least, and I'm sure Elan would appreciate the extra men around. It'll be easier for you to channel Clarine's Emogic too. Once we know where the Tyrdens are, we can reach them faster than they'll have time to react. Then we can all go home."

Home. The word sounded strange in his mind. Would he be able to go home? After traveling all the way out here, home was such a distant memory that it may as well not have existed. If only he had become a Regret Emogician so he could see the future and know exactly what needed to be done to kill the Tyrdens without issue, if only his one regret had done that for him...

Interlude 2

The Prophet of Regret

Roderick sat at his desk in the forward command post of southern Parasten reading through his officers' reports. Everything was progressing smoothly with the war, aside from minor setbacks. The biggest nuisance was Arkonia still harassing their military convoys throughout Parasten despite the efforts made to stop them. He wasn't set on pushing into Arkonia itself, there just wasn't much that interested him in their land or people. It was Elyssanar he wanted on its knees, and Parasten was just a stepping stone along the road. Why Arkonia felt the need to be an aggressor was beyond him.

There was good reason to attack Elyssanar, besides his personal vendetta. The western mountains were the largest source of gold, silver, copper, and lightstone, but their potential had scarcely been tapped into. As far as the Elyssanarans were concerned, such metals were mostly vain and not worth the trouble, so they didn't mine more than they thought necessary. Roderick knew better. The things he'd seen which copper alone could accomplish was reason enough to take control of those mountains. If only Royce would realize their utility as well, but his delusions of grandeur blinded him. Even so, he was sure he could make Royce useful once Elyssanar had been dealt with. He had a knack for making people useful. It was a decent enough substitute for not being an Emogician.

The door to his office opened slightly and a soldier's head popped through. "Sir, there's someone here who says he was sent by Royce. He's not one of ours."

"Is he armed?" Roderick asked, turning to the door.

"No. He's a Regret Emogician from Arkonia."

Roderick dropped his officers' reports as his hand jerked towards his belt knife. How had an Ark gotten through... no, there was no question. If it really was a Seer, there was nothing that could be done. This was it. He might as well have been dead an hour ago.

"Show him in," Roderick said, hoping his voice betrayed no hint of hesitation as a shaky hand grasped the hilt of his belt knife.

The door opened wide, letting a man in plain clothes stride in. Nothing about him appeared threatening, but looks were always deceiving when it came to Regret Emogicians. And *always* was not a word Roderick used lightly. The door closed behind him.

Do I even need to say anything? Roderick was about to open his mouth to speak the words, but the man beat him to it.

"No, you do not," he said casually. "But frankly, I actually quite like the sound of your voice. It has a *seasoning* to it. Seeing as you're a man that's to the point, though, I will keep this short and—"

Roderick wasted no time unsheathing his belt knife and throwing it at the man in one swift motion. He evaded it as though he were merely leaning over to inspect the rugs.

"—to the point, indeed," he continued. "You may know me as the Seer. Hilariously original, I know, but some traditions are more difficult to part with than others. I stumbled upon your brother as he was out digging ditches in the most spectacular fashion I'd ever seen. We had a little chat, and I saved him from an attempt on his life in the spur of the moment. He wasn't all that grateful despite it, though."

"He isn't the grateful type," Roderick said cautiously.

The Seer smiled, though it didn't touch his eyes. "Indeed. I have known a number of people who've had gratitude pursue them all their lives, and I imagine those prone to Rage can run awfully quick.

Though if you ask me, it's a miracle any Gratitude Emogicians exist at all."

Roderick frowned. "You said you'd keep this short." Why was he giving him the opportunity to speak at all?

The Seer gave a slight bow. "Of course, my deepest apologies. I do tend to get carried away as there is always so much that can be said. Not that it necessarily *should* be said. Well, rest assured, I'm not here to kill you. In fact, I have a proposition for you. More of a request, really. You might say, a demand. What do you call something that you know is already agreed upon when the proposition has yet to be made? A precognition? A foreordained will? Regardless, the terms are simple. You have little love for your brother, yes?"

Roderick narrowed his eyes. This was starting to feel like one of the most pointless conversations he'd ever had, but his hands had yet to stop shaking. "Do you even need to ask?"

"I've never asked before, have I?"

Roderick stared at him before letting out a short laugh. "Just how far into the future can you see, Seer?"

"Far enough to be useful. Your answer? I did say I like the sound of your voice."

There was no use trying to get anything out of him that he didn't want to reveal. But there was no way he didn't already know Roderick's answer, unless Roderick was stubborn enough not to truthfully answer that question under any circumstance. Was he? It was certainly a secret that was best kept as such. Controlling Royce was critical for the war effort.

"Royce is a good boy," Roderick answered slowly. "For the time being."

The Seer's head tilted forward. "In that case, this is my precognition." Reaching into his pocket, he took out a letter and handed it over.

"Why a letter?"

"I prefer all my demands in writing, in case you ever need to refer to them again."

Roderick opened it and read, then gave the Seer a confused look. "A mere footman's salary?"

"I have few material wants. It is enough for me to be at your disposal however I see fit, and the way I see it, your goals are my goals."

"Everything in my being screams not to trust you."

The Seer chuckled. "Because you shouldn't. If I had wanted you to trust me, I wouldn't've made my way in here announcing what I am. But you aren't the trusting type to begin with."

"And what am I to you?"

"You are an adequate means to an end. That is more than can be said for most. As such, you have my undying loyalty. But something must eventually be done about *him.* The little stunt with Irostead may have been a necessary demonstration, but he seems far too inclined to perform another, don't you think?"

Roderick leaned back in his chair. "I'm compelled to agree. But we will need him if Elyssanar is to be conquered."

"No argument there." The Seer extended his hand. "When the time is right."

Roderick stared at the hand and half wondered if he was about to make a deal with Hell himself. There was no controlling this man, not without knowing how far ahead he could see. But there were ways to determine that, and Roderick was confident that if the necessity came, if this arrangement turned sour, he could figure out some way to deal with him.

He took the Seer's hand and shook. "When the time is right."

The Seer smiled; it still didn't touch his eyes.

CHAPTER 22

Norwood

Dowyr felt like he was being watched as he crossed the frosty Norwood streets. But then, he felt that way ever since they arrived in Norwood the previous morning. It didn't help that most of the Company was gone, with no friendly soldiers to hide between. There were only ten of them now.

Himself, Weynon, Garec, Elethe, Clarine, Donnan, Sirona, Alann, Boughton, and Henric. The best infiltration team they could have, and it had worked so far. Getting into Norwood was easy. A bit of telepathy and sensory manipulation work, and they were accepted within the city walls in no time. Though the walls weren't really walls, more of a rough palisade that the Kircans had thrown up. Parasten's cities never had walls.

The Parastenians themselves were just as welcoming as those in Leife, though perhaps a bit more deflated in their posture. Garec had found a decent inn to use as their hideout. The Blinking Weaver, an odd name, and practically in the middle of the city. Norwood wasn't nearly so big as the capital of Elyssanar, but the central area could have competed with it for amount of activity with all the music, dancing, shops, and general chatter. The innkeeper—a fat, balding middle-aged man with a broad smile that left his face all wrinkly—had claimed that this was hardly a fraction of the activity Norwood would normally reach. War and the winter had dulled things down. Dowyr could scarcely believe it, especially considering half of their young men had also been taken away.

Today he was going around trying to find Kircans to read their minds and figure out where this Colonel was, or better, where he was going to be. Difficult with the bustle of such a city. Luckily, according to Elethe, there were no other Empaths in the city. They were able to detect one another with no channeling involved, though couldn't tell how powerful they were. An odd quirk to Empaths. Henric and Donnan would have been trying to use their Emogic to try and locate the Colonel, but Garec wanted to keep as low a profile as possible, and there might be other Seducers and Ghosts among the Kircans. Mind Intruders were rare enough that it was unlikely to encounter another.

And so Dowyr tried his best to blend in with the other Parastenians and discreetly mind-read any Kircan soldiers he noticed. Except *every single one of them* was apparently a nobody who knew nothing. Or rather was never thinking about anything. Somehow, he needed to find one that was important and thinking about important things, but they were probably all in important places he wasn't allowed into. Sneaking into them using sensory manipulation would only work if there were a small number of people that needed to be channeled to.

What he'd give to be a Class 3.

Why wasn't Elethe doing this? He could stay at the inn and just be channeling for her wherever she was in the city. Instead, she stayed with Sirona in their room, and Garec let her get away with lazing about. So not fair.

As he entered a busier part of the city, he noticed a middle-aged man carefully removing a road stone and replacing it with a blue-colored one.

Stricken with curiosity, Dowyr approached him and channeled, "*What are you doing?*"

The man looked up at him and smiled. "You haven't heard? We're having flightstones installed on all the busy streets. They're not charged yet, but once we get them all in place and ready to go, you'll no longer have to worry about navigating through large crowds or wagons blocking the way. You can just fly over them. Won't that be neat?"

Dowyr nodded, mildly surprised someone had even thought of such a thing. If anyone were to, of course, it'd be a Parastenian. Though after giving it slightly more thought, he wondered if allowing anyone to fly over busy streets would be all that safe. And how high would the flightstones allow them to go? What if someone didn't land before getting out of range of the flightstones?

He didn't want to bother the man with such questions and left him to his work. Surely the Parastenians had thought of that and had solutions to prevent any accidents. Maybe nets would be enough.

Suddenly a young man appeared running from around a corner, shortly followed by a group of pursuing Kircan soldiers who managed to pin him to the ground right in front of Dowyr. The man let out a pained grunt and looked at him, a fire in his eyes.

One of the Kircans noticed Dowyr watching and waved a club at him. "Piss off, you ugly whelp!"

Dowyr turned back and ran, but only so far as to get out of sight around another corner. Norwood had plenty of corners. He peeked back at the soldiers as they arrested the man, then, hoping no one was paying attention to him, followed them. There were only four Kircans, so he began to channel and make himself disappear from their eyes, but maintained his distance in case more soldiers appeared.

It was difficult to keep up with the bustle of crisscrossing city streets, but eventually the crowds lessened as they got closer to where the Kircans had set up headquarters. Dowyr continued to follow until the soldiers came to an inn that had a dozen more soldiers hanging around it. Too many to channel towards unnoticed.

With a sigh, Dowyr turned back. Another dead end. But then he froze as an odd sensation came; his Emogic surged within him, as if he were bursting with it, overflowing with power. He looked back and for a moment locked eyes with the man being arrested, desperation in his eyes. The man had to be a Booster, there was no other explanation. But what did he expect Dowyr to do? Bust him out of prison? He couldn't... no, with this much power, he *could*. Perhaps he knew something about the Colonel too, or someone else in the inn.

Heart racing, Dowyr let out the Emogic boiling within himself and split it across all the Kircans. Once satisfied that he had them all, he hid past a corner and channeled to make himself disappear from their minds, then carefully went out and headed for the inn. This was *too easy!* It must've been what being a Class 3 was like, or maybe a Class 4. Dowyr couldn't tell how much power he held. He laughed, careful to make sure no one could hear him either. To the Kircans, it would be as if he didn't exist.

Feeling confident, he dashed to the inn door. A Kircan stood right beside it. Dowyr made a face at him, then slowly opened the door enough to peek in and channel to another handful of soldiers.

This door isn't opening, and no one is coming in, Dowyr thought, making it the reality to everyone he was channeling to.

Slipping inside, he crept forward, trying to stay light on his feet. Any noise he made might still be heard by anyone he wasn't channeling to that might be out of sight. While it might be taken for whatever noise the soldiers were making, he didn't want to take any chances.

The common room of the inn had been converted into a barracks, with the bar area as a small armory. There were cots spread evenly across the floor with only a couple tables and chairs.

"Vanov!" a soldier barked, making Dowyr jolt. "It's time for your shift at the courthouse."

"Yes, Sir," replied another soldier. Dowyr sighed with relief that he was channeling to them both. "I get a share of the women being hauled up there, right?"

He and a few others around chuckled while Dowyr pressed on. His Emogic connection to the soldiers who arrested the man was leading upwards. Going down a hall that lay straight ahead, he came across a staircase and prepared a flow of Emogic for anyone who might be at the top. He went up, one step at a time, heart thumping. No extra soldiers were at the top, but the ones arresting the man were there, opening a cell door. One of the four soldiers—the one who'd yelled at Dowyr—walked into the cell, shoving the man inside, while the remaining three headed right for Dowyr. He sidestepped them, still invisible to their eyes, then went to the cell door. The entire second floor of the inn had been converted into a makeshift prison, with wooden doors replaced by iron bars. Rudimentary containment, all things considered. Without voidstones, a handful of different Emogicians would have no issue escaping. But Parastenians weren't really known for fighting back and escaping their captors.

Dowyr made it look to the soldier that the cell door remained closed as he opened it and entered. The arrested man was on the floor, but he glanced at him, a spark of hope in his eyes.

"Already thinking you'll be able to escape?" the soldier sneered. "You'll be lucky to get out the front door." He spat towards the man and just missed his foot, then turned back and made the motion for opening the cell door even though it already stood open. Walking out, he made the motion of closing and locking it. Dowyr grinned, then made sure to close the door enough to ward off any suspicion from someone he might not be channeling to.

Turning his attention to the man, he finally got a better look at him. He looked maybe just a few years older than Elethe, and probably could've passed as Weynon's brother or cousin with that same sandy blonde hair. A bit lanky though; maybe that was why he hadn't been taken away like a lot of the other young men.

Dowyr held a finger to his lips. *"Don't speak,"* he channeled, causing the man to blink. *"I can't stop anyone I'm not channeling to from hearing you."*

How am I supposed to talk to you then? The man thought.

"You just did."

The man gaped for a moment, then understanding came. There was something strange about his thoughts. Dowyr could hear a second voice in them, but he couldn't quite make out anything it said. It made him uneasy.

"Why did they arrest you?"

I killed a soldier.

Dowyr frowned. *"Aren't you a Parastenian?"*

The man looked confused. *Yes, and no. That should be obvious. Are you not a Parastenian?*

"I'm from Elyssanar." The man looked even more confused. *"It's a long story. Look, I'm trying to figure out where the Colonel is. If you help me, I'll help you escape."*

The Colonel? He stays at the courthouse on the Broadway. I could show you.

Dowyr grunted. Well, that was easy. Maybe too easy.

"How do you know he's there?"

Everyone knows. Did you just get here?

Dowyr took a deep breath. None of them had thought for a second to just ask a Parastenian where the Colonel might be. Of course, they didn't want to arouse suspicion for what they were up to in the city, but these were Parastenians. It wasn't like any of them would ferret them out. What an absolute waste of time.

"Whatever, let's go. Try not to make any noise. I think you should come talk to my Captain, I bet he'll want to know your story."

The man nodded and got up. *I'll follow. My name's Gwyn, by the way.*

"Mine's Dowyr. You'll keep channeling at me, right?"

Gwyn nodded. Dowyr gave a thumbs-up and peeked out the door. No guards. The Kircans probably assumed any Parastenian prisoners would never try to escape.

They weren't wrong, but that didn't change Dowyr's mind about them being complete idiots. Whoever allowed this deserved a scalding earful about proper security.

He still maintained his channeling to everyone downstairs and outside the inn. It was amazing how easy it was. He didn't feel tired at all. Gwyn stayed close behind as he made his way out, eyeing the soldiers skeptically. Dowyr opened the front door an inch and checked for any new faces. Channeling another couple streams out just to be ready, he went out and casually walked down the street. He maintained his Emogic almost the whole way back to The Blinking Weaver, not so much out of necessity, but simply because he could.

Upon entering, he spotted Weynon sitting at one of the tables with Donnan. They looked up at him and then to Gwyn with consideration.

"Need to talk to Garec," Dowyr channeled to them, putting a tone of urgency into it.

They stood and went upstairs. Dowyr motioned to Gwyn and followed. Garec was sitting at a small table in his room, Elethe across from him. There was a thickness in the air between them. He wondered what they'd been talking about.

"Who's this?" Garec asked.

Gwyn frowned. "You're a Voidspeaker."

Garec's eyes widened. "You're a Booster. What's going on, Dowyr?"

The others looked at Gwyn in surprise. Weynon especially looked enamored.

Dowyr made sure to channel to everyone in the room, and was frustrated by how much it took to do so now that Gwyn wasn't channeling at him. *"I rescued him from prison right after he got put there. He told me where the Colonel is."*

"Courthouse on the Broadway," Gwyn said. "Not far from here."

Garec grunted. "How do you know?"

"Everyone knows. Not really a secret since they invaded."

Garec looked at Dowyr questioningly. "And you weren't able to find this out sooner?"

Dowyr shrugged. *"Not my fault people weren't thinking about it when I channeled at them. Should've had Elethe do the mind-reading. She could've learned it."*

Garec sighed. "Doesn't matter. Now we know. Thank you for your help, Mister...?"

"Gwyn, Sir."

"Thank you, Gwyn. You're free to go."

Gwyn didn't move a muscle. "Why are you all here?"

"That's none of your concern."

"Certainly, but you are quick to let me go so easily when I could rat you out to the Kircans, so I assume you're here to help my people."

Dowyr looked uneasily between Gwyn and Garec. Gwyn looked resolute, though maybe even resigned to whatever might happen next. Garec had an unreadable expression though. Whether he might let Gwyn live or kill him, Dowyr couldn't tell.

"If that is what you assume, then you should feel content knowing that is the truth and it is best you stay out of our way."

"He's said you'll fail, hasn't he?"

Garec stared at him for a moment then leaned back in his chair. "So what? He's a liar."

Gwyn nodded. "You're here to kill the Tyrdens aren't you? You need the Colonel to tell you where they are."

Nothing about Garec's expression or posture changed, but Dowyr caught Donnan looking between him and Gwyn meaningfully.

"Did Heaven tell you that?" Weynon asked.

All eyes turned on him, but he didn't notice, being so focused on Gwyn. Dowyr had to look away out of embarrassment. It was typical that a Booster would have that sort of effect on him.

"No," Gwyn said. "It just seems like the only sensible conclusion to what's in front of me."

"Everyone out except Gwyn and Dowyr," Garec said softly, but there was a tone to it that got everyone moving on the instant. Even Dowyr almost ran out the door despite hearing his name.

An uncomfortable silence followed as Garec stared down Gwyn, eyes weighing. Then he signed to Dowyr, *do you trust him?*

"*The Kircans arrested him, and he trusted me enough without knowing anything about who I am to rescue him.*"

That's what concerns me.

"*I read his mind. He genuinely wants to stop the Kircans. He even killed one, that's why he was arrested.*"

Garec narrowed his eyes at Gwyn. "You killed one of the Kircans?"

"Yes," Gwyn said coolly. "To save a young girl from being... harassed."

"So you've abandoned the Way of Paradise."

"Yes. My Apex was only a few months ago. I kept it hidden because I was afraid of what others might think or how they'd treat me differently. It wasn't long before I came to realize that the Way is... not what the world needs right now. He is very persuasive, if rather cryptic."

Garec snorted. "I'm not surprised. So now that you know why we're here, what will you do?"

"Let me come with you. I will help however I can in making sure the Tyrdens die. My people will hate me, but I can live with that knowing I played a part in saving them."

"What Class are you?"

"I don't know. Probably somewhere between Class 2 and 3. I haven't tested my limits."

"*He's at least Class 3,*" Dowyr channeled. "*I say bring him with us. With our smaller numbers, it'd almost be like having a backup Elethe.*"

Garec nodded. "Alright then. I will allow you to join us on the condition that you listen to me and do everything I say. You have my word that I won't order anything of you that I wouldn't do myself."

Gwyn put a fist over his heart. "I swear by the Sentinels I will do as you say, or Hell take me."

Donnan burst through the door causing Dowyr to jump.

"Kircans are stirred up," Donnan said. "Barged in searching for someone broken out of jail. They looked ready te tear apart the common room."

Garec gave Dowyr a meaningful look.

Dowyr sighed and channeled at Gwyn. *"Gonna need you to channel at me again. I'll get rid of them."*

"Get everyone but the women together in here," Garec said to Donnan. "Make sure Sirona knows what's going on, she should be able to handle the Kircans."

Dowyr split his channeling as he felt his Emogic surging again and was almost giddy at the ease of it. Making sure all three of them heard, he channeled, *"Make sure to line up against the walls too."*

Carefully opening the door and glancing down the hall, he tiptoed out towards the top of the stairway into the common room while Donnan went to gather the others. One of the Kircans was shouting at the innkeeper. Preparing a number of Emogic streams, Dowyr went down and channeled as quickly as he could at everyone he spotted, making himself vanish from their minds before they saw him. There were about a dozen of them, none he recognized.

"I harbor no Parastenian killers in my doors, good sir," the innkeeper said, oddly calm for what he was up against. "As I said before, you are welcome to search the rooms and see for yourself, but please don't disturb my honest patrons."

The Kircan sniffed and motioned to his men. They started right toward Dowyr. He darted back up the stairs, making sure he wasn't heard, and saw the rest of his group entering Garec's room. He made them vanish from the Kircan's eyes too. There was nothing going on in the hall. No sound, no movement. Dowyr slipped into the room, and as instructed, everyone was standing with their backs against the walls. Still maintaining his channeling at the Kircans, he made a hushing motion, then went to Weynon and stood against the wall beside him.

Garec made a motion to catch his attention before signing, *how many?*

About a dozen, Dowyr signed, though he could have easily channeled it too. *Hopefully they leave soon.*

Garec nodded.

They waited.

The Kircans could be heard outside the hall now, opening doors and checking rooms. Their own door opened and two Kircans marched in, looking around warily. Everyone held their breath. The Kircans saw and heard nothing. This room was empty.

They left, and everyone let out a soft, slow sigh. Despite knowing his channeled deception would keep them hidden, Dowyr's heart pounded in his chest.

It wasn't long before they heard them talking with Sirona a couple rooms down. Dowyr's heart pounded even more for that. There was little he could do to prevent the Kircans from hurting any of the women. Perhaps he might create some sort of distraction that pulled their attention away, but that could just as easily create more unwanted suspicion for the inn.

The talking continued for a short time, but there was no shouting, no screaming. A door closed. Footsteps in the hall.

Twice more Kircans entered the room, different soldiers each time. One of them took a long sniff, and Dowyr's heart skipped a beat. He hadn't thought of altering what they smelled. But thankfully nothing came of it.

It felt as though hours had passed by the time the Kircans left, but in reality it had maybe been fifteen minutes. Even for that long, Dowyr was amazed he had been channeling to so many people and felt no trace of fatigue.

Once satisfied with how far the Kircans had gotten, Dowyr released his channeling and gave Garec a thumbs-up.

"They'll be on the lookout for you," Garec said, looking at Gwyn.

"Yes," Gwyn said. "But you are leaving once you know where the Tyrdens are."

"That is going to be the hard part. I want to be as discrete about getting the information as possible."

Donnan snorted. "No kidnapping for once?"

"No," Garec said dryly. "I'd rather not have the entire regiment here bearing down on us, much as I think we could outrun them. We'll need Dowyr and Elethe to get the information. Gwyn, do you know if the Colonel has a routine that involves leaving the courthouse?"

Gwyn shook his head. "Everyone says he never leaves. He seems to have a serious contempt for the sun."

"What, is he a vampire?" Donnan asked.

"It wouldn't surprise me."

"I could get the teens inside," Henric said. "We go late when there's fewer guards, I work some Emogic, and they let us in."

"*I can get us in myself,*" Dowyr channeled to everyone, and was again annoyed at how much effort it took now that Gwyn had stopped channeling at him. "*Or if not by myself, with Elethe's help, it shouldn't be hard.*"

Garec folded his arms and looked lost in thought for a moment. "I wish we had some way to lure him out. I don't like having you two walk straight into a badger's den alone. Almost prefer Henric's suggestion, but that sensory manipulation is hard to beat."

"I can watch them as they go," Donnan said.

"No, Elethe said there's another Ghost here. I don't want to risk it, night or day."

"*We'll be fine,*" Dowyr channeled. "*She's Class 3.9, after all.*"

"I can channel from here if she ever needs my Emogic," Boughton said.

Garec sighed. "I'll go talk to her. But if she doesn't agree, we find another way."

CHAPTER 23

What Boredom Can Do

"I can't believe I agreed to this," Elethe said.

Dowyr glanced at her from his seat by the window. He had been watching the courthouse from the second floor of an inn across the street. Elethe sat next to him, also watching. It had been simple getting the room without paying, making themselves invisible to the innkeeper as they entered and went upstairs. Thankfully none of the other patrons noticed their fraud, too wrapped up in dance and conversation with each other. Parastenians could be so unaware of their surroundings to the point of hardly noticing they were occupied by Kircans.

"You could always change your mind," Dowyr channeled, and he meant it. A part of him wished Garec had chosen another way, one where he didn't feel so annoyingly self-conscious. At this late hour he probably could have done everything alone. How many people could possibly be in the courthouse? And it's not like he *needed* Elethe to get the information from the Colonel. Garec wouldn't accept that, though. Wandering the city was one thing, but infiltrating a building with few ways of escape was another.

"So could you," Elethe said.

Dowyr rolled his eyes. *"I bet you'd love that."*

Elethe was silent for a moment, focused on the courthouse. "No. I wouldn't love that."

"Oh. Well, I just farted."

Elethe sniffed then cleared her throat. "Yep." She slowly stood up and walked a few paces away before taking a deep breath and coughing.

Dowyr grinned to himself, keeping his eyes on the courthouse. The sun had been down for two hours at least, but there was plenty of commotion still, even in the cold. The noise from the common room was often loud enough to reach his ears. Torches and fires glowed across the whole city, and even a few lightstones.

Movement in one of the courthouse windows caught his eye. The room beyond it brightened as someone was moving around inside. Two someones, though it was hard to tell if they were soldiers or otherwise at this distance. It wasn't long before they exited the room and came out the front doors. Two soldiers, replacing the ones that had been standing guard for the evening.

Finally.

"*Time to go,*" Dowyr channeled.

Elethe came back to the window and saw the new soldiers. "We should wait five more minutes, just in case."

He got up and started putting on his coat. "*Five minutes isn't going to change anything, let's go!*"

She gave him a sharp look. "I'm not leaving until I feel good about it."

"*Whatever, you do you. I can handle it myself anyways.*"

He marched for the door.

"Dowyr, no!" She ran in front of the door to block his way. "Don't be an idiot."

"*Fine. I'll just stare at the wall until you're ready.*"

He went over to the actual door and stood in front of it for a moment, long enough for Elethe to look confused as to why he'd do such a thing. Then, to her perspective, he walked right through the wall. He stopped channeling and made his way down the hall.

Elethe finally stormed out, absolutely fuming. Dowyr smiled and waved but didn't slow. She caught up next to him, looking ready to slap his nose off.

Nobody in the common room paid them any mind. The innkeeper was too busy with another patron to notice two faces he'd never seen before coming down the stairs. Just a couple of teenagers going out for a walk, that's all they were.

Stepping into the cold, Dowyr gave himself a second to breathe out and watch the vapor in front of his face. For the brief moment, he felt like his younger self, awed by the world and its mysteries. That awe had driven him to read everything in the library he could get his hands on. He had to know how the world worked.

The vapor dissipated, followed by the next puff, and he came to himself, looking both ways down the Broadway. A wide street, still with plenty of activity between shops and spots where there were fires burning to eat and dance around. There was more light by fire than lightstone. Parastenians loved fire. None of the books had ever told him that. They had hardly said anything of people from Parasten or Arkonia or Kircany. What a waste of space all those words about Elyssanar were taking up. It made him wonder what the other nations were really like.

"Are you going or not?" Elethe asked from behind with a touch of irritation.

"*Yes*," Dowyr channeled, starting his way toward the courthouse. "*Just got caught up with how much I hate the cold.*"

He kept channeling a stream of Emogic for Elethe to Match and channel at the new guards at the courthouse, and everyone else on the street for that matter. There was no way to tell what she made them see, though. Dowyr did his best to avoid bumping into anyone passing by.

For how colorful all the other buildings in Norwood were, the courthouse was strikingly painted white, making it stand out among all the hues of blue, green, and yellow surrounding it. Even the conical chimney covers were plain, at least as far as Dowyr could tell. It was too dark to be sure.

They strode up and entered the courthouse without so much as blinking. It was warm inside, though there were no fires in sight. A dim amount of light came from lightstones hanging from the ceiling and wall-stands. Dowyr and Elethe moved slowly so as not to brighten them, looking in all directions for any signs of movement.

"*There's a Ghost here,*" Elethe channeled, a whisper in Dowyr's head.

"*Is he astral projecting?*" Dowyr channeled.

"*He was a second ago, but I think he was looking outside, not in here.*"

"*Maybe you should channel at him just in case.*"

She gave him a level look. "*Boredom doesn't do anything if he's astral projecting.*"

He blinked. "*How do you know?*"

"*That book you read forever ago. I read your mind, remember? I know because you know.*"

He mentally slapped himself in the face. She was right. He must've been so distracted he couldn't remember, and if the pounding in his chest was any indication, it was hard to think about anything except what they were doing. A Ghost might make things problematic unless they got the jump on him. Hopefully, wherever he or she was, it would be nowhere near the Colonel.

"*So, uh, I'll follow you,*" he channeled, slinking back behind Elethe.

She rolled her eyes and pressed onward. The halls and rooms they passed were spacious, but with how little light there was, darkness made everything feel squeezed tightly together. Nobody else inside was stirring. They came to a stairway leading up to somewhere more well-lit. Elethe went up, Dowyr keeping at her heels as quietly as he could manage. Reaching the top, there were two hallways, one stretching forward and the other off to the right. Elethe went right.

"*Do you know where you're going?*" Dowyr channeled.

"*Of course not,*" Elethe channeled. "*But it's away from the Ghost.*"

Coming to a set of two open doors, Elethe entered the door on her left. It led onto a balcony with rows of seats overlooking complete darkness. When they went into the other door, it also led to the balcony, though a separated section.

"Must be the courtroom," Dowyr channeled.

They left and found more empty rooms and offices. Some of them looked like converted living spaces with a mattress and blankets stuffed into the corners. The fact they hadn't run into anyone else in the building yet was starting to make Dowyr nervous. Where was everyone? Did the Colonel not have anyone else around with him?

"Chill, dude," Elethe channeled. *"You're starting to freak me out."*

"Well excuse me, princess," Dowyr channeled. *"I'm just a simple Mind Intruder that can't sense what people are feeling or channeling."*

He grunted as he felt something invisible slap his face that made no sound. He had expected her to do as much.

"If you can sense people's emotions, couldn't you tell where people are in the building?" he asked.

Elethe gave him a look that accused him of being an idiot. *"You realize that most of the time people aren't feeling much of anything, right? And it's hard to tell the distance from others unless the emotion is strong enough. The Parastenians also kind of drown out a lot. Buncha weirdos."*

Dowyr nodded. *"Maybe we should go find that Ghost. They might be with the Colonel."*

"I guess that wouldn't surprise me. Just stay quiet."

"Sure, just don't use my Emogic to slap me."

Elethe ignored him and moved back towards where they'd come from. Coming to the top of the staircase again, they went down the other hall. It was brighter than the other, and Dowyr was grateful for the carpeted flooring keeping their footing silent. Any other time, he might have admired the beauty of the courthouse, from what he'd been able to see so far, but he didn't give anything a second glance that didn't look like the silhouette of a person.

They checked every door they passed, first listening closely before cracking them open to check for anyone inside. Dowyr's heart pounded each time, and he breathed a sigh of relief when they were found empty. He was surprised that none of the doors screeched or creaked, but then Parastenians seemed to be auditory purists. No unwanted sounds allowed in their cities and towns. All of their instruments were tuned to perfection, always.

Then one of the rooms wasn't empty. A Kircan slept inside, a single dim lightstone outlining his body.

"*Is that him?*" Dowyr channeled.

Elethe stepped into the room and channeled to the Kircan. After a moment she shook her head. "*No, he's a... uh oh.*"

A stream of Boredom surged from Elethe in random direction so quickly that Dowyr hardly saw it before Elethe dove at his chest, knocking him to the ground just before the room's floor fell into darkness with a thunderous crash. He raised his head and looked back through the doorway, eyes wide. Now the room was just walls and a ceiling.

"*The Colonel is the Ghost, and he's seen us,*" Elethe channeled.

Dowyr wanted to run, but she still pinned him down. "*Are you channeling at him?*"

She nodded. "*I know where the Tyrdens are now. Let's get out of here.*"

She scrambled off him and pulled him up into a run. As they rushed down the hall, Dowyr glanced back and saw the Colonel coming out from another room. A balding, wretched looking man if he ever saw. The Colonel marched over to the doorway of the room with the missing floor and peered downward, then frowned.

"You're still alive, aren't you?" he sneered loudly.

"*He's astral projecting again,*" Elethe channeled.

"There you are!"

Dowyr barely had enough time to stop in order to avoid plummeting to his death as the floor in front of them collapsed. Elethe had been able to slow down sooner, and she grabbed onto the back of his coat, pulling him away from the hole.

We're going to die, Dowyr thought with grave sincerity. He turned to the Colonel, who slowly walked towards them.

"Nowhere to run now," he said.

Elethe put herself between Dowyr and the Colonel, her body trembling. Then the Colonel stopped, fear filling his eyes, and he began screaming, louder and louder. He flailed his arms, then fell to the ground and flailed his legs, convulsing. His screams were that of absolute horror and pain, as if he were being ripped apart. Dowyr covered his ears and shuddered as he realized that might be exactly what he was feeling. Elethe was crying. She looked ready to empty her stomach. An eternity seemed to pass until the Colonel's arms and legs fell to the floor, unmoving. Was he dead? Dowyr couldn't tell.

With the immediate danger dealt with, they rushed back to find another way out. Dowyr heard soldiers shouting from downstairs, unsurprisingly. Anyone else in the building or even outside nearby would've heard that scream. He tried to focus on keeping his legs moving.

They came across the room the Colonel had come out of and entered. It was a spacious office with part of it converted into a living space. Two glass balcony doors offered them some hope for escape. Before opening the nearest one he peeked out the window and spotted Kircans running to and from the building. It didn't look like there was any way down from the balcony. Elethe opened the door and crouched down to avoid any eyes on the street.

"There's no way down," Dowyr channeled.

Elethe looked at him. *"We're not going down."*

She stopped channeling his Emogic and a second later began floating in the air. Dowyr felt a sudden new sensation; he knew how to fly. There was no explaining it, it was just as if he could always do so, and so he did, floating closer to Elethe.

"Let's go," she whispered, then froze, grabbing his shoulder and looking back into the room.

Dowyr followed her gaze and saw what she was staring at. A small group of terrified young women, huddled together, hands bound, barely clothed. They stared right back at them.

"Can you help us?" one of them breathed, desperation in her voice.

Dowyr looked back to Elethe, his heart feeling like it was going to explode out of his chest any second. "*What do we do?*"

"That... that man won't hurt you anymore," Elethe said, voice trembling. "But you... you have to help yourselves."

With that, she turned and launched into the night.

Dowyr clenched his teeth and channeled to the women, "*I'm sorry.*"

A pang of guilt coursed through him as he turned back and let himself follow after Elethe. They should have been able to do something for them, but soldiers were coming, they were trying to avoid notice, and... he hated that he thought of this question; could all of those women be trusted?

The frigid air quickly distracted him from all other thought as he caught up to Elethe, but it wasn't long before they landed behind The Blinking Weaver, and thankfully it was dark enough that it looked as if no one had seen them land.

They came around the building and found Boughton waiting for them at the front. He ushered them inside and followed as they made their way to Garec's room.

"Thanks for the lift," Elethe said.

"Close call?" Boughton asked.

Elethe didn't answer.

"*We should probably leave tonight,*" Dowyr channeled to them both.

Elethe grimaced but nodded. Boughton merely hummed in response.

They found Garec pacing in his room with Donnan and Gwyn sitting at the small table. All eyes turned to Elethe when she entered.

"Did you learn where they are?" Garec asked, then, noticing her expression, strode up to her and took her by the shoulders. He looked her in the eye. "What happened?"

Elethe completely broke down at the question. She embraced him and wailed into his chest.

Garec held her gently and said, "Everybody out."

CHAPTER 24

The Third Torments

Garec brushed Elethe's hair gently as she shook in his arms. Everyone had left. He'd heard the innkeeper out in the hall asking what the matter was, and Donnan was able to reassure him that everything was fine and being taken care of. Elethe had stopped crying, but something must have gone horribly wrong for her to still be shaking so violently. Had she failed to learn where the Tyrdens were? He braced himself for the bad news.

"We didn't have a way out, so I learned what he was most afraid of," Elethe whimpered. "I made them real. The... the monsters. They ate him, limb by limb. I knew it wasn't real, but he believed, I could tell from... oh Heaven... I can still hear his screams. And the... the wom... I couldn't..."

So that had been why the Kircans were suddenly mobilizing in the streets.

"You did what you had to," Garec said softly. "It's something every soldier learns to do eventually."

"I think I... k-killed him."

Garec's heart skipped a beat and he pulled back to look Elethe in the eye. "Are you absolutely certain?"

She looked at him, eyes still watering. They were different from this morning, haunted by imaginary monsters. "I don't know, I used telepathy to check... and there was nothing."

Garec tried to remember if it had been written that Mind Intruders could kill with their Emogic. There was only the memory that they could be extremely dangerous given enough intelligence to use their Emogic the right way, but nothing about the Emogic itself being capable of killing someone. But then the effects of using Boredom to do something that extreme had never been documented, to his knowledge.

"Listen to me," Garec said slowly. "Whether he is dead or not isn't your fault, it is his. He chose his path and dealt with the consequences. May Heaven rest his soul if that is what he deserves, but it does no good to dwell on it. Remember why you're here."

Elethe sniffed and shook her head. "I want… I want to go home."

Those were not the words he wanted to hear, but he had made a promise to himself that if she wanted to go back, he would let her go back. Yet his heart froze in that moment, and the words she would want to hear got caught in his throat.

"The Kircans will be on high alert," Garec said, heart pounding. He made a good show of being calm and collected, so he thought. Would she notice? "You should get some rest. I don't think they'll come back here for us. We'll see how safe it is in the morning."

Elethe's face darkened, but she nodded slowly. Garec led her back to her room and was mildly surprised the hall was empty. He would have expected at least Dowyr to be loitering around, maybe trying to listen in. The noise from the common room had quieted as the patrons began discussing what had gotten the Kircans running around so frantically.

Sirona gave Elethe a worried look when she answered the door. Garec exchanged brief words with her to make sure Elethe got some sleep, and for the rest of them as well. Clarine was sitting by the window, peering down at the streets as Kircans rushed by. She looked at Garec with sunken eyes.

"We know where they've been taken now," Garec said, trying to put some hope into his voice. "It shouldn't be much longer before we find them."

Clarine nodded gratefully, and Garec left, closing the door. He let out a long sigh and nearly opened the door again. Elethe still hadn't said where the Tyrdens were, or if she knew. She would, he was confident of that, but not knowing gnawed at him. It was an effort to force himself to refuse bothering her more, especially after what she'd been through. Instead, he went to the room across from his and knocked. Weynon opened the door and stepped aside to let him in.

"How are you doing?" Garec asked him.

Weynon nodded. "I'm okay. Worried about him." He looked at Dowyr, who sat on his bed staring at the wall. "He won't tell me what happened."

Garec pat his shoulder reassuringly and went to sit down next to Dowyr. The boy didn't even look at him. Garec tried to see what might be so fascinating about the wall and failed.

"*You're wondering if I know whether Elethe knows where the Tyrdens are,*" Dowyr channeled.

"It would be good to know," Garec admitted. Had he used telepathy on him?

"*Nope, I figured that out on my own. Hah. Yeah, she knows. At least that's what she told me.*"

"Would you tell me what happened?"

Dowyr shrugged and finally looked at him. "*We looked around the courthouse for a while. The Colonel found us first. He was a Ghost. Tried to kill us by dropping the floor. Then he screamed, and screamed, and screamed until he dropped. I think Elethe killed him.*"

"Can Boredom do that?"

"*Yes.*" He'd never seen Dowyr's eyes so serious before. "*I read about it once. Boredom can overload someone's senses enough to cause brain damage, to the point of killing them. It's something that I've tried to forget about. We also found some Parastenian women in the Colonel's room, and...*"

I couldn't do anything to help them. We just left them behind. I hope they'll be okay. I... I really hope."

Garec decided there was something fascinating about the wall after all. He had no words for the women. At least they would be better off with the Colonel dead. Maybe.

"Elethe wants to go home."

"What?" Weynon asked. He had gone to a chair beneath a light-stone to read his copy of The Five Sentinels. Putting it down, he got up and came closer. "She can't go back, we need her."

"I promised her if she wanted to go, I would let her go."

Dowyr gave him a curious look.

"Why would you do that? She's the only way we'll—"

Garec held up a hand. "We can survive without her. With Heaven, anything is possible."

Weynon frowned and looked to the door. He marched towards it. "I'm going to talk to her."

Before Garec could react, Weynon froze for a moment, then walked right into the door and rebounded onto the floor. He shook his head in confusion, then looked at Dowyr accusingly.

"Why?" Weynon asked. "If she leaves us... Yeah, but, it's different..." He stood up and gave Garec a grim look, then marched back to his chair. "Fine."

Garec sighed and turned back to Dowyr. "Thank you. But I'm confident that Elethe will decide to stay in the morning. Let me handle it and everything will turn out right."

Dowyr nodded and turned back to the wall that so fascinated him. *"I'm sorry for how I've treated Elethe through all of this. For my behavior overall. I'll try to do better."*

"We all will. And we'll win." Garec pat Dowyr on the back. "Get some rest. Whatever happens tomorrow, you'll need your strength."

*

Dowyr managed a few fitful hours of sleep. They'd been full of dreams; being kidnapped by Kircans in the night, the Colonel chasing after him and the floors falling into an infinite darkness, screams ringing in his ears. He awoke with his heart pounding at least twice, and a furious chattering was happening in the back of his mind. A prayer. It went on and on through the night and his dreams, faint in the background. There were no distinct words he could recall, only the general sense of a plea for help, for safety, and to know what to do. Dowyr blinked his eyes and violently shook his head to make it stop, and then had to wonder why.

Because it's stupid, he told himself. *It doesn't change anything. Stop thinking about it.*

He got out of bed and went to the window. It was still dark out, though there were plenty of oil lamps illuminating the streets. A light snow fell. His eyes fell on someone standing next to one of the lampposts, a woman, whose gaze met his own. His breath caught, wondering if she might be a Kircan soldier, unlikely as that was. Staring directly at him, she made the hand-sign for *safe*, then turned and disappeared down an alley.

He blinked and turned back to climb into bed. He could hear Weynon breathing softly and wondered if he was awake. Channeling telepathy, he tried to listen to Weynon's thoughts, but there was only the unintelligible buzz of dreams. Sometimes he was able to make out what someone was dreaming, though it was unpleasant more often than not. He sighed as he closed his eyes and flexed his fingers and toes. A sense of aloneness enveloped him, the same aloneness he had often felt lying in bed at the orphanage. There was nothing waiting for him after this was over. Perhaps he'd be hailed as a hero for helping stop the war before it really began, or perhaps not. He could die. What had happened only hours ago reinforced that idea, though it didn't bother him too much. Without anyone back home waiting for him, there wouldn't be anyone to mourn him. Weynon would be upset, but he was young. He'd be okay after a little while. Or

Weynon would die as well. That idea certainly bothered him. There was a slight appeal to having absolutely no one around to mourn him, but there was just no abiding the thought of Weynon dying. No, they were both going to be safe. The strange woman in the street signed so.

Dowyr let out a soft chuckle. He was becoming as superstitious as Weynon.

*

Elethe was going to leave. She kept telling herself that, and that she had made up her mind about it already. So why, at this early hour, was she awake and still thinking about it? Part of her wanted to scream, but Sirona would wake up and give her the rough side of her tongue for doing so. Not to mention waking and bothering Clarine was the last thing she wanted to do.

Poor Clarine. Elethe had hardly spoken to the woman since she joined the Company, mostly since Garec wanted to keep them separated as often as possible. Clarine still didn't know Elethe was a Class 3.9, and still thought Dowyr was supposed to be her Booster. The woman had become hardened steel ever since that first Kircan ambush that felt like it had happened months ago. It sickened Elethe to have to participate in that lie. Sirona had been livid when she learned what Garec had Dowyr do, yet she said nothing. No one did. The entire Company went along with it, and she couldn't blame them. That didn't stop her from hating the situation.

She felt a small spike of anxiety from nearby. Garec's room, she suspected. He must be awake, worrying that she wanted to go home. She could tell that he was afraid when she told him that. She could tell he wanted to delay her into changing her mind. And every second of knowing that tormented her, making her rethink the decision and try to reinforce it, only to come back to the promise she had made to herself that she would see this through to the end. But how could she? The weight of it all, of killing the Colonel, especially the way she did it, of deceiving Clarine, of leaving those women behind. It was too much to bear. She hadn't trained for this as an Emogician. Yes, all Emogicians trained to always keep their emotions under control, but it was no easy task for an Empath. Especially one that wasn't trained to be a soldier by any means.

I'm going to leave, she told herself again. Gwyn was powerful enough to make up for her absence. She wasn't needed now that he had joined, and...

I promised both Dowyr and Weynon...

Well, those promises were reliant on her being in a situation where she could save only one or the other. If she left, it wasn't like she'd be breaking any of their promises. She could avoid having to choose one or the other entirely.

That hadn't been what she promised in her heart, however, and it gnawed at her. If she left, and the mission came to ruin, or either of those boys didn't come back, or her uncle, she would never be able to forgive herself. What if Gwyn couldn't be trusted? She didn't know him. Though being a Booster and a Parastenian, she had to give him some credit.

No, none of that mattered. The pain was too much. She was leaving, that was the final decision.

Wanting to cry out in frustration, she slowly climbed out of bed and went to the window. It was still dark, but by the lamplight she could see the streets below and that a light snow fell. Standing below a nearby lamppost was a man. Elethe's breath caught. He seemed to be staring right at her. No, he *was* staring at her. Eyes locked on hers, he hand-signed, *safe.* Then he turned and disappeared around a corner. Elethe blinked, rubbing her eyes. Something about that moment almost didn't feel real. Was she dreaming? Had there really been a man there?

Turning back and climbing into her bed again, she had the sudden urge to wave her hand in front of her eyes. It was too dark to make out anything except its silhouette. She closed her eyes and waved her hand again, still sensing an impression of where her hand was, like a faint glow. She had never understood why she could sense it like that with her eyes closed, but something about the man under the lamp-post made her think of that sensation.

You're tired, Elethe told herself. *Just go to sleep. Leaving in the morning.*

Sleep did come, though with what the morning brought, she almost wished it hadn't.

CHAPTER 25

An Acceptable Fantasy

Dowyr shifted uncomfortably in his chair at Garec's table, wondering why the Captain had asked him to be present while he spoke to Elethe. He hadn't asked him to read her mind or talk to her or anything like that—obviously she would know if he tried—but simply to be in the room. Elethe looked none too pleased at his presence either, though she said nothing. After telling Garec where the Tyrdens were—a Kircan city to the south-east called Florissant—they just silently stood in the middle of the room, staring at each other, not even bothering to glance in his direction.

"You've made up your mind," Garec said matter-of-factly.

Elethe nodded, then nodded again as if to herself. "Yes."

Garec cleared his throat and reached into his coat pocket. He took out the letter he had received back at Fort Calhoun and held it to Elethe.

"What's this?" she asked, cautiously taking the letter.

"It's from Eala. Read it."

"Out loud?"

"No, just read it."

Her eyes scanned the letter and slowly began to glisten.

"I want you to take the letter back to her," Garec said.

"Take it back? Why would..." Elethe shook her head, then again more vigorously. "No. No!" She flung the letter back at Garec. "You're taking it back yourself, you stupid uncle!"

Dowyr looked around in any direction he could think of to avoid watching the two of them. Why on earth had Garec told him to sit here and listen to this?

"I can't," Garec said, more calmly than Dowyr believed he felt.

"Why?" Elethe screamed. "You're going back, we're all going back."

"You don't understand. I walked away."

"But you two were perfect together."

Garec took a deep breath. "Not anymore. Not after I knew what I had to do, what it would take. She wouldn't want me back."

"I don't believe that. Why else would she send a letter? Light! Is this what you've been anxious about this whole time? Is this what you regret? You learn you're going to be a father, and all you have to say is that you walked away?"

Dowyr gaped at Elethe, then at Garec, who stood unnervingly still and indifferent. He was *what?* What kind of man did that? Not that the idea of a parent abandoning their child was alien to Dowyr, but he wanted to know. There had to be an understandable reason.

"It's better that way," Garec said.

Elethe clenched her fist. "Better for who? Eala? Knowing her I'll bet if I came back with this letter in hand she'd try to chase you down all the way to the capital of Kircany, and I wouldn't even try to stop her!"

Garec seemed to relax, surprisingly. He even smiled briefly. "She would. But her brothers have better sense than to let her. It's better for everyone. Her, me, the baby."

Elethe's arms sagged at her sides. "You don't mean that," she sobbed. "You can't… stupid… why does everyone think things are better without them?"

Dowyr cringed inside when he realized that was meant for him as well. While he believed it was true, he shouldn't have told her. And now he wondered if his own parents had thought he was better off without them. They couldn't have known he was a mute and thus destined to be ignored all his life. Or maybe they thought *they* would be better off without *him.* Maybe they were right.

Elethe wiped at her tears and drew herself up. "I won't let you go like that. I won't if I have to drag you back to Eala myself! I don't care that you're using this to manipulate me to stay, or that you're using him!" She flung an arm in Dowyr's direction.

His eyes bulged and he nearly knocked his chair backwards. "You're what!?" he tried to say out loud, though it came out as a garbled croak.

Elethe glared at him. "What, like you didn't know?"

"*KNOW WHAT?*" Dowyr channeled to them both. "*I don't know why I'm here, I just want to go back to sleep! For a hundred years! No more screaming, no more killing, no more strangers signing at me through the window in the middle of the night.*"

Garec turned his full attention to him. "You saw someone signing to you last night?"

Elethe gave Dowyr a curious look. "Someone signed at me too."

Garec's head whipped back to her. "What? Why didn't you tell me?"

"I forgot about it until now."

"*It was a woman, right?*" Dowyr channeled.

Elethe looked between him and Garec. "No, it was a man. He looked right at me through the window and signed 'safe'."

Garec again turned to Dowyr. "You saw a woman?"

"*It looked like a woman. She also signed 'safe', looking right at me. She disappeared around a corner right after. I almost thought it was a dream.*"

Elethe nodded. "Me too."

Garec's eyes narrowed and he strode out of the room and across the hall to Dowyr and Weynon's room. They followed him in as he approached Weynon, who sat on his bed reading The Five Sentinels. His eyes darted between the three of them.

"Were you awake at any point during the night?" Garec asked.

Weynon paused for a moment then shook his head. "No, I slept through it all. Did I miss something?"

Garec frowned. "No, nothing. Never mind. Get dressed and something to eat, we'll be leaving soon."

He strode back to his room, and Weynon gave Dowyr a questioning look, to which he shrugged and followed after Garec. Elethe seemed to hesitate before following.

Once the door closed behind them, Elethe spoke with an unusually nervous tone. "So, um… he… I'm pretty sure he was lying."

The air felt a little colder at the words. Garec froze in place, and a chill went down Dowyr's back. Weynon didn't lie about something like that so casually. Hell, besides jokes, he never lied about *anything*. It just wasn't who he was.

"How do you know?" Garec asked.

"I could feel him become agitated the moment you asked your question. Or scared, something like that, but whatever it was, there was something he remembered when you asked and it triggered an emotional response. He even immediately channeled to calm himself down to keep it from showing."

"Maybe he saw someone too, but doesn't want to worry anyone," Dowyr channeled, thinking it could be the only reasonable explanation.

"Maybe," Garec agreed, though he glared at a random corner of the room as though lost in thought. "We need to leave. Now. I don't care what these strangers signed to you, this city isn't safe anymore. The Kircans have probably lost sleep trying to figure out what happened last night. Elethe, get Sirona and Clarine ready to move. Dowyr, you get ready yourself."

Elethe took a deep breath and seemed to steel herself. "I hope you know that this conversation isn't over. I meant what I said, I won't let you abandon Eala or your child."

Garec gave her a solemn look. "We all do what we must."

Dowyr scampered back to his room to put on warmer clothes. Weynon was already dressed and had grabbed them some buttered cornbread from the kitchen to scarf down. The Parastenians made far better bread than Elyssanar, and cornbread was their specialty. Dowyr swore to learn how they made it if he ever returned.

He still wasn't sure what to think about the matter with Garec. It was cruel of him to leave his family behind, but he genuinely seemed to believe it was for the better. If he had been Dowyr's father, it easily would've been preferrable for him to stay. But then, it wasn't for him to judge, sharing such feelings of self-loathing.

Wanting to forget the whole ordeal, Dowyr returned to Garec's room with Weynon and waited. Within a few short minutes, everyone else had gathered their things and entered. The women looked haggard but prepared to face Hell himself if he came thundering down on the city. The men looked ready to spit in his face.

"We have to leave our horses behind," Garec said. "The Kircans will likely be suspicious of anyone going out, so until we can manage to get replacements—*if* we can anyway—we'll be having Boughton and Clarine help us fly out of here fast enough to avoid notice. I've spoken with the innkeeper about the horses, and he'll make sure they're returned to Leife. I've left a coded letter with my horse so the rest of the Company will know what's happening."

"What's our next stop?" Henric asked.

"Florissant is our target. It's the main staging area of Kircany's armies and where they're keeping prisoners of war." Garec gave Clarine a significant look. Gwyn looked somewhat confused by the exchange, so Dowyr channeled and explained they were also rescuing Clarine's children. Best that he bought into the lie now.

"We'll go east until we reach the Missionary," Garec continued. "There's a large trade post on the river called Ravenport. Henric, I'll need you to get us passage on a boat with either a Puffer or a Sogger. That way it should only be a week at most to reach Florissant."

Henric nodded. "Easy enough."

"Why are we taking a riverboat when we could fly there really fast?" Weynon asked.

"Ye really want te be flying at that speed in this cold?" Donnan asked.

Weynon frowned. "I guess not."

"It's less about the cold and more about the risk," Garec said. "We might be a small group now, but the closer we get to Kircany, the tighter their reign gets over the skies. Just because we have Clarine doesn't mean they won't have their own Sprinter and Scout teams. Not to mention it will be better to enter Florissant through its heart on the river. The prisons are likely to be located near there."

"How do you plan to rescue my children?" Clarine asked.

"It'll be rather simple," Donnan said. "With the help of Gwyn, Henric, ye, and I will infiltrate it. They're likely te have voidstones inside, but Gwyn can Boost ye from outside te let the four of us search for them quickly."

As they discussed the infiltration plan, Garec discreetly signed to Dowyr, *link.*

He did so and asked, *what is it?*

She still thinks you're a Booster, right? Garec asked.

I assume so. Dowyr frowned. It hadn't been too difficult to maintain his distance from Clarine. He'd managed to spend hardly any time within her line of sight up until now, which had almost made him forget to channel to her and make her see his mouth move whenever he said something.

Good. While Donnan's group is chasing the shadow of Hell, the rest of us will be going after the Tyrdens under the guise that it's another possible location for where Clarine's children will be. We'll need you to figure out exactly where they are.

Okay. Dowyr stopped the link from letting any more of his thoughts through. He hoped figuring out their location within the city wouldn't go like it had with the Colonel. They hadn't meant to kill him. Yes, he was a disgusting man, but there would be no prevention of suffering from his death. If anything, the Parastenians would be blamed and severely punished. The prospect of them being to blame alone would be appalling enough.

Don't worry, Garec sent. *We're going to end this, then we'll all go home. You can end the link now.*

Dowyr did so and quietly took a deep breath. Home. What was that? A place of fantasy. He wasn't old enough to own property. What would it mean to be a war hero with no home to return to? Was he to simply return to the orphanage? Would Garec let him choose to go somewhere else? He had no doubt there would be someone among the Parastenians who would take him in. That could be a happy life. He could help them rebuild from Kircany's invasion. There was nobility in that, and it would relieve some of the pain for what he had done on this bloody journey. Or perhaps he could make it down to Arkonia as he intended and start an orphanage of his own.

Fantasies. Until he lived through this, it was all fantasies. He could die, and why not? Why not just die? There was nothing wrong with that. It would be a sufficient punishment for the things he'd done; the lies, the death, the suffering. To stop existing, for the suffering to be over, that was an acceptable fantasy. But only once the Tyrdens were dead.

Yes. Once the Tyrdens were dead.

CHAPTER 26

Murderers of Murderers

Dowyr huddled next to Weynon as they sat below deck of the riverboat they'd been granted passage on, trying to avoid thinking about how sick to his stomach he felt. It was a somewhat tight space, which necessitated huddling close to one another when everyone was occupying it, but there was also the frigid air that made him grateful for it. Weynon was asleep, his head leaning against the wall. They'd all needed to get used to sleeping that way, though the soldiers adapted faster than everyone else.

Everything had gone as Garec planned. They'd flown out of Norwood and nearly frozen their hands off before finding a village that they were able to get horses at, with some help from Dowyr anyway. From there they reached the Missionary River and, with Henric's charming help, found a boat with a Puffer at its helm that channeled the winds to speed them down the river faster than was natural, much to the displeasure of Dowyr's stomach.

Boats are worse than horses, he thought sourly for the hundredth time.

It had been a week since getting onto the river, and Garec said they should be getting close to Florissant. Everyone had stayed rather quiet for the journey, and there was a heaviness to the air. Dowyr chalked it up to the cold, but a nagging voice in his mind said otherwise. *The mission is almost over,* the voice said. *We're going to kill or be killed.* And he desperately, guiltily, wished it was the former. There was no guilt for the life of the Tyrdens. It was his own life and what he'd done to get to this point that weighed on him. Why had all of this been necessary? What did the Tyrdens really want from war? Something that would've made leveling the entire city of Irostead necessary, that would've made taking away the young men from Parastenian cities and villages necessary, except he couldn't think of anything that would. Only a raw hatred of life or a twisted religious fervor would give someone reason to destroy the lives of so many Parastenians.

Why did such people have to exist? There was a reason for everything, scientifically speaking. There had to be. But he could not, for all the books he had ever read, understand.

Elethe came below deck, her arms crossed to keep her hands warm. If Dowyr hadn't known better, he would've thought she was frowning at him, but that frown seemed permanently affixed to her mouth since leaving Norwood. She came over and sat up against him, leaning her head on his shoulder. A week ago he'd have been shocked from her doing the same, but now he was merely grateful for more body heat. More *eventual* body heat; he could feel how cold her ear was through his coat.

He glanced around to make sure Clarine wasn't in sight then channeled, *"You shouldn't stay up there for so long."*

"I know," Elethe mumbled. "Can you keep channeling? I don't feel like talking out loud."

Dowyr gave her a mildly skeptical look. *"But you still feel like talking?"* He wondered if she had some ulterior motive in using his Emogic, but then it wasn't like he couldn't cut her off, so he kept channeling.

"Talking is better than listening to all this silence," she channeled. *"It's like ever since we got on the river, everyone's emotions have dulled. It's so quiet, except for flickers of anticipation."*

"Must be nice compared to before."

"Yes... and no. It feels like when you've done something so wrong or embarrassing that nobody wants to even look at you."

"Ah, well, I wouldn't know what it's like for nobody to want to look at me."

She reached over and gave a soft knock on his skull with her fist. *"That kind of sarcasm isn't funny."*

"No, but my face is."

Elethe snorted, and there was even a glimpse of a smile.

"I love you," she channeled.

"That kind of sarcasm isn't funny either."

"I know. I've never been very good at being funny. My older brother is the one with the sense of humor, but it never rubbed off on me, unfortunately."

"You have an older brother?"

"Had. He passed away a long time ago."

Dowyr frowned. *"I'm sorry."*

"It's fine. I'm mostly over it."

"How did he die?"

A vision began to play out in front of Dowyr's eyes. There was a teenage boy, maybe only a year or two older than him. He shared Elethe's eyes and nose, but the rest of him looked like a younger version of Garec. The vision then showed him with a group of men trying to restrain a horse that was putting up a wild fight. He had a rope around one of the horse's legs, but then his foot got caught on something and he stumbled. The horse kicked, and he flew to the ground head-first, and didn't move after that. The vision faded.

"That's just how life goes sometimes," Elethe channeled. *"One little unexpected kick and..."* She sighed. *"Mostly over it. He's the reason I had my Apex, you know. All the emotions at the funeral swirling around. I was so overwhelmed I ran away, but no matter how far I ran, it wasn't enough. That's always been the price of my strength."*

Dowyr grimaced, unsure what to say.

"You don't have to say anything," Elethe continued. *"I'm just glad I can still cling to the memory of him."*

He looked at her. *"Are you using telepathy or was that an Empath thing?"*

She smirked. *"Neither, I could just tell."*

He rolled his eyes and laid his head back against the wall. *"The Sisters back at the orphanage seemed to be able to do that sometimes too. It must be a woman thing."*

"Damn right. Or at least that's what I'd like to say, but it's a people thing. You're just not a people person."

Dowyr made a noncommittal hum and looked over at Weynon to make sure his hands were still covered.

Elethe sat up and gave him a thoughtful look. *"No,"* she channeled. *"That's not it. That's what you think about yourself, but really, you know and care more about people than anyone realizes. You even care about the other kids at your orphanage, but you try not to show it. People don't understand you."*

That came like a gut punch, but he dismissed it with a huff. *"Yep, and I don't care."*

"Do you care if Weynon understands you?"

"Shut up, he's different. Why does it matter anyway? Growing up I learned pretty quick that nobody would understand me, especially without learning all..." He took his hands out for a moment and wiggled them. *"And it's better that way. Honestly, I'm so sick of Elyssanar. Sick of its preachy, holier-than-thou dimwits that barely do themselves what they demand of others. None of them actually cared about me, they just cared that I lived and thought how they wanted me to live and think. But I showed them, and eventually they all gave up on me!"*

She frowned. *"Do you hate them for it?"*

He scowled. Why was she grilling him about this? It was getting annoying. *"They're not even worth putting in the effort to hate. They don't care a lick about me, and I always thought Hell put it so eloquently: swing back the sword that pierces you."*

"But even then, it still hurt when they left you alone."

Dowyr wanted to jump up, storm out, and be done with it all, but his legs were stiff from the cold and he couldn't get them to do what he wanted. His heart pounded so hard he wanted to scream, not even knowing whether for anger, frustration or, or...

"*You aren't even supposed to know that!*" he channeled. "*You ripped that information out of my head like it was nothing, like you didn't even know what you were doing. Why are you even asking me about it? Since you already know the answers, what else do you expect me to say?*"

"*You're right, I didn't know what I was doing. I often wish I could take that moment back because I know how invasive and wrong it was. But right now, I don't care, because I want you to know that I understand you.*"

Dowyr clenched his jaw. She understood him? She had barely made the choice to. Her knowing anything was more like an accident, and now she wanted to pretend that understanding him was somehow meaningful or significant. He gave a long sigh.

"*So what?*" he channeled, ready to be done with the conversation.

Her shoulders slumped and she leaned back against the wall. "*I don't know. Read my mind if you want the answer.*"

"*No, I want you to tell me.*"

Elethe turned away. "I already did," she mumbled.

What was that supposed to mean? She hadn't explained herself at all, and now when he actually wanted her to respond, she was done talking?

No, he didn't care, he was done with the conversation too, and forget about reading her mind for an answer, even if she was fine with it. It was a waste of time trying to understand the mind of a woman.

He noticed Henric sitting with the other officers nearby giving him a curious look.

That looked like an intense conversation, Henric signed.

Dowyr shook his head and signed, *infuriating is more accurate.*

Want to talk about it?

"*Hell no,*" Dowyr channeled.

Fair, Henric signed with a slight smile. *Sleep. Keep up strength.*

Dowyr gave a short nod and leaned back against the wall, closing his eyes. Sleep was still difficult to come by, and the anticipation that they would be in Florissant when he opened his eyes was overwhelming. They would become murderers of murderers and call themselves heroes. Maybe he'd feel better about it if it wasn't so cold.

What in Hell's name did Elethe mean? No, no, he was going to stop thinking about it. She hadn't even said anything in response to his 'so what', just to read her mind as if that was the answer. Had she meant that something she'd said before was the answer? It was going to drive him insane.

Garec came below deck, his head wrapped in a long scarf so that only his eyes could be seen. He pulled the scarf down from his mouth.

"Florissant is in sight," he said loudly for everyone. "We'll be there within the hour. Be ready."

He gave Dowyr a significant look, which Dowyr understood to mean *he* was the one who needed to be most ready. It was his job to figure out exactly where everyone needed to go, after all.

Elethe didn't even react to the news, just sat there, shivering alone. Garec came over to her and put his scarf around her neck. Weynon stirred, rubbing at his eyes.

"Are we there?" he mumbled.

"Yes, almost," Garec said. "Thank you for all your help with the wolves and horses, even if it didn't amount to much."

Weynon shivered. "Wolves… they're still following us, I think. I saw them watching us yesterday."

Garec looked at him. "Did you talk to them?"

"I told them to stay away, but they wouldn't listen. They're worried about me, I think. They can smell Royce in the direction we're going."

"That's all the confirmation I need." Garec gave Weynon a soft pat on the shoulder. "Well done. I want you and Sirona to stay in the ship while we go after the Tyrdens."

Weynon frowned. "I want to help." His face darkened as he looked up at Garec. "I want to go after them too."

Garec stared at him for a moment and sighed. "You'll stay close to me and do exactly as I say."

Weynon nodded fervently.

"Good. Be ready."

*

Royce lounged on a plush chair in his meager quarters, staring at the dwindling flames of a brick fireplace. Above him levitated a couple of fist-sized rocks as he channeled the least bit of Rage to spin them about in various patterns, faster and faster. He was quite enthralled with patterns. There was always a new one to discover, to solve as though it was a game or puzzle, and victory was his when the pieces were set in their proper place. That was the whole point of this war. When the pattern of the world revealed itself to him, he realized its pieces were scattered, chaotic, without meaning. They needed to be rearranged to make sense, to bring balance.

He wanted to scream with impatience.

The main door to his quarters swung open as a man in plain clothes marched in, eyes set with determination.

Royce scowled at him. "I said—"

"That you didn't wish to be disturbed," the Seer boomed over him. "Obviously that shouldn't apply to me. No, it's not about your brother, and it's not something trivial, but you will have a devious plan and I, of course, wish to see it through."

Royce clenched his jaw. The rocks in the grasp of his Rage cracked. "I hate—"

"It when I do this, yes. I know. There is a group arriving on a ship within the hour from Elyssanar, they have come to kill you and your brother. They have a Class 4 Empath and a Class 3 Voidspeaker among them."

Royce had levitated a glass of wine over to himself as the man talked and was mid-sip when he mentioned the Class 4 Empath. Wine was no easy thing to remove from clothes.

He ignored the mess and stood up, letting the wine glass fall to the floor. "They have a *WHAT?*"

The Seer looked down at the wine puddle seeping into the rug with a blank expression. "Yes, indeed. I appreciate your gratitude, however long in coming it may be. Your brother need not be informed. When the last flame in the fireplace goes out, send Doom Company of Fourth Battalion to surround the prison. Half of the Elyssanarans will be there. They have a high-Class Booster to bypass the voidstones and are looking for something that's not even there. Yes, that's ridiculous, but it doesn't matter. They will surrender. The other half of their group will come straight here. Light a candle after I leave, they'll be in this room when it goes out."

Royce tapped his foot impatiently. "And I assume the Empath and Voidspeaker will be among them? Why haven't you told me what to do about them?"

"You like puzzles, and your solution will be adequate. I leave it to you." The Seer gave a slight nod of his head.

Royce sat back down and let his rocks fall into his palm, now merely pebbles. He shifted them around each other, listening to the slick, grinding sound.

"Simple puzzles," Royce said. "Their strengths cancel each other out. An arrow should work."

The Seer tilted his head again. "As imaginative as you are cunning. I will return when there is something else that begs your attention. Oh, and, don't channel until they're dealt with."

"I'm not an idiot."

"It needed to be said."

The Seer turned and exited the room, leaving Royce grinding his stones for a moment before he took a candle from the mantlepiece and used the fireplace to light it.

He did not like the Seer. Despite his uses, there was an arrogance to the man beyond salvation, and it always felt like there was something he left out. For having someone around who could see the future, there were too many surprises for Royce's liking. There was little to trust about an Ark, even if he had pledged his loyalty and services to their cause. He still refused to properly name himself. The Arks had a strange way with names and always wanting to be steeped in mystery. Simply another chaotic pattern in need of his hand. Still, the Seer had foreseen and prevented a number of attempts on Royce's or Roderick's life, so his presence was deemed a necessity. But Royce couldn't make himself fully trust him. It was too strange for a man with that kind of power to request only a common soldier's wage. Some game was being played, some pattern being woven by him, and Royce couldn't tell what it was. Perhaps he was too much of a risk to keep around. But how does one capture a man who can see the future?

It dawned on Royce that it was a game of Kings. Only when the pieces were all put in the right place at the right time would the Seer become cornered, with no way of escape.

Now, where to put the first piece...

CHAPTER 27

Mightiest of All

Time seemed to slow and yet blur together all at once as Weynon emerged from below deck and stepped onto the docks of Florissant. There were piers as far as the river bends would let him see with boats of varying size and shape docked at nearly each one. More idled on the other side of the river, and there were three tall arching bridges in sight before the city hid the rest. People noisily busied themselves unloading or loading the boats. Some fished or loitered around blocky gray warehouses, all wearing thick fur coats. The sun hung low in the southern sky with only a couple hours of daylight left.

Weynon had to resist the urge to channel and seek out sources of emotion that any animals or other creatures might be giving off. He reminded himself that there was so little during winter it was probably pointless, even more so being in a city. The wolves wouldn't have followed. They knew to avoid cities, especially ones that housed men like the Tyrdens.

Donnan's group split off, taking along everyone except Weynon, Garec, Dowyr, Elethe, and Sirona. Garec had wanted Sirona to stay at the docks, but she wouldn't have it and insisted on coming.

"In case anything goes wrong," she said.

Weynon watched the other group as they made their way towards the prison. The captain of the ship had told them where it was. After they were gone, Dowyr and Elethe were able to mind-read a few dock workers to get the basic layout of the city and shared it telepathically.

It was a somewhat odd sensation to suddenly know exactly where you were in a city you had never been to before.

The Tyrdens were staying at a small fort in the central part of the city, and the plan was just to have Dowyr and Elethe work their Emogic to get them inside.

"Simple and straightforward is usually the best way," Garec said.

As they navigated through the city, it seemed to hold true. No one spared more than a glance for their little group. Weynon wasn't sure whether it was Dowyr and Elethe's doing or if he needed to keep pretending he was any other boy in the city with nothing worth being suspicious about. Normal boys walked like this, right?

"Relax," Garec muttered.

All of them except Sirona gave a start. But Weynon *was* relaxed!

Garec hadn't even looked at them and spoke like he'd just seen them all jump out of their coats. "Light. Elethe, do you know if there are any other Druids in the city?"

"No, I don't think so," Elethe said nervously.

"Weynon, calm everyone down."

Glancing around at passersby as though they might be able to see what he was able to do, Weynon channeled a stream of Peace to everyone, including himself, and their shoulders relaxed. Yes, now they looked like they were walking more casually. Dowyr even began to hum softly to himself. Weynon recognized the tune from the music the Parastenians played back at Leife. It was a nice reminder of what they were here to protect, especially when Weynon noticed his surroundings. The buildings here weren't anything like the ones in Parasten. There was no color to them, no life. They were all straight lines and hard edges, as if imposing themselves upon reality. Weynon tried to hold himself higher, calm and confident in the face of their brutal imposition.

It almost felt like that was all he had left. So much had gone wrong, so much of the plan changed, but perhaps Heaven needed it to be this way for them to succeed. It was difficult to accept. Why had they needed to go through so much? There was evil that needed to be destroyed, the path should have been so much easier.

Suddenly he was aware of Elethe walking beside him, lightly touching his shoulder. "It's gonna be okay," she whispered.

Weynon nodded. "I know. I think."

"You really did see someone out the window that night, didn't you?"

If Weynon hadn't been channeling, his heart might have skipped a beat. It figured that she would've been able to tell, but even so, he couldn't bring himself to say anything.

"You don't have to tell me," Elethe assured. "I just want you to know I'm going to keep you safe, no matter what."

Weynon nodded again and tried to put on a reassuring smile. It was all he could do to try and forget about it. He wondered why she had waited until now to mention that night. There was no explaining what he had seen, what he had felt; a dread that chilled him to the bone. Channeling Peace was the only thing that was able to keep him moving.

The small fort was soon in sight. They marched right up to it and past the guards at one of its gates. Beyond was a small courtyard with what would've been a garden during the warmer seasons, but everything besides the ground where soldiers and servants tread had a layer of snow coating it. The main building of the fort was a plain, large gray block about three stories tall if the arrow slits were anything to go by. Garec was keeping a sharp eye on them, though Weynon saw no eyes peering down himself.

There wasn't any activity in the courtyard at all besides themselves. A heavy wooden doorway into the fort stood unguarded.

"I don't like this," Garec said.

"Someone was just channeling inside," Elethe said.

"Royce?"

"No, it wasn't Rage it was... I'm not sure. It was only for a moment. But I can feel anticipation from someone too."

"Like from all of us?" Sirona asked dryly.

"From inside, duh."

"I doubt it's anything to be concerned about," Garec said. "There's no way anyone knows who we are and what we're doing here. Let's go. You kids stay right on my heel."

They did so as Garec moved up to the door and drew his dagger. He pushed it open slowly, peering around inside before entering and letting the rest of them in. Inside was a small chamber with another door on the far end and two hallways stretching opposite directions a short distance into more rooms. Lightstones mounted evenly along the walls gave plenty of light. Nobody else was in sight. Despite channeling Peace, Weynon's heart was pounding in his chest.

Garec went to the far door and lightly put his ear to it. He motioned Elethe over. *Someone inside,* he signed. *Can you channel at them?*

Elethe stared at the door as though she was looking through it then gave a nod. *Royce,* she signed. *Alone. He can't hear or see us.*

Garec gave them all a smile. "This is where it ends."

He opened the door and the five of them strode in. A young man sat on a plush chair in the middle of a large room with an extravagant bed, colorful and complicated rugs spaced about, and a large brick fireplace decorated with brass embossing. The young man, Royce, was facing the flameless fireplace and staring intently at a candle on the mantlepiece. Garec moved towards Royce, and the candle went out.

"Welcome," Royce boomed, causing Garec to stop mid-step. "Or should I say that you're very unwelcome?"

An explosion of stone came from behind them, sealing the door. Weynon might've jumped at the sound, but his channeling helped keep his and the others' wits about them. Garec bolted forward, dagger in hand. Ten paces from Royce, an arrow came out of nowhere and struck him in the chest. He stumbled to one knee, grasping at the arrow.

"No!" Elethe cried, rushing toward him and Sirona chasing after.

Weynon cut his channeling, too stunned to continue. What was happening? Were they about to fail?

"Yes, I know you're here," Royce continued as though nothing were happening. "However you might be concealing yourselves, this was always going to be the inevitable outcome."

Another arrow came, and Elethe yelped as it grazed her arm.

"Where are they shooting from?" Sirona asked.

"I don't know!" Elethe said, eyes darting wildly. "I can't sense anything. Hurry up and heal him!"

"I have to get the arrow out first. *Light,* it's wedged deep."

Weynon forced his legs to move. He felt Dowyr try to grab him, but he slipped away and charged at Royce.

"You should say your final prayers," Royce said. "Not that they'll be heard. Just wasted breath. Ultimately, from the beginning to the end, I am the mightiest of all."

Two more arrows came, one just missing Weynon, the other striking Garec's right shoulder. He gasped and dropped his dagger, letting it clatter to the floor. Sirona and Elethe were trying to help him up and pull the arrows out.

"Channel so I can heal him too," Elethe said.

"I *am* channeling!" Sirona said.

"I don't see it!"

Weynon ignored them as he scooped up the dagger and made a mad dash towards Royce. Another arrow zipped past his ear, but he didn't hear or notice it. Fixated on his target, he jumped, stabbing at Royce's neck. Steel met flesh, and out came a gurgling croak. Weynon looked up and saw Royce's shocked eyes. Who was this? This was just a young man. He was the evil to be destroyed?

"What?" Royce gasped, then collapsed forward, blood spurting from his neck.

Weynon stepped back from the corpse, leaving the dagger embedded in its oozing resting place, and all else became a blur as he stared at it. They had finally won. He heard doors bursting open, shouts, screams. One was Dowyr's garbled cry. Was one his own? There was blood on his hands. He shook them, but it did not come off. He wiped them on his coat, but it did not come off. They had finally won. A voice rung in his mind, pleading, but he might as well not have heard it. Turning his head, he saw another corpse with an arrow sticking out of its back. Where had Elethe and Sirona gone? They should've been celebrating, and yet for some reason he didn't really want to celebrate. He wondered why. They had finally won. Something struck him on the head. He was so tired. The floor came crashing forward.

Finally, Weynon thought, *I can go to sleep.*

CHAPTER 28

Festival of Atonement

Dowyr laid on the top of a bunkbed staring at the dark ceiling of his prison cell. A prisoner for true, this time. No visiting days, no Emogic lessons, no religious lectures or sermons to endure, just a space to exist in and do nothing. He might've laughed at how familiar it felt to the orphanage or the Academy even still, but he thought he wouldn't be in the mood to laugh ever again.

Elethe and Sirona were gone. Garec was dead. He hadn't seen nor heard about any of the others. Weynon shared his cell, but that didn't seem like much to be happy about. The kid spent most of his time sleeping, or maybe pretending to sleep, and even while he was awake, he wouldn't speak. He barely even moved. Dowyr would sign something to him, and it was like his eyes glazed over. At one point he even slapped Weynon trying to get his attention, and he simply chuckled as though it were a great joke.

It made Dowyr want to scream, though he wasn't sure if out of frustration or fear.

The only source of light in the cell came from a single lightstone attached to the middle of the ceiling and whatever illuminated the hall outside the iron bars, which wasn't to say much. He'd need to run in circles for a short while for there to be enough light to make out every detail of the room. At least it had plumbing.

While staring at the ceiling, he wondered what was happening in the rest of the world. It had only been a few days since Royce's death, but that news had to have traveled swiftly. Would the war end? They'd have to be mad to go on without him. That was the only solace Dowyr had. So many lives saved, ones that would never know him. He was happy for them, and they were better off not knowing him anyway, so he told himself.

The echo of footsteps getting nearer caught his ear, and he turned to the iron bars. A lone man in plain clothes stopped in front of his cell and opened the door. Dowyr didn't recognize him. Weynon stirred from his bunk below.

"Happy Festival of Atonement, children," the man said with an overeager voice. "How appropriate it is to take the darkest day to think back on past mistakes and how one might atone for them."

Oh no, a preacher, Dowyr thought, and signed something particularly vulgar at him.

The man continued without any indication he noticed. "Which is why, after much reflection, I have decided to give you the option of freedom." He stepped aside from the door and motioned to it.

Dowyr blinked and looked at the open door. Freedom? There had to be a catch. Regardless, he didn't care, and laid his head back down.

"Goodness me, do you not want to be free?" the man asked.

"I like it in here," Weynon said, the first words he'd spoken since killing Royce.

"Do you now? And your friend, too?"

Dowyr gave an apathetic thumbs-up.

"Hmm. Unexpected, and yet, understandable. Might I share the room with you a little while?" The man sat down cross-legged, back against the iron bars. "I've grown tired of my conversational partners as of late, and talking to children has always been somehow refreshing."

Dowyr gave him a questioning look, realizing his accent wasn't from Kircany. Who was this strange man?

Weynon made no further comments. Dowyr looked down at him and saw he simply laid in his bed, staring upwards. He didn't even look Dowyr's way. It sent a shiver up his spine.

"What an odd lack of reaction," the man said. "I truly can't tell whether you are bothered with my presence or not. You, on top, you cannot speak?"

Dowyr looked at him and shook his head. *Only sign,* he signed.

"I see. Speaking of which, you may know me as the Seer. I see too much. Many things, webs and weaves and patterns and possibilities I see before me, and so strangely in here I see nothing but what is only now and has been. It is a curse. Not to see so little in here, but to see too much out there. I would give it back if I could, but I must make use of it."

Dowyr frowned at him. A Seer, or a Regret Emogician. Now things were beginning to make sense, some of which being the nonsense he was saying. But if Royce had a Seer on his side, how had they managed to kill him at all?

"I see questions in your eyes. Lay them before me, and I will answer."

Why? Dowyr signed.

"You will need to be more specific, unless you wish for me to talk until the end of time. Don't tempt me, I will do it."

Why did you let us kill Royce?

"Ahhhhh, that is a terrible question," the Seer said, nodding thoughtfully. "It implies I was in control—true, yes—and that I was helping Royce to begin with and then changed my mind—also true. Why did I let you? I simply did not want to do it myself."

Dowyr scowled at him. Did not want to do it himself? And so he allowed Garec to be killed and for them to be captured and imprisoned. It made his offer for freedom even more shallow.

"Yes, I am to blame for everything," he said. "Except the war, of course. That was certainly all the Tyrdens' doing. I am merely along for the ride."

Liar, Dowyr signed. *You're up to something more.*

The Seer shrugged. "Every man is up to something more. It doesn't take a keen eye to see that, unless the average person is much more stupid than I feel comfortable believing. And that would be saying something. I've heard about you, you know. That you remember everything you've read. It should be obvious to a boy like you just how stupid the average person is. The pain of that burden is unbearable, isn't it? You feel like you're trapped. Nobody understands you. It's easier to be distant. You convince yourself that, somehow, if only somebody came and set you free, others could see just how great you are. But that is the clever self-deception of the intelligent. Your own wits betray you, convincing you thoroughly of foolishness, and no one could tell you otherwise, for they are so utterly beneath you. You tell yourself that they cannot comprehend the machinations you've so carefully concocted in your mind. Your brilliance becomes your truth. But even the stupid can smell narcissism. That is always the trouble. More questions?"

Who told you about me?

"If we wish to be technical about it, you did, but you also did not because it never happened."

It dawned on Dowyr that this man had foreseen their interaction, perhaps in dozens of different ways. Hundreds. He could learn things from people without ever talking to them.

"A curse, certainly. It means none of my conversations are ever truly real unless I intend them so. But real conversations are dangerous. They can wander around without a point and touch things that shouldn't be touched. Or simply be terribly dull, and make no mistake, that is one of the worst dangers of all. To be dull, boring, predictable. I want to die just thinking about it. You're not in the mood for a story but I'm going to tell you one anyway. Don't worry, it is short. There once lived a man who ate, drank, worked, slept, and then died. The end. Now you can say you have heard the tale of ten million men. Incredible that you didn't even have to meet them. Here is a question for you, one I have not asked and so I do not know the answer. You must leave some surprises for yourself, you know. What is it that you are afraid of sitting here in this cell?"

It was difficult to keep up with the man and how much he said, but Dowyr pondered on the question. Death first came to mind, but he was quick to dismiss it. Death would have been preferable. It had been what he hoped for once the Tyrdens had been dealt with in the first place. And now, after being put in prison, there was nothing that had threatened to kill him, the guards had brought him food, and he had access to water. But to live with only that for the rest of his life? He was afraid of that. There was nothing honorable about such a life. Nothing useful.

The open cell door invited him out.

He refused its call.

I am afraid of what's out there, Dowyr signed.

"That's not good. But it is understandable. The world is so big, and we are so small and fragile. Even a man such as Royce fell to a child with the smallest of blades. A fitting end, as his ideas were too big for his head. But overall a rather disappointing answer, I was hoping for something more dramatic from you. Maybe your friend has a better answer? Though I find it rather difficult to get him to speak, so I won't press my luck."

Weynon still laid in his bed staring upwards, but at the Seer's remark he turned his head. "I'm not afraid of anything."

The Seer's eyes narrowed. "Now that... is what I call a bullshit answer."

"So what? You talk too much. It's annoying. Leave me alone."

The Seer gave a short whistle and stood up. "As you command, milord. Still, this was most fascinating. Two boys, one afraid of everything, the other afraid of nothing. This tickles me in such a way I might call fate, but I know better than to believe in such a thing. You could even say I *know* it doesn't exist. But I suppose I do need to be going now, there is much to do. And next time, despite the fact there won't be one, don't be so hasty to chase off a clever man. It's always worthwhile speaking to a clever man. Don't forget to think upon your sins and the ways you can atone for them, it is the appropriate holiday for such things. Fare thee well."

The Seer left, leaving the cell door open behind him, though it was only a moment before one of the guards strolled by and closed it. Dowyr sighed and moved to lay back down, but a voice caught his ear.

"Weynon? Dowyr? Is that you over there?"

CHAPTER 29

Sacred Games

Dowyr scrambled off the bunk and up to the iron bars. He hummed in response to the voice that had called out.

"I thought that was you," Henric said. "So they got you too, huh? Damn. But Royce is dead at least. What about the others? Is Garec here?"

Dowyr wasn't sure how to respond. His head wouldn't fit through the bars, and he couldn't see far enough down the hallway to spot Henric. He reached his hands out and signed, *can you see?* But there was no response. He let out a groan.

"Oh, right. Click your tongue once for yes, twice for no. Can you do that?"

Dowyr clicked his tongue.

"What's with Weynon? Is he there?"

Tsk.

"Is he not speaking?"

Tsk.

"Do you think he would tell me why if I asked?"

Dowyr grimaced. *Tsk tsk.*

"Well... I suppose I can only imagine why. Is Garec here?"

Tsk tsk.

"Is he... dead?"

...Tsk.

There wasn't a response for a moment. "Elethe and Sirona?"

Dowyr hesitated. *Tsk tsk tsk.*

"You don't know?"

Tsk.

"Snakes. They better be okay. Gwyn is in here with me. Donnan and the others were taken somewhere else. I'd been wondering how they knew we were here. They took us completely by surprise, but I suppose that Seer fellow explains everything. Odd man. Rather scary if I'm honest. Even with Royce gone, a man like that on Kircany's side... I'm not sure our mission meant anything. Maybe we saved some people. I hope so."

"Henric, you need to tell him the rest," Gwyn's voice echoed.

There was a long silence that followed. The rest? Dowyr perked his ears to make sure he wasn't missing anything, and then the bleak words of Henric came.

"Clarine is dead."

If a guard had come in at that moment and stabbed him, he imagined it would have felt less painful. No, was it pain he was feeling? It had to be, as it brought him to the cell floor, slumped against the iron bars, his head ringing.

I've killed her.

No, this couldn't be pain, it was something deeper. A bottomless pit of nothing, its maw reaching out to consume him. He knew nothing about this woman, had no cause to feel anything for her beyond pity that he tricked her into helping them.

I've killed her.

She was a means to an end, a nobody who risked nothing save her own life, despite not knowing that herself. Why could he not feel anything? His body felt like a blazing fire that burned cold, his skin prickled all over. Would her children ever learn what happened to her?

Oh, Light, I've killed her.

He wanted to scream. His mouth gaped open, urging it to come out, but his throat burned as though molten iron had been poured down it. The same emptiness that filled his soul was the only sound he heard.

He looked to Weynon, eternally staring upwards at nothing. At nothing, he thought again. At *nothing*. No, how could it be that was where his gaze laid? Not him, never, it had to be impossible. There had to be something up there to look at, something that might be able to fill the bottomless pit before him.

"It was quick," Henric continued. "I don't think she suffered. But... I suppose this entire time she was suffering. I'm sorry we brought her along at all. I'm sorry I didn't say something to Garec, but... well, that's that. May they both find peace in the embrace of Paradise."

"We couldn't even find her children," Gwyn said.

Dowyr began to cough and wretch, but nothing came out. It was as though his insides had been consumed by a void. The taste was so bitter, he desperately wanted to throw it up, to spit it out. He tried to spit, but his mouth had gone dry.

"Aaahhh!" he cried, echoing through the prison.

"I understand that cry," Gwyn said. "My heart has made it every morning and night in the days we've been in here. I don't want to be a prisoner for the rest of my life. I've had only such a brief time being able to hear Heaven, and now I can't hear anything. I've prayed, begged, to hear him again, and there is only silence. I wonder what I've done, or what I must do in order to hear again. How do I atone? What sort of sacred games must I play? The last words I heard from Heaven were, 'it should not have been done this way, but the fault is not yours'. I was confused by what he meant. What should not have been done? I've laid awake thinking about it. Our search of the prison? Or our attempt at killing the Tyrdens? That must've been it, because we didn't get Roderick. I cannot blame any of us for what has happened though. It was that Seer fellow. Clearly from what he told you he wanted Royce dead. I wish he hadn't been too cowardly to do it himself. He used us to pay the price, and... I don't know if my complaints are worthy enough to be heard by you. I joined with you so quickly with dreams of avenging my people. Now my people are avenged, and for that I am happy, but some part of me knows Heaven is not pleased. I wish I had gone with you instead. Perhaps if I had, something might've been different, better. Perhaps it should have been me to kill Royce."

"What's this about my brother?" a new voice called.

Dowyr tried to peer as far down the hallway as he could, and saw a man dressed in fine coat and britches looking into Henric and Gwyn's cell.

"*You* should have been the one to kill him?" the man asked, though there was only silence in response. "Maybe you think you had the right to, but if any man had the right to Royce's life, it would be me."

"Roderick, I presume?" Henric said. "Have you come to torture us?"

"Hah, no," Roderick said. "Not even worth my time considering. I'm here merely to sate my curiosity about the boy who *did* kill my brother."

"I don't think you'll get much conversation out of him."

"Really?" Roderick walked down the hall and stopped in front of Dowyr. "Were you the one who did it?"

Dowyr looked up at him but made no other motion.

"Leave him alone," Weynon said. "It was me."

"Me who?"

Weynon turned his head to Roderick but said nothing.

"Don't tell me you're an Ark. I'm already dealing with one too many."

"No. My name is Weynon Rozbury."

"Weynon Rozbury. So, you're the one who stole my brother's life from me? I'm not sure I can believe it."

"It was me." Snakes, his voice had no emotion at all. "Garec was hit by an arrow and dropped his knife, so I picked it up and put it in Royce's throat." He lifted a hand in front of his face. "Still some blood left over."

Roderick sniffed. "What an... interesting stroke of events."

"Are you upset I killed him?"

"In a matter of speaking, but I will consider what you've done as a favor. Royce was a good boy, but I could always tell there were things that irked him that most others would have brushed off. I wasn't around for his Apex and thank the Light of Heaven every day for it. It was clear to me he'd gone mad ages ago, but he still had his uses for the sake of war. Frankly he will continue to have his uses."

Another man came walking up beside Roderick, and Dowyr couldn't stop himself from gasping. It was Royce.

"When people are convinced of the power you hold, they will always treat you as if you have such power," Roderick continued. "Whether or not you truly have it becomes irrelevant. Not to make it sound like such a phenomenon is profound, it's rather pathetic. People are idiots and it disgusts me. If they knew better, they wouldn't deserve what's coming to them."

"Okay, whatever," Weynon said, looking back to nothing.

Dowyr looked at him wide-eyed. How could he not react? Had Royce been healed? It couldn't have been an illusion, or another Mind Intruder making him see Royce. The voidstones would prevent channeling of any kind unless a strong enough Booster was outside the prison. He had no way to ask Gwyn if he could tell unless he got Weynon to ask.

No, there was no way it could truly be Royce. Death was permanent, and he'd seen the life go out of Royce's eyes more closely than he'd like to admit. Dowyr pinched himself, half seriously wondering if he was dreaming.

"I'm surprised that is all you have to say," Roderick said. "You've come all this way, killed my brother, and now see that all your effort was in vain. Do Elyssanarans train their Emogicians to be so… indifferent?"

"Leave him alone," Henric said. "Kid's been through Hell's Gate. He's probably in shock."

"Indeed? This was an enlightening conversation, Weynon. Perhaps we'll speak again."

Roderick and Royce left, and Dowyr listened to their footsteps. Two sets, and in a short time, none. It didn't convince him that was truly Royce, but he had to know one thing.

It was difficult getting his legs to work again, but he pulled himself up using the iron bars and stumbled over to Weynon, who thankfully turned his head to him.

I need you to ask Gwyn if he felt another Booster channeling, he signed. "Why?" Weynon asked.

To know for sure that man wasn't Royce.

"He wasn't. I killed him. Isn't that all you need to know?"

Dowyr grimaced. He wanted to shake Weynon, and thought perhaps he needed as much, but decided against it. He only hoped that they wouldn't start hearing of towns and cities being buried underneath mountains.

For now, he climbed back onto his bunk and wept for the woman he'd killed and never known.

CHAPTER 30

To Be Gods

After the first week of being in a cell, Dowyr and Weynon were let out for daily lunches in the prison mess hall. They found Donnan, Boughton, and Alann there, who were as happy as could be to see them alive, but the smiles didn't last long as they sat together at a table and shared their stories. Donnan looked ready to snap some-one's neck when no one knew what had happened to Sirona or Elethe. They were silent at news of Garec's death.

"It's not your fault, sir," Henric said. "I don't think there's anything we could've done. They've got a Seer."

"I know," Donnan sighed. "We've spoken. More than I like te think about. Perhaps I can get a letter te Eala, let her know... Zion damn them. He was a good man. I believed in his mission, but I often wor-ried that Hell had misguided him in his methods. I should've done more te reign him in. Are ye alright, Weynon?"

Weynon had been silent for the entirety of their reunion, picking away at his food. He'd finished before everyone else and simply sat staring at his empty plate.

"I'm fine," Weynon said without looking up.

Donnan gave Dowyr a quizzical look, but he could only shrug in response.

"If ye say so," Donnan said with a frown. "Henric starts pickin' on ye too much, let me know."

Henric snorted. "I wouldn't do that. Not after what he's been through. Maybe we should talk of lighter topics for now."

"Aye."

Weeks began to pass, and then months. It was hard to notice for Dowyr as being in prison felt somewhat like being frozen in place. Nothing got worse, but nothing got better. Weynon never showed any sign of the passage of time changing him back to his usual self. Dowyr went to bed every night wishing he had told Clarine it was all a trick he played on her before any of them had left the boat. Why hadn't anyone told her the truth? He asked the question every day, and every time he knew how simple the true answer was. They hadn't thought of that. Everyone was so engrossed in the lie they had forgotten it was a lie, and she paid the price.

Spring came, and news of the war trickled into the prison. Kircany was being harassed by the Arks in southern Parasten to little effect. Though hard to believe, it was rumored that groups of Parastenians were attacking Kircan caravans in northern and central Parasten, but mostly unsuccessfully. Roderick had his eyes set on Elyssanar, and they were taking it city by city with essentially no effort. The Elyssanarans were surrendering in masses it was said, with no battles or lives lost. If there were battles, they were wildly fought skirmishes. After five months, as summer quickly approached, news came that the capital had been taken. Yet not even that roused Weynon to comment.

Lunch that day was eaten in silence, though Donnan looked of a mind to say something.

"I wonder," he finally muttered, "were I te be one of the Sentinels, could I stand by and watch as this happened?"

"If any of us were to be gods, I don't know that we'd find ourselves able to think on such a small human scale," Gwyn said.

"Why would we not be able, Parastenian? Did Heaven speak te ye of this?"

Gwyn frowned. "I'm not a Parastenian anymore. And no, he didn't. But in the short time I was able to hear him, I came to understand that he doesn't think small. He doesn't love small. He doesn't favor small. What I mean to say is, Elyssanar isn't special."

All eyes turned to him, including Weynon's. Gwyn shrunk back an inch.

"And so Kircany is?" Donnan asked.

"No," Gwyn said firmly. "That's the point. No one country or people is."

"Then why do ye think this has happened? Is it because Hell has found victory?"

"It's because Heaven doesn't care," Weynon said, and all eyes whipped around to him, though he didn't flinch.

"Of all the lads te say something like that, I never thought it would ever be *you*."

Weynon's gaze returned to his plate. "Well, it's obvious to me."

Dowyr gaped at his friend. He wasn't sure he knew him anymore. What had been going on inside his head all this time? There was no knowing while stuck in this place, at least not while he refused to speak his mind. Not that Dowyr had tried to ask very often, or at all he admitted. This sort of conversation wasn't one he was interested in, though Donnan's initial question did make him wonder what he would do if he had so much power.

"I think it's best we just leave it be," Alann said. "There's no knowing the full mind of Heaven. Even for a Booster."

And that was the end of the conversation. But they raised a solemn cup to their homeland, a silent cheer, a silent hope.

Later in the evening, Dowyr laid on his bunk, imagining sketches on the concrete ceiling. Over the months he had mentally inscribed faces upon it, of the rest of the Company, of students and teachers at the Academy, of the Sisters and orphans. Even some of the preachers he'd come to particularly hate. Why not? Perhaps something undeservingly terrible had happened to them. He left out Clarine, though. There was too much guilt to even remember her face. Special spots were given to Garec, Elethe, Sirona, and the other officers left behind.

He set them firmly in place across the ceiling in his mind. It didn't matter that he didn't have something to truly etch them into the ceiling with, they were there.

He jumped as Henric's voice came. "Are you boys awake?"

Tsk.

"Good. I wanted to say I'm sorry. I wish Garec hadn't dragged you two into this. We didn't know at first, but eventually everyone in the Company learned that he'd stolen you away from the Academy. By then, it seemed too late, and you both looked happy to be along for the ride. Heaven was right. It shouldn't have been done this way."

"Stolen away? You mean kidnapped?" Gwyn asked. "He kidnapped them to bring them here?"

"He stuffed us into barrels," Weynon said.

"Snakes and—"

"I don't care anymore." Weynon's voice rose with each word. Dowyr had never heard him sound so heated. "I don't care about *any* of this. It was all pointless! Heaven was never with us to begin with. He's abandoned us, or maybe even caused the Kircans to do this. I don't know. But it's obvious my prayers meant nothing, my devotion meant nothing."

"If you believe in the meaningfulness of those so, it is thus," Gwyn said softly.

"Taking a verse from The Five Sentinels and changing it a bit doesn't make it true."

"Then what is true?" Gwyn asked.

"I've laid here wondering. Are any of the Sentinels true? *No,* I think, *they've forgotten us, they no longer care.* Are the Snakes true? *No,* I think, *we are the Snakes.* Because the only thing that is true is our suffering through time, and we are the cause of it. There's no end to it, and it's all for nothing. It's all pointless suffering, and no justice for it. That's the only truth."

Dowyr listened closely to his friend, and while part of him shuddered that it was Weynon saying such things, another part of him was saying, *don't you believe this too?*

But could he believe that anymore? Once he had thought it obvious, life was full of suffering for little to no reason. He had been born mute and ugly with no memory of loving parents, and not even pity had brought anyone to love him. When he finally stopped chasing after the acceptance of others, the freedom of pointlessness allowed him to live as he pleased. He believed he could live with anything. But now he had come face to face with the grim consequences of his actions, the death of an innocent mother. He couldn't accept it as pointless. He couldn't accept no justice. Not for her, not for himself. There was nothing left of his life he could find contentment in if it was pointless. There had to be a point to what he'd gone through, to what he'd done.

Royce is dead, he thought. That had been the point. But that didn't satisfy him. Clarine and Garec were dead too. Perhaps even Elethe and Sirona. Why them, and not him?

"Maybe you are right," Gwyn said. "But I do not believe that. I cannot. I cannot even abandon the Way of Paradise, not completely. I still find the idea of eating meat rather disgusting, and I still hate killing. I see the face of the man I killed every night I close my eyes. I hadn't really meant to kill him, but I knew the right thing to do was stop him, no matter what. I don't think it's possible for us to exist on this Earth without killing. There will always be those who want to inflict it for their own gain, so there will always be a need for those who arise to put a stop to it. But I'll always prefer that to be done without lethal force if possible."

"I wouldn't mind settling down in Parasten if there were more who thought like you do," Henric said. "I often wonder how things might be different if they hadn't stood aside. Could what happened to Irostead have been prevented? I don't know, but I wish they had fought. Now their deaths fight for Kircany. Elyssanar has fallen more out of fear than bloodshed. I'm not sure which is worse. I can't imagine what you've been through, Weynon, and so I hold no fault towards you for thinking that way, but I reject your vision of the truth. Yes, there is suffering, and much of it could be pointless. But my suffering in here is not pointless. My suffering is not meaningless. You aren't who determines that, nor my abusers, but myself. I have used it to my advantage to free myself. My body is in prison, but my soul is free."

Weynon scoffed. "Your soul is trapped in your body."

"Not when I dream. Not when I see with my mind's eye. Not when I let my emotions flow outward. And you don't need to be able to channel to do that."

"Whatever."

Henric sighed, and there was silence.

Dowyr climbed down from his bunk and walked up to the iron bars to look out into the hall. He saw no one and hummed.

"I wish you could speak with us, Dowyr," Gwyn said. "You rescued me back in Norwood, and I feel as though I should know you better. I really don't know much at all."

Tsk.

"I'm glad I've at least had all this time to catch up on learning signs like my mother wanted when I was younger. Wish I had you teach me during the boat ride, I'm sure it would've been faster."

Tsk. How Dowyr wished he could speak. Back at the orphanage he hadn't cared about not being able to speak. There was little of value to communicate with the other orphans, and they left him alone anyway. It had been as much a prison there as here, but now he wanted nothing more than to speak. Weynon would turn his head to see what he signed, but with his eyes turned towards nothing most of the time, he'd been hesitant to bother signing anything at all to him over the months.

A guard came around one of the corners, banging a thick stick on the iron bars as he walked. "Lights out. No more chatter."

Dowyr sighed and climbed back onto his bunk. Sleep was not coming easily.

To be a god, he thought. *The only war I'd allow would be against anyone who abandons their children. Or those who take others away from their children. And... no, I can't have them killed. I don't want anyone to die. Maybe I'd just...* He wasn't sure.

CHAPTER 31

Real Justice

Dowyr ate separately from the others today. Being around them and their lunchtime chatter was usually the highlight of his day, but today he wanted to be alone to think over his meal, so he sat at an empty table as far as he could from anyone else. Which wasn't to say very far, and there was still plenty of chatter reaching his ears.

Ultimately it wasn't that helpful for him to think. His thoughts were scattered. Everything that was being said around him crossed his mind, everything that had been said during his time with the Company, and even some conversations with pastors and preachers back at the orphanage. It all jumbled together, and he desperately wanted to make sense of it all.

One word repeatedly leapt into his thoughts. *Justice. Justice. Justice.* The word never went anywhere. It played like a chorus of the dead demanding retribution. *Where is justice?* he wondered. *What is justice?* But no answers came. He once thought he knew, but his old answers had been sucked into the void.

A man came over with his plate and sat down across the table. He was plain looking, barely into his middle years, and gave Dowyr a single glance before digging into his food.

Dowyr looked to the table where Weynon and the others sat and locked eyes with Donnan, who gestured that he was keeping an eye on him.

You should eat, the man signed as Dowyr turned back. *A boy your age should not leave his food untouched.*

Dowyr blinked at him, but he supposed it wasn't that odd another prisoner noticed he used signs.

You don't have to sign, I can still hear, he signed.

"I know," the man said, taking another bite of his bread. "My point still stands. Why aren't you eating?"

Dowyr shrugged uncomfortably and glanced towards Donnan again. *I'm hungry for something else, I guess.*

"Something beyond food?"

Dowyr frowned. *What does it matter to you?*

"The things we hunger for beyond food matter a great deal. And in a place like this," the man looked around emphatically, "one can find himself needing them more than ever. So, copper for your thoughts?" He pulled a copper coin out of his sleeve and flipped it to Dowyr, who barely caught it.

He looked over the coin with curiosity. It wasn't from any nation he knew of. A small image of an ancient building was carved into it, and it seemed to have words surrounding it, though he didn't recognize the language. The coin was in perfect condition. He put it down and signed, *what's your name?*

"Leone. May I ask yours?"

Dowyr Mawkin. It had felt like years since he last introduced himself with his joke of a last name, but he wanted to see Leone's reaction.

He merely smiled. "It is good to meet you, Dowyr."

Where is this coin from?

"Far away. But I can tell that is not the real question on your mind. If you tell me, you can keep the coin, and perhaps one day discover its origins."

Dowyr looked at the coin and shrugged. Figuring there was no harm in it, he signed, *is justice real?*

Leone set down his fork and leaned back in his chair. "Real like that coin is real, or real like how a story represents reality?"

I don't know. Either way, or any way.

"Do you not believe it is in any way real?"

I believe people pretend it's real so they can kill or imprison others. But that doesn't make it actually real.

"I am real justice."

Dowyr gaped at him. It was said so plainly that he wasn't sure if it was a joke. *That makes no sense,* he signed.

Leone smiled. "How else might justice be actually real? I am real, I am justice. Now you don't have to believe in a pretend justice, you can simply believe in me."

But that doesn't mean anything to me. It doesn't tell me what justice is.

"You asked if justice was real, not what it was. And wouldn't you think by asking whether it was real, you already had some notion of what it was?"

I don't know. When I think about justice, I can only see it as what everyone pretends at. Punishing criminals.

"And criminals are determined by the law. Do you believe the law is real?"

Dowyr covered up his thinking by taking a bite of food, and inwardly chuckled knowing he could chew and sign at the same time. *It's as real as the people who enforce it.*

"Ah, so you see, justice is enacted by people, and I am a person. I am real justice."

Dowyr tried to hide his frustration by eating some more, though Leone seemed to see through it and gave him an unusually sad look.

"A boy your age shouldn't have to be struggling with something like this. It isn't easy. But you are clearly very smart. I'm sure you will come to understand what I mean."

Dowyr sighed and shrugged. He continued to pick away at his food.

Leone clasped his hands over the table and leaned forward. "I have a question for you now. What would you give up to be able to speak?"

Dowyr narrowed his eyes. *Give up?*

"Sacrifice, let go of, rescind ownership, whichever you prefer. If you could give up something of yours in exchange for your voice, what would it be?"

Does it look like I have a lot of possessions?

Leone pointed a finger at him. "Perhaps not in the traditional sense. But there are still the clothes you wear, the food you are given, the light in your cell, your wits, your physical health. Are any of those too important to give up for your voice?"

Dowyr looked down at his plate and was surprised at how much he had eaten. *I don't know. If I were to give up anything in here, I guess my Emogic. Doesn't really do anything for me.*

Leone nodded. "Doesn't seem like much of a sacrifice in here. What would you choose if you were out there?"

Dowyr hummed. *Still my Emogic. Nothing good ever came of having it.*

"I'm sorry to hear that. Maybe there will be some good yet to come." Leone looked up at a distant prison guard who was making eye contact with him. "And now it looks like my time has come."

What do you mean?

"Oh, these people don't want to keep me around. One too many mouths to feed. But I am glad to have had the pleasure of speaking with you here, Dowyr."

Dowyr grimaced. *They're executing you? What for?*

Leone stood up with a chuckle. "Isn't it obvious? Pretend justice." He came around the table pat him on the shoulder with a smile. "Think on what I've said. Remember, I am real justice."

Dowyr stared after him as he walked to the guard and was taken away. He caught Donnan's eye again and noticed him sign, *everything okay?* Dowyr nodded and went back to finishing his food.

Later, back on the bunk of his cell, he added Leone to his ceiling of mind sketches. It seemed appropriate. A strange man he wished he could have had a longer conversation with after thinking about what he'd said. Mostly because it still made no sense to him. The kind of justice Dowyr wanted couldn't be a *person*, unless by their existence justice was done for everyone, somehow. But that was impossible.

In this life, Dowyr thought. *But if there was a next one... if Heaven were real... he could be justice. Then there would be justice for Clarine and her family. For Garec, and Elethe, and Sirona. And also... justice for the things I've done. But then what? I stay in this cell waiting to die? I can't live that way. I don't know how to free my soul from this void.*

He sighed and pulled his blanket over him. Perhaps in dreaming he would find some freedom.

His mind drifted, and at times he thought he'd fallen asleep, but then his eyes opened and searched the dark cell before closing again. His ears twitched, and he thought he heard distant footsteps, then they were gone. He dreamed of Leone being hung from a tree, of Elethe dancing with him around Parastenian fires, of the Colonel she had killed in Norwood chasing him through burning buildings, of Weynon sitting on a golden throne in the middle of a forest surrounded by wolves trying to talk to him.

"Dowyr, Weynon, wake up," they said. The words repeated, only this time it was Elethe's voice. Something shook his shoulder.

"Come on, I'm getting you out of here."

Dowyr sat up, rubbing his eyes. The lightstone was brighter than usual. No, there were two lightstones, one close to his face. His eyes focused on the most beautiful thing he'd ever seen.

"Hurry and get up, we don't have barrels to throw you into this time," Elethe said.

CHAPTER 32

To Remember

Dowyr still felt as though he was dreaming as Elethe led him and Weynon through the prison corridors. Weynon hadn't even said anything when he learned what was going on, he simply got up and followed.

"We have a boat waiting at the river," Elethe said. "Don't worry about the others, we're rescuing them too."

They passed unconscious prison guards along the way, which Elethe assured weren't dead, just asleep. It wasn't long before they made it outside, the city dimly lit by moonlight and street lamps. Dowyr tried to channel, but the voidstones apparently still affected the area around the prison.

After making it down the street a short way, Elethe slowed their pace. "Dowyr, can you channel for me just in case?"

He tried to channel again, but there was nothing to grasp and pull out. No Emogic. He stopped in his tracks, shocked.

"What's the matter? Just channel a little, we're out of range."

"I can't," Dowyr said without thinking, and gasped at the sound of his own voice.

Elethe gaped at him, then spun around, eyes searching wildly. "Where'd Weynon go?"

Dowyr realized Weynon was no longer behind him and scanned the streets, but it was too dark to make out anything farther than twenty paces.

Elethe looked on the verge of panicking. "I can't sense him any-where. Did you see anything?"

Dowyr ignored the question and the surprise of his newfound voice, bolting back down the street they'd come from. He couldn't let Weynon run off like this, not after Elethe and the others had put in the effort to rescue him, and especially not after how much he had changed. Where would he go, anyway? The kid couldn't take care of himself on the streets, not even with Peace.

Elethe chased after him, breathing hard and sniffling. The two of them looked down every street they passed, desperately searching, but Weynon was nowhere to be seen, and they could hear nothing but themselves.

Rounding a corner, they ran headfirst into two adults, a man and a woman. Dowyr would've yelled in fear, but the woman's hand im-mediately clasped over his mouth, and the man's hand over Elethe's. It was only a brief moment of panic before Dowyr recognized the woman from the night before leaving Norwood. The woman who had signed to him in the middle of the night. He hadn't gotten a clear look at her face back then, but something about this woman gave off the same feeling as the one from that night. Elethe stared at the man with the same recognition. They both put a finger over their lips be-fore letting go.

Who are you? Elethe signed.

Not safe, they both signed. *Go to the river.*

I'm not leaving my friend behind, Dowyr signed, not caring whether they were two of the Sentinels themselves.

Not safe, they signed again.

A third person appeared, another woman. Tears were streaming down her face. *Weynon is lost,* she signed. *You will not find him. Go to the river.*

Go to the river, they all signed.

The signs rang in Dowyr's mind like they had been spoken. He wanted to push past them, to run and find his friend, but the words pulled at him. *Weynon is lost.* Not lost as in not knowing your way home, but in not knowing your way anywhere. Dowyr understood, but it did not stop his eyes from welling up.

He turned to Elethe and spoke softly. "I don't think we can find him. We'll just get lost ourselves. And... I think Weynon only wanted out of the prison, not to come with us. He's changed."

Elethe hesitated, looking up at the man again who stared down at her with a sympathetic look. "I... I guess we all have. Okay."

She turned back, pulling Dowyr by the hand. When he looked back, the three strangers were already gone, like a dream. *Not safe.* He wondered if that's what they'd signed to Weynon that night so long ago. Something made him doubt it. He wouldn't have lied about something as simple as that. Would he?

They continued on to the river and reached the boat without seeing anyone else on the streets. Upon boarding they were greeted by Sirona and a few men from the Company, and shortly after Donnan and the rest were brought onboard too. Donnan attacked Sirona with a bear hug at the sight of her, to which she responded with a punch in the gut—that Donnan had no reaction to—and a chiding remark for getting himself thrown in prison. More hugs and handshakes were exchanged as old comrades were reunited, and Henric introduced Gwyn to the men who had stayed behind in Leife.

"Where's Weynon?" Sirona asked.

Everyone stopped to look around. Not seeing Weynon anywhere, their eyes fell on Dowyr.

Dowyr took a deep breath. It was an effort to hold back from crying. "He didn't want to come."

Everyone was silent.

"So he's still at the prison?" Sirona finally asked.

"I'll go get him," Donnan said, striding off the boat, but Elethe grabbed his arm.

"He came out with us and disappeared," she said. "He's long gone by now."

Donnan's arms trembled. "Snakes." He slammed a fist against the boat railing, splintering a handful of it. "Why?"

"I wish I knew," Dowyr said.

Sirona took a knife from one of the men and clasped her hair into a ponytail before cutting the tail off and throwing it into the river. "We'll properly mourn his loss another day. Let's get ourselves to safety first."

Donnan hesitated only a moment before pushing the boat off, and they began heading up the river at a steady pace. Elethe took the knife from Sirona and cut her own hair too.

Dowyr went to the front of the boat and watched as the blocky outlines of buildings passed by. His breath caught as he saw one that wasn't like the others. It was taller than the Academy back in Elyssanar, with three triangular spires that pierced the sky, and many smaller ones topping its walls. Elaborately carved stonework marked every inch of it, as though it was a work of artistic embroidery, and a massive circular stained-glass window reflected trace amounts of light. The only similarity to its surroundings was the same feeling of a forced presence, as if to say "Here I am, look at me!", but with an air of beauty instead of oppression. It made Dowyr want to see what secrets were hidden within and understand what the Kircans did with such a building. Who were these people, and why had they gone to war? For all the time he had spent in their prison, he hadn't tried communicating with any of the other prisoners to learn about them. It almost felt like a waste to leave.

He pinched himself, still wondering if he was dreaming, and remembered there was a reason he needed to leave and return to Elyssanar. Clarine's family needed to know what had happened. Weynon's family. If he could find any of them, that was. He stared hard down the passing streets, still hoping that he might catch a glimpse of Weynon around one building or another. He never did though, and let himself weep for his friend. He even thought of praying for him, but the right words wouldn't come to him. What did it mean to pray? Despite knowing what The Five Sentinels had to say about it, he felt clueless. There had to be more to it than what words in a book could describe.

"I am real justice," he muttered to himself, and realized that was what he needed to be. People could play pretend justice to hurt others, but not him. Justice had to be what stopped people's suffering, and he would become the force that did so. Perhaps he was deluding himself, but he didn't care. It was all he could offer of justice to this world. The next world would have to take care of the rest, if there was one. He wanted to believe there was.

Elethe came up next to him with a curious look. "So, what happened? How did you get your voice and lose your Emogic?"

Dowyr shrugged. "I don't know... I guess I sacrificed one for the other. Does my voice sound... okay? I can't tell."

She gave a short smile. "I like it better than the other one. Why sacrifice your Emogic though? I thought you'd always wanted to be an Emogician."

"I did, but... I had a lot of time to think and feel guilty for what I'd done with my Emogic. If I still had it, I don't know that I wouldn't continue using it selfishly, hurting others in the process. I'd rather have a real voice and see what good I can do with it."

"That makes sense. I hurt others using it too, so... I guess it's for the better."

Elethe seemed to hesitate for a moment, looking around and taking a deep breath before tackling him with a hug.

"What...?" Dowyr managed to ask as it felt like his lungs were being crushed.

"Sorry," Elethe said, still holding him but easing her grip. "Just caught up in all the emotion of the moment, I guess."

Dowyr then remembered their conversation from months ago when they were coming down the river. Her answer to his 'so what?' had come to mind while in prison a few times, but only now did it become clear to him what she meant, what she had already said that was the answer.

"You meant it when you said you loved me back then."

"…Yes," Elethe said, still holding him.

Dowyr could feel her heart racing. He sighed and hugged her back. "I'm sorry. I don't think… I can feel the same way. Not yet."

"I know. I'm not asking you to. But… can I just hold you a little longer?"

"Yeah."

A soft, cool breeze blew against them. Dowyr wasn't sure whether he should've let go first, but she had asked to hold on, so he figured it was best to let her decide when to let go.

It then occurred to him that this was the first time he had ever been hugged. A real hug, like the ones he'd seen the other children at the orphanage receive. This girl actually loved him, holding him so close. So close he could still feel her heart racing. The thought began to sink in, and he unexpectedly felt tears sliding down his face. What was happening? He didn't deserve this. And she deserved better. Yet, she held on.

It wasn't until her heartbeat slowed to a relaxed, normal pace that she let go. Dowyr quickly turned away to hide his tears and wipe his face with a sleeve, though it didn't do much good.

"I'm sorry I wasn't able to keep my promise with saving Weynon," Elethe said. "I wanted to save you both, but…"

Dowyr shook his head. "It's okay. At least you were able to keep your promise to him. I just hope, wherever he ends up, he'll be safe."

Elethe nodded and looked ahead, brushing hair out of her face. The back of it was much shorter since she cut it, but still long towards the front. It was a rather odd look, and yet it also suited her. Dowyr probably needed a haircut himself.

"So where are we going?" he asked.

"Back to Leife. The rest of the Company is still there. Sirona and I were able to make it back and plan a rescue. We'd been waiting at a town upriver for the right moment. News came that Elyssanar had completely surrendered, and we figured that was it. Sorry we couldn't have come sooner."

"Don't be. It would've been a lot colder out."

Elethe snorted. "Right."

"What were you planning to do once we got back?"

"I don't know. Arkonia is still fighting, but... I've seen enough of war. I want to go home, find my Aunt Eala, tell her what happened to Garec. Maybe do what I can to help take care of the baby while living with whatever Kircany has in store for Elyssanar. The rest of the Company can do what they want. What about you?"

Dowyr took a deep breath. "I'm going to find Clarine's and Weynon's family and let them know what happened. Probably beg for their forgiveness too. After that, maybe take back my country from that future-seeing bastard, if I don't die trying."

"By yourself?"

"Yeah, unless someone wants to help. I think I'll ask the Parastenians if they want to."

Elethe rolled her eyes. "I doubt it."

"Why? I don't plan on killing anyone."

"Then... what are you planning to do?"

"No idea, but I'm sure I can figure it out on the way."

Elethe was silent for a moment, staring at him. "Alright," she sighed. "Since you'll clearly need more brain power, I'll help too."

He nodded. "Cool."

"Really, Dowyr? That's all you got? 'Cool'?"

"Okay, very cool. And... don't call me Dowyr anymore."

"What? Don't tell me you had an Ark in there giving you stupid ideas about names."

"No, but I'm serious. I don't want that name anymore."

"Fine, should I just stick with 'alien' then?"

"Pfft, no. You can call me... Leone."

"Huh. Why Leone?"

Leone smiled. "To remember."

About the Author

These 'about the author' sections are always so dry they leave something to be desired. 'Christopher was born in such-and-so place and enjoys doing x, y, z' blah blah blah, screw this. What if we mix it up a bit? You want to know something about me? I'll tell you stuff about me if you tell me stuff about you.

Shoot me an email at CJAuthorGraham@gmail.com.

Cat and/or dog pics are encouraged.

Or you can go to cjauthorgraham.com